THROUGH
HER EYES

a novel

AVA HARRISON

Through Her Eyes: A Novel
Copyright © 2016 by Ava Harrison
Published by AH Publishing

ISBN: 978-0-9963585-3-8

Through Her Eyes
Cover Design: By Hang Le
Photographer: Jenny Woods
Interior Design: Champagne Formats
Editor: Chelsea Kuhel (www.madisonseidler.com)
Line Editor: Brenda Letendre, Write Girl Editing Services
Content Editor: Jennifer Roberts-Hall, Indie After Hours
Proofreader: Shawna Gavas, Behind the Writer

DEDICATION

To the ones who helped me grow along the road to finding me.

Special Content

To receive the full experience of this story, please follow @ ChasePorterPhoto on Instagram when prompted in the book.

PROLOGUE

I WAS A HORRIBLE person.

Truly.

But I had goals, and he didn't fit into them.

I didn't know how to take back the words I'd said. They filtered through my brain like a bad dream that I just couldn't awaken from. Just when they started to slowly slip away, they resurfaced. Rooted so deeply in my psyche, there was really no place for them to hide.

If only I'd known the ramifications of my actions. If only I'd known how my decisions would hurt me beyond repair.

But at the time, I couldn't let him halt my progress. I was so close . . .

"Are you in love with me, Aria? Do you want to be with me?" Parker asked, and my heart completely stopped. I had waited so long to hear those words, for him to see me as more than a friend.

"No. I don't want to be with you," I replied. Even as the words left my mouth, I knew they were a lie.

I didn't just love him. It was so much more than that. So

1

much more than love. He was my rock, my friend. He was the lifeline that ran through me.

At the time, I thought I had no choice . . . I thought he would be able to see that after everything I'd been through I needed to succeed. I needed to make up for the loss of my brother Owen. In the end, though, my decisions were always toxic.

Toxic to him.

Toxic to Owen.

Toxic to everyone.

"No, I don't love you."

Those were the last words he heard as he turned and walked away.

My heart tightened in my chest as the words replayed over and over again that afternoon. A record skipping that I just couldn't turn off.

Then the phone rang.

Three words were uttered.

Three words that changed my life.

The phone slipped from my trembling hand, and I dropped to the floor.

I couldn't swallow. I couldn't scream.

Cemented in place.

My shoulders curled in, and I clutched my stomach through dry heaves.

I'd lost my soul mate, and now I'd lost my future.

Everything I'd worked for crumbled, and it all no longer mattered.

Inhale

CHAPTER ONE

Twenty-six days later

STILL FEEL THE loss of his presence in every breath I take. The emptiness is unbearable. I'm not broken. I'm ripped in two. Severed completely. A blanket of darkness has been draped over me, and no matter what I do, I can't see the light. I can't remember the last time I felt whole. The moment Parker walked out of my life, I knew a part of me would be forever changed. At the time, I just didn't know how much.

You can never really know how your life will be impacted when you lose a part of yourself. You think you know, but in truth, once a laceration starts to form, once your soul begins to tear, there's nothing more you can do. What are the options?

Drown yourself in pity?

Drink yourself to oblivion?

Give up on your life?

And that's where I find myself twenty-six days later.

Giving up on my life.

Starting a new one.

I'm swimming in a sea of color. Red, yellow, blue . . .

An endless ocean with no bottom.

Waves of people push past me like the rolling tides of a rough day at sea. The swirling of their bodies brings disarray. Faces come into focus, then distort as they slip away. Some linger like a strong gust of wind, others a soft caress, but the darkness brought on by the bodies is frightening to me. As if parts of me are floating. Being tossed around by forces beyond my control. This is my personal hell, and I'm scared. Scared of drowning and scared of who I will take down along the way.

After what seems like forever, I've broken through the crowd. A light sweat breaks against my brow. Quickly, I gather my belongings from security. I need to seek some refuge from the chaos. With two hours to kill, I make my way to the first class waiting area. An added bonus to my impulse purchase. Normally I wouldn't splurge on a first class ticket, but when I called this morning it was all that was available. Against my better judgment, I'd reached into my pocket and pulled out my parents' credit card and made the purchase. I hated giving them something to hold against me, but I couldn't see any other way to leave this quickly. Luckily that was all I'd need from them, as I'd saved for years to pay for the rest of this trip I was supposed to take with Parker.

As I enter, I'm transported into what should be a calming atmosphere. Serene music plays gently over the speakers, but it does little to calm my nerves. The tingle in my chest is still present. *What am I doing?* At the time, this all made perfect sense. After another night in which sleep evaded me, I thought I knew what I was doing. *This is what Parker would want.* Now, sitting alone, rubbing the back of my neck to loosen the corded muscles, I wonder if I'd been rash. Maybe this wasn't the right solution?

But how can I not leave?

How can I stand to be here anymore when he's not with me? Staying in New York is no longer an option. I'm being dragged down here. The demons that haunt my mind suffocate me. I've been living in a fog the last few weeks, my reality so far away.

Drowning.

Emotionally defeated.

That's what I'm doing here in New York. I'm gasping for air while I wish for Parker to come back to me. This trip is my salvation. Like an eraser, I hope it will wipe away the previous twenty-six days and allow me to make it right.

My cheeks burn, and my shoulders slump forward. I know that one day the fog of my oblivion will recede, and reality will come crashing down on me, but that day won't be today.

My cell phone vibrates in my pocket, and my jaw clenches. I pluck it out, slide my finger across the screen. Before I can even say hi, my friend Sophie's voice echoes through the earpiece.

"I saw your text. What are you doing, Aria?" I purse my lips at her question.

"Looking for happiness. Trying to make it up to him," I reply under my breath.

"You're what?"

"I'm looking for something to make sense of the confusion in my mind. I don't know. I can't even breathe anymore. I need to find my happiness again and find myself. That's what he would want. It's just . . . how do I find happiness if I'm not sure where to look?"

"That's the thing, Aria. You can't *find* happiness. It's not something you can walk into the grocery store and buy. You need to learn to love yourself and realize that some things are beyond your control. What happened with Parker isn't your fault, and until you realize that, you will never find what you're looking for. "

"Easy for you to say. You're always happy. Your life's pretty perfect. I just . . . I can't do this without him, Soph."

"I know you miss him, but I don't understand. How can you leave right now?"

"I can't be here. You have no idea how hard it is to be here when I can't talk to Parker. I just need to get away."

"He's not gone, Aria."

"He might as well be. It's not like he'll talk to me." I cast my eyes downward. My gaze lands at my feet as I let out an audible sigh.

"Have you told your parents you're leaving?"

"No."

"Don't you think you should mention it to them?"

Hell no. The fact is, I'm afraid of *her* reaction. Being around my mom is like waiting for a bomb to explode . . . or *im*plode. No, she won't care. Her only love is the bottle. And Owen. But since he's gone, she only has time for the amber liquid that brings her solace. And my father . . . he won't even notice I'm gone.

"Why? It won't change anything. I'm still planning to leave, and it's not like they'll care. It never concerned them where I was. Parker was the only one who gave a damn." It's a sad truth, but it's my truth, unfortunately. Without Park, I have no one. As much as I love Sophie, our friendship is only a few years old. She doesn't understand the history.

"I care," she says, and she does. I know this. She just isn't who I need right now. There's only one person who can calm me, and he isn't here to soothe my nerves. Parker would know just the right thing to tell me, the perfect joke to make me smile and if I started to cry, he's the only person who would hold me just the right way to stop my tears.

"That's different." I lower my head and stare off across the floor. My vision focuses on a piece of lint. The need to mentally distance myself from this conversation takes over.

"How is it different?" she asks, pulling my attention back.

"Park was the only one here for me after Owen was gone. He brought me back to myself. He taught me how to breathe again. Without him, I can't even exhale. I'm not sure how to do it again."

There's a pause on the phone line. All I can hear is the steady rhythm of Sophie's breathing. "Where are you planning to go?" she finally asks.

"On our trip. The one he planned."

"You can't keep running away, Aria."

"Don't you see? I have to go. I can't stand the uncertainty. I can't stand the waiting to see what will happen. I can't stand the fighting that's going on here. I need to leave."

"This is what you always do, Aria. When things get hard, you run. You did it in college when you avoided speaking to your parents rather than confront them for how they treated you, and you're doing it now." Her voice is serious, and I hate myself for putting that tone there.

"I . . . I just can't be here, okay? Please support me on this," I stammer.

"Is there anything I can do to convince you to stay?" She lets out a long breath that makes my heart lurch in my chest.

"No." There's nothing anyone can do to change this. Other than a miracle or divine intervention, I'm getting on that plane.

"Do you want me to come along?" There's no mistaking the concern in her voice. I hold my breath, then let out a long, painful exhale.

"This is something I need to do alone."

"Listen, babe, I know you're sad, but you really can't—" Knowing what she's going to say, I cut her off before she can finish.

"I just feel so displaced in my life without him."

"So you're just up and leaving?" she asks. Placing my finger nervously in my mouth, I think of how I should answer.

"This is what he'd want. I feel like I need to do this to make up for . . . "

"Make up for what?"

"Nothing. Plus, being here right now is tearing me in two." I feel dead inside, but I don't need to tell her that. That will only worry her more.

"And you think running away will fix that?"

"Yeah, I do. Parker always said I needed to do this, so I am."

"Aria, I don't think that's what you need. I think you need to see someone. Talk about your emotions. I don't think traveling around Europe will help you." She's probably right, but then I have to admit what I did, and that isn't going to happen.

"I love you, Sophie, but nothing you can say will change my mind. I'm getting on this plane." I smile weakly to myself. It's true—nothing will change that I need to do this. If not for me, then at least I've got to for Parker.

"Will you promise to call me, at least? I'm freaking out

that you're doing this."

My shoulders tense, and I knead my temples. I have to tell her, but I can't think straight.

"I'm actually considering going off the grid for a while. I need to get away from everything here, and I don't think having constant updates will help me."

"That's insane! Have you lost your mind?" She'll never know how lost I am. I don't even think it's possible to make her understand how I feel. This is the only option.

"Yeah. Yeah, I have." My voice cracks into the phone.

"I'm so sorry, babe. That was insensitive. Just . . . please, Aria. What if something happens? Won't you want to get back? Please can you just check in? Check your texts. Okay?" she pleads, and I know she's right. I have to check in just in case there's any news. I have to keep in contact. It's only right to reach out to Sophie. Ever since I met her in college, she has been there for me. Through every fight with my mom and every tear I shed over Park. The least I can do is keep her from worrying too much.

"You're right, I'll send the occasional text checking in. It might not be every day, okay? I need some time to quiet the voices wreaking havoc in my brain. I have to try to find me." I'm not completely sure how I hope to accomplish this, but I need to get away and change something, and at least this is a start. "But I promise to check in."

"That works for me. Also, can you promise me you'll be safe?" I think I can hear her sniffle in the phone.

"I promise. Of course I will be. It's not like I'll be staying in a shady youth hostel like in one of those horror movies where they kill all the tourists." I laugh, an attempt to lighten the mood, but it comes out spotty as I hold back the tears threatening to expel. "God, I just wish he was coming with me. This was his plan." The thought of going alone terrifies me, but as Parker often told me, 'Sometimes you just have to face your fears.' This is what he'd want, so I'm going to do it.

"I know, honey. It will be okay. You will be okay." I don't think I'll ever be okay again. A person can only break so many times before they can no longer be mended. But still, a sliver of hope lives within me, or I wouldn't be setting off on this trip.

"Promise?"

"Promise."

"Okay, I have to get going, Soph. I'll keep in touch and please if anything at all happens. If I need to come home for any reason, text me and I'll get on the first plane. Okay, I do have to run. Love you."

"I love you, too," I hit the end button. I reach into my oversized carry-on bag and pull out the New York City postcard I bought in the gift store. Growing up, Parker and I always sent postcards. When I was away at camp, I waited for them to arrive. Tales of his summer travels around the globe . . . Going on a safari in South Africa, hiking the Andes, and dancing in the streets of Rio during Carnival. The list went on and on . . .

Parker and I lived very different lives. While he traveled the world with parents who doted on him, I did not. After my brother's death, I was ignored. Shipped off to camp. My mother was shipped off to a posh "spa" to dry out, and my father lost himself in running his empire. So, I collected postcards over the years from far off places I could only ever hope to travel to.

I pull out my pen and write.

Dear Park,

I know you won't speak to me, but I wanted to tell you I'm leaving. I can't stand the uncertainty, the not knowing. I feel like I'm suffocating. I lied to you when I said I didn't love you. I do love you. I was just too scared and not strong enough to admit it. But I'm going to change that. I'm going on our trip to learn to be the person you love. Two nights in London, then off to Castello Del Nero. Exactly as we planned. I know this is my fault, but I hope one day you can forgive me.

Yours always,

Ari

I rock back and forth as I clench the postcard between my fingers. It slips from my trembling hand as a scene from so long ago plays before me.

The light trickled in through the shades pulled up haphazardly in Park's room. His tall, lanky body stood only a few feet away. I smiled at him, and he smiled back at me as I made my way further into the room.

"Your mom let me in. What are you doing?" Parker stood in front of the far wall of his room. His hand lifted as he poked something on the wall.

"I'm plotting all the places I'm going."

"What do you mean?" I tilted my head to the side to get a better look, but I couldn't make out what he was doing. I took a few steps closer.

"This summer when you're at camp, my parents are going to take me to Europe with them. It's our big summer adventure.

It's going to be unreal."

From my new position, I looked again at the wall, which was no longer blocked by his stance, and noticed a large map taped to it. Red, green, and yellow pins were spread across in no particular pattern.

"So, what's all this mean?" I gestured to the map.

"Green is where we're going, Yellow is where I want to go. Red is where I've been."

"Wow, you're going to all these places in Europe? Your parents are so cool. Mine just ship me off." And that was the truth. Ever since Owen died, there was no room for me in their house, their lives. Not that there ever really had been.

"One day, Aria. We'll go together. All these places, all these adventures, they will be ours. You and me, kid." My heart crushed to my chest at the reference . . . kid. That's all I would ever be to him . . . Owen's kid sister.

"Good afternoon passengers. This is the pre-boarding announcement for flight 595 to London Heathrow. We now invite those passengers with small children, and any passengers requiring special assistance to begin boarding at this time. Please have your boarding pass and identification ready. Regular boarding will begin in approximately ten minutes time. Thank you."

Swiping the tear dripping down my cheek, I make my way to the plane. Before I get on, I head over to the woman smiling brightly behind the boarding counter.

"Good afternoon. How can I help you today?" She smiles brightly at me as her fingers lightly tap on the computer in front of her.

"I know this is a strange request, but I wondered if you

wouldn't mind sending this out for me?"

"That's no problem at all." Reaching across the counter, I hand her the postcard. My movements are hesitant as an aching feeling grows in my chest. I wish I were able to say goodbye in person, but this will have to do. She looks over the image of the lights of the Brooklyn Bridge glimmering against the backdrop of New York City.

"It will go out tonight." The corners of her eyes crinkle as she turns around and glances at the mailing address and postage. "Should be there tomorrow."

"Perfect. Thank you so much."

When they call first class, I move toward the jetway. With each step I take, I watch my feet hit the dull, grey pathway leading up to the plane. The continuous clatter of my rolling bag's wheels squeaking against the floor echoes in the narrow corridor as I make my approach. Once on board, I make it to my seat, but like some cosmic comedy, fifteen minutes later everyone is directed to deplane . . . *mechanical issues.* I wonder if this is divine intervention. Maybe I'm wrong to run away. Maybe I should face what troubles me.

My heart thrums to the beat of my steps as I exit the plane. My gaze looks past the seats and in the direction of the airport exit. The hair on the back of my neck stands on edge. *Maybe I shouldn't be going. Maybe I should face my fears.* My body turns toward the exit and with slow steps I begin to head away from the gate. From the corner of my eye I see a couple embrace and my stomach drops. *No. I have to leave.* Reluctantly I sit and my knee begins to bounce uncontrollably as I continue to take in the room around me. Airports are like no place else in the world. Joy, fear, trepidation, and in my case, sadness, fill the room.

Everyone has a story.

I look over and see a young girl. She appears to be about four years old. Her chestnut hair is pulled up into two lopsided pigtails, and she bounces up and down in her seat. Our eyes meet, and I see hers light up with excitement. They twinkle a delicate shade of green that reminds me of a child's watercolor painting. The emotions radiating off her could be contagious, but I don't feel the same way she does. For the first time in forever, I feel something other than the sadness that has been burdening my heart. My feelings match her eyes—green with envy. I'm jealous of a little girl. Her life is so innocent and she has yet to feel real pain.

"Our apologies for the delay everyone, but Flight 595 to London Heathrow will now begin the boarding process. We'll start with our passengers with small children and anyone needing special assistance followed by our first class passengers."

And just like that, my fate is sealed.

A new adventure.

A new beginning.

Seated in my cocooned bubble, I lift my head from my hidden nook and pop up to look around. The Virgin Atlantic plane reminds me of a spaceship. Futuristic seating and neon pink lighting runs throughout the length of the interior. In the front of the plane, they even have a full service bar. Seems a bit silly to me, but to each his own. Moving my eyes to the entrance of the plane, I watch a steady stream of passengers entering. A cute waitress dressed in a red, seventies style dress guides the excited passengers to their seats.

I feel robbed of the excitement.

Reaching into my purse, my fingers touch the cold surface of my phone. I need to turn it off, but before I do, guilt creeps upon me. I really need to send Sophie a text.

I know I'm being selfish for making you worry. I know you want to be there for me, and I really appreciate it. I promise if I need you, I'll call. Love you.

Acidity burns in my stomach. The fear of the unknown claws at me. I have a basic idea of where I'm going, but all in all, I'm fucked. Park and I planned this trip. Well, he planned it. He'd already been everywhere so planning our adventure was a no-brainer to him. All I did was buy a few more pins and stick them securely in the map. That was my contribution to the big trip. My way of claiming the places I dreamed to go. Places we could witness together for the first time.

As I settle back in my seat, the white noise of passengers talking hums in the background. Pulling the shade up, I glance out the window and notice rain has started to fall down the pane. This afternoon when I left, the sun poured brilliant rays of burnt orange across the city, and now it's as if the heavens are crying for me. My hand clutches my chest. My heart thrums heavily. *It feels like it might explode.* The flow of the oxygen I'm inhaling feels restricted as the plane's tires move. I want to grab for the oxygen mask and breathe in heavily, but I know that's just crazy. It would get me a one-way ticket right off this plane, and I need this. I need to get away.

"Ladies and gentlemen, this is your captain speaking. We're currently number one for takeoff."

His words become a distant noise as my pulse picks up. I share a glance with the passenger in the seat across from me.

White knuckles. She's as scared as I am. Great! If this plane bumps up and down, I won't be the only one screaming. She digs inside her purse, pulls out a little white pill, and places it under her tongue. *Traitor.*

My stomach drops as the weight of the moment hits me. I'm doing this. I'm really doing this. My hands become sweaty, and I clench my fists. My eyes shut out the outside world, and I try to take calming breaths. My foot taps as I wait.

We begin to take flight.

Park.

As if my soul is tethered to his back in New York, my emotions pull and snap. The strength I'm trying to hold onto comes crashing down. I'm suffocating. Silent sobs join the moisture caressing my cheeks. I clench my eyes shut to stop the onslaught of emotions that threaten to expel. I hear his words as clearly as the day he spoke them.

"Ari, as my friend Everest always says . . . stay in the present, don't live in the past. Be strong. Be you."

When I'd first heard those words, they'd angered me. Once again, Everest was interfering in Parkers life, and mine. But now I had no choice but to heed his words.

Inhale.

I. Can. Do. This.

I can be strong.

Even if I have to do it *alone.*

CHAPTER TWO

Twenty-seven days since I spoke to Parker

3 8,880 MINUTES SINCE I said those horrible words to him. We have arrived at Heathrow. *London.* I made it. I pick up the phone and begin to dial, but the ghost of my words makes me stop. Shaking my head, I begin to place it back in my bag, but not before I look one more time at the picture of Park. I pinch the bridge of my nose and close my eyes to think. When I reopen them, I turn my phone off.

My heart pounds as I reach overhead to grab my bag and make my way off the plane. With each movement I make, the fluttery feeling in my stomach gets worse. I walk through long corridors and brightly lit hallways. Each twist and turn makes this seem more real. A whiff of an airport restaurant filters through my nostrils, and my stomach turns. *How do I get out of this airport?*

I pick up my pace and search for the baggage claim because I know I can find a ride from there. I make my way through the cavernous room. There is no reason to pause, as I didn't even check a bag. All I have for this adventure is a small rolling carry-on. Packing light is key when your journey is not planned. How do you even know what to bring when you don't know where you will be? Hell, I don't know where I'll end up. London isn't my final stop, merely my layover. Pretty great layover spot if you ask me. I figure I'll stay two nights and see a few sights, using Parker's stories as my guide.

The cab ride into London is everything I expect. My cabbie is a complete gentleman, and he doubles as a tour guide and historian. By the time we arrive in Mayfair, I'm officially an expert on London and know its complete history. I also know the hottest bars, the most classic places to drink tea, and all the best restaurants.

The driver turns down the street and pulls up to the legendary Brown's Hotel. *Wow!* I think as I take in the façade. It drips with English elegance, which makes complete sense, as it's the oldest hotel in London. My lips turn up for the first time in twenty-four hours. By habit, I reach for my phone in my purse, but before my fingers grasp it, I decide against it. *Nope. No phones.* Shaking my head, I decide I'll shoot Sophie a text later. I'm too tired and drained to deal with any questions she might reply with.

A young man in uniform reaches for the door. I admire his elegant gray suit. *Smart.* My eyes move upward, and I take in his matching top hat. To an American seeing this for the first time, he could have easily passed for one of the best-dressed men on Savile Row. As he opens the door and welcomes me, I'm completely taken aback by his pleasant and friendly demeanor.

"Welcome to the Brown's Hotel. Will you be checking in?" I nod my head at him and my lips part slightly.

"May I help you with your bag?" He walks toward me, his hand outstretched.

"No, I have it, but thank you so much." Making my way through the doors, I head towards the front desk. There I'm greeted by a giant smile and a name tag. Mary it reads and she's the definition of hospitable, beaming at me from behind the counter.

"Good morning. Welcome to the Brown's Hotel. How can I be of service to you today?

"Hi. Good morning. I have a reservation under the name Bennett."

"Yes, Miss. Bennett. I have your reservation for a queen room for two nights, is that correct?"

"Yes, that's right."

"Let me grab your key. If you need anything—dinner reservations, a car—please let me know. It would be my pleasure to assist you."

After she hands me my key, she names the services the concierge can help me with. My body relaxes as relief courses through my veins.

Opening the door to my room, I place my belongings on the carpeted floor and make my way inside. I throw myself onto the queen size bed sitting in the middle of the room. My eyes run over the lush surroundings as I settle in. This really is perfection. Parker was right. Park . . . *Shit!* As my body begins to sink into the mattress, I realize just how exhausted I've become.

I'm drained, weathered and beaten.

I lost myself somewhere and this trip is my chance to find it, being tired is my cross to bear.

So, what's the first thing you do when you're trying to

find yourself when in a foreign country and staying at a luxury hotel? Break open the mini bar. *Oh, who am I kidding? I'm a classy girl.* I reach for the phone.

"Room service, please." My fingers tap anxiously on the table as I wait to be connected.

"Hello. May I please have a bottle of Bollinger? One glass—"

"There will be only one of you?" she inquires.

"Yes, that's correct."

"So, first things first. We go to London, kiddo." Park smiled at me. At seventeen he was finally filling out to match his tall frame. He was so handsome, I only wished he would see me as more than his best friend's little sister. While he'd grown into his looks, I wasn't much to look at. I was way too tall and skinny at fifteen to be considered attractive. Gangly, like a giraffe. I had no shot at Parker looking at me the way I saw him look at other girls.

"We'll stay at the Brown's Hotel."

"Not the Ritz?" I winked at him.

"Nah, Aria. The Brown's, it's right down the road in May-fair. Only seconds from Bond Street, but it has this classic charm. You will love it. I can already see you sitting there at The English Tea Room. All prim and proper. So you."

"What are you trying to say, I can't have fun? I have a stick up my ass?"

"No, of course not. Just, this place is right up your alley, that's all. Don't get so sensitive. You know I love ya." My insides warmed.

"You're like the sister I never had." And then they froze. My breath came out heavy as I swallowed the lump in my throat.

"Okay, Park. The Brown's it is. High tea at four o'clock. I'll wear an ostentatious hat to match the giant stick up my ass." I stuck my tongue out at him and hoped that would take away the uncomfortable feeling hanging in the air.

Shaking my head, I walk across the room and into the bathroom . . . the loo. I'm in England, after all. Fifteen minutes later, while barefoot and wrapped in only a towel, a soft knock sounds through the room. I pull the towel a bit tighter and make sure it's secure before I reach out to open the door. Naked and dripping wet is not the impression I want to leave on the room service guy.

An older gentleman in a black suit steps into the room. When he walks past me, he barely glances my way. I want to thank him for leaving me with what little dignity I have left which the tiny towel only covers. He makes his way further into the room and efficiently sets the bottle in a bucket of ice. The desire to give him a big kiss as he uncorks it and pours me a glass floods me.

Champagne . . . *finally.*

After he finishes and shuts the door behind him, I pick up the glass.

"Cheers to myself." Sighing deeply, I lift it to my mouth and feel the bubbles as they caress my throat. The crisp smell tickles my nose when I swallow. The champagne infiltrates my body and proceeds to drown out my thoughts. They have become a soft hum. Through the reflected glass of a large, ornate mirror across the room, I catch a glimpse of myself. Exhaustion reflects back at me. Complete and utter exhaustion.

I wake a while later with a jolt. A faint ray of light peeks in through the sheer draperies adorning the windows facing

Albemarle Street. The champagne must have gone straight to my head. I peer at the clock and notice it's already three o'clock in the afternoon. *Shit.*

I almost slept the whole day away. For the life of me I don't know what to do with myself now. Straightening my clothes that are now wrinkled from sleep, I decide to leave the confines of my room and see London. *I just wish I wasn't alone.* Fabulous . . . It's been a whole two seconds, and I'm depressed. This trip is supposed to enlighten me and pull me out of my misery. It's meant for me to atone and then find my happiness again. Instead, I'm sitting around being sad.

I decide to spend the next few hours taking in the sights. I walk through Bond Street and then hop a cab, continuing my trek around London until I see Buckingham Palace. Unfortunately, I slept through the Changing of the Guard, but even viewing the grand structure leaves me completely breathless. It's awe-inspiring.

Timeless.

Like a typical tourist experiencing London for the first time, I have to visit everything, including Big Ben and Parliament. My heart tugs in my chest as I remember all the times Park and I got stuck driving around in circles back home because we'd missed our exit on the highway. We would always quote our favorite movie "Look kids . . . There's Big Ben . . . Parliament . . ." We would laugh for hours. My eyes fill with tears at the memory, but I wipe them away.

The glimmer and flair of Piccadilly as the sun starts to set for the day is like being home. It reminds me so much of Times Square at night, of the time I went to see Wicked with Park for my eighteenth birthday. Thinking of him makes my heart hurt. Would he forgive me?

I'd been selfish, stubborn, and blind. Not having Parker is my fault. My shoulders drop forward. I should have fought for him. At the end of the day, that's all he wanted. That's all anyone ever wants, to know someone would fight for them. God, I hope deep down, wherever he is, he knows I'm sorry. The only thing that keeps me sane is that tiny sliver of hope.

I suck in a breath as sadness coils in the pit of my stomach. Thoughts of home hurt too much. I can't allow myself to go there. There will be a time I'll have to deal with my emotions swirling inside me, but I'm just not ready. Right now, all I'm ready for is to drown myself and my emotions in a drink. It scares me how often my thoughts turn to that vice. Must run in the blood? *I'm nothing like my mother, and I'll never be.*

Searching for a bar, I make my way down Oxford. I pass through the Marble Arch to a little street called Seymour Place. The street is eerie, as the day has now turned to dusk and it's completely empty. To think, this is just steps away from the buzz of Edgware Road. My skin pricks, and my neck tenses as I take in my surroundings.

The dilapidated state of the buildings only adds to the spooky feeling of the dimly lit street. A few feet up ahead I notice three wood planked picnic tables, a green awning, and the words 'The Carpenters Arms'. Just what I was looking for—a hole in the wall pub. I scrunch my nose as I walk through the alley toward its unobtrusive entrance. The pungent smell leaves little to be desired as I make my way down the narrow passage. Gathering my composure, I tentatively open the heavy green door and step into the cozy wood paneled bar. I find it's quite charming despite the shoddy location. It gives me the feeling of family. Of laughter and celebrations. This is the quintessential pub feel I was looking for.

Perfection.

Now for a drink.

I scan the room for a place to sit. I notice three men in business suits. They look completely out of place. My God, are they all wearing the same suit? My eyes roam their finely tailored three-piece ensembles cut slim to their bodies. I can't help it when my mouth drops open. Are they all drinking the same drink? Each man has a dark ruby red drink before him. So dark the drinks almost appear black. *Guinness.* Seriously, do they also share one brain? A giggle bursts from my mouth, and I bite my lower lip to stifle another from breaking loose. My feet start to ache from all the sightseeing today, so I'm pleased to spot some open stools at the end of the bar.

"What can I get for you, love?" the bartender asks as he lifts an eyebrow at me.

"Umm . . . a pint please." *When in Rome or in this case, London.*

"Pint of what?" He chuckles.

The men sitting next to me chuckle as well. They're obviously amused by my choice of drink. *Rude much?*

"Guinness, of course." That sets off another round of laughs from the peanut gallery to my right.

"You sure that's what you fancy, love?" the bartender asks. He bites back another snicker as the men continue to cackle at me.

I consider whether I should just ignore them, but against my better judgment, I find myself doing quite the opposite. I turn my body toward them as I speak.

"Find something funny?" I focus on the man sitting directly next to me.

"Aye no, nothing at all," he replies.

"How come I think you're laughing at me?"

"Well you're quite a pretty little thing to be drinking a Guinness. I fancy you more a champagne drinker." His eyes glimmer as he speaks. They are the perfect shade of hazel green, almost like moss in springtime. He's very handsome in a refined, British way. As if he's a noble or part of the royal family. It seems he would better fit in a private club in Covent Garden.

"I didn't think they would have any," I bite back. There's no hiding the annoyance in my voice.

"That will be three quid," the bartender cuts in. I welcome the distraction and dip my hand into my pocket.

"Put that on my tab," the handsome stranger interjects. Shaking my head adamantly, I try to refuse. I'm here to sit at the bar alone and drink, not chat with him, but Mr. Suave will have nothing of my rejection and proceeds to force me to accept his gift. I keep my eyes on him as I grab the frothy drink now sitting in front of me. Tipping my head, I bring the glass to my mouth and take a big gulp. Big mistake. Huge. I instantly start choking and gagging. It tastes like the piss I imagine they scrape from the bottom of a urinal.

As I catch my breath, the bartender nods and places a glass of white wine in front of me. Needing a chaser and to never again look at that disgusting monstrosity the British call a 'stout,' I guzzle my drink like I'm a starving woman having my first meal. I force myself to look up and meet the eyes of the stranger.

"So I was a forgone conclusion?"

"I wouldn't say that." His eyebrows waggle, and I roll mine in return.

"Then what am I, just a typical tourist?"

"You're certainly a lot easier on the eyes than the usual sort we get in here." He leers at me. A wicked gleam crosses his perfect features as his gaze travels up the length of my long and lean legs. I can almost hear the dirty thoughts running through this stranger's mind.

I can tell this man is trying to charm me, but unfortunately for him, this is as far as he will get. I might as well have some fun before I break the news to him.

Biting my lip seductively, I lean in, running my tongue against the seam of my mouth. His Adam's apple bobs as he takes a big gulp. He ate it up. Hook, line, and sinker. His eyes dilate as I speak.

"You're dreaming that I'll come home with you, aren't you? Well, you better wake up," I deadpan. I grab my glass and chug the remainder of the wine.

"You slay me." He chuckles as his eyes sparkle. All I can do is shake my head at him.

"Excuse me, sir? Can I have another glass of white wine, please?" I definitely need a new glass, and when that one is done, I'll need another.

After my latest glass is done, I stumble into the bathroom. I glance at my reflection in the mirror and start splashing water on my eyes. I'm a mess. A horrible person. No matter how much I drink, when I look in the mirror, I can't change the reflection that stares back at me. No matter how far I go, I'm still there staring back at me, reminding myself of what I did, who I hurt, and what I let myself become. I can't hide from myself. My hollow eyes always stare back. My brown eyes have become so dark they're an abyss of nothingness. *This whole trip was a bad idea. I won't find what I'm looking for.*

I can't even stand looking at myself. How am I supposed

to tolerate trying to find me?

No.

It's too late to turn back, and there's no way I can face what is waiting for me at home. So I head back to the bar and order one more round. The handsome stranger has abandoned his pursuit of me. I'm relieved. I'm used to people leaving me, and learned that it's easier to push them away first. My brows knit together. He's much better off. He would have eventually gotten the memo that I'm toxic. That's me, the toxic girl who ruins everything around her.

I glance up at the ceiling and try to hold back the tears that threaten to flow. As I begin to lose my battle, I'm handed a new glass of wine. I make swift work of it, sigh loudly as I lift it to my lips, and set it down it again. The liquor hits me right upside the head and makes me feel woozy. I whimper as the room starts to spin.

"What's got you so sad, love?" The bartender studies me as he speaks, his eyes trailing over my face.

"I don't know what you're talking about." *Walk away bartender, walk away.* I silently pray. You do not want to know the depth of my misery.

"Not often do you have a beautiful American in here all alone, throwing back drinks." I rest my face in my hands and groan to myself.

"That bad?" the bartender observes.

"Worse," I mutter through my clenched teeth. I bend forward and rest my head on the bar. The tightening in my chest increases.

"So, where you from?" he asks.

"New York." I raise my chin and rub at my temples.

"And what brings you to our lovely establishment?"

"I hurt someone. Then shit happened. Then I ran. Apparently, that's what I do. Aria Bennett, serial runner. I thought maybe if I did this, he'd forgive me. Can I have another—" I hiccup.

The bartender hands me a fresh glass, and I take a giant swig.

"H-h-h-heeeeey!" I hiccup again. Why can't I stop hiccuping? A laugh bubbles up and escapes my mouth. "This isn't wine. Whaaat d'ya think ya doinggg?"

"I figured you could use a water. So, who did you hurt, love?"

"Everyoneee. Who didn't I hurt?" My hands grip the glass goblet tighter as I lift it up in the air. "Okay, sir. Time for more wineeee." The chairs start to tilt, or maybe it's the walls. Rising to stand, I stagger forward, but land back in the seat instead.

"I think another glass of water would do you some good."

"I'm no better than my mom," I mumble. "She's a drunk. Hateful bitch. Drunk. God, is she evil." I laugh. My hands swing forward and almost spill my water.

"Seriously. Sheee devil." The bartender walks away.

"Heeey. Wheeeere d'ya think yeeeeer goin'?"

"I'm going to call you a cab, love."

CHAPTER THREE

Twenty-eight days since I spoke to Parker

WAKE UP EARLY to acidity trying to fight its way up my throat. My body reminds me of how my first night of my adventure played out. Guinness, wine, darts, wine, a second attempt at Guinness, and another wine chaser. Room spinning. Home. *How the hell did I get home? Not sure.*

All I remember is hugging the toilet.

My stomach revolting.

Knowing this is karma.

Laying back in the bed, I cover my head with the blanket and curse my life. *Never drinking again.* My brain pounds as I try to decide how I'll spend my day.

Museums?

Sightseeing?

Hiding under the covers and pretending last night never happened?

Bingo.

That's how I'll spend the day. I reach across to the bedside table and dial zero.

"Good Morning, Miss Bennett. How may I be of service today?"

"Can I please be connected to room service?"

"It would be my pleasure." The phone rings twice.

"Room service. How may I help you?" his soft British accent pounds on my hungover brain.

"May I please have eggs, toast . . ." I think for a minute to decide what else would make me feel better. Grease. "Also bacon and orange juice. Oh, and can I also have two Ibuprofen?"

"But of course, Miss. Bennett. Please give us thirty minutes."

"Thank you." I hang up the phone and walk across the room, picking up the complimentary postcard the hotel has placed on the desk in my room. My hand can barely write from my exhaustion, but I push through the pain.

> *Dear Park,*
>
> *This trip is off to a rocky start. I can barely get out of bed. I might have gone overboard my first night in London. I'm doing a piss poor job of finding myself. At least I saw a few things yesterday, or this stop would have been a complete waste. Tomorrow, I'm off to Tuscany. I wish you were here with me. Having tea at The English Tea Room doesn't sound so great without you, nothing sounds that great with you not here. Without you by my side, without you next to me.*
>
> *I know you want me to experience life, but it's just so hard alone. I wish you were here. I miss you.*

All my love,
Ari

I drop the pen, and head back to the bed. My body flops down with a loud thud. My eyes flutter shut, and I begin to fade back into my sanctuary waiting for my hangover cure to arrive. I can't remember the last time I was this sick. Not since high school probably? It must have been the time my parents left me all alone on my sixteenth birthday. God I remember it so clearly. I'd broken into the liquor cabinet and started guzzling an 18-year-old scotch. At the time I'd no idea what the numbers meant. I'd picked it up because the bottle was prettier than the rest. After downing the burning liquid, I stumbled outside to look at the stars. As the night sky twinkled above me, a feeling of nausea wretched through me. Parker had found me there. He held me as my body shook with sobs and my stomach emptied itself. I remember how the grass cushioning me tickled my knees as I kneeled, letting go of everything I'd consumed in my misery. In Parker's arms I felt safe and when he eventually went and got me a change of clothes . . . loved. After he cleaned me off, he brought me inside my empty house and sat with me while I slept, making sure I was okay. Protecting me from everyone, everything and most importantly protecting me from myself.

CHAPTER FOUR

Twenty-nine days since I spoke to Parker

'M ABOARD MY plane to Florence after a horrible attempt to wake from the dead this morning and make myself presentable for the nine a.m. flight. Despite spending my last day in London hungover and in bed all day ordering room service, I'm still not feeling any better this morning. I drank way too much two days ago. Being drunk is starting to become a coping mechanism I'm all too familiar with. I need to cut it out, but when the emotions begin to grip at me, I can't help but reach for the bottle. It's fine. I have it under control. I'll never become her.

Never.

The flight is bumpy, and I pray to a higher power that we don't crash and burn. I also have to fight off the feeling that I'm about to be sick, which is always unpleasant. When I arrive at the airport—happy to still be alive—my ride doesn't show, and I'm forced to take a cab to my hotel. Check-in runs smoothly, thank God, and I hurry to my room, shut my eyes, and close out the hell of a morning I had.

I find myself hours later sitting down to have a yet another drink. *God, I really am no better than Mom.* I want to curl up with the shame of it all. But a drink certainly held the possibility of brightening my mood.

Just when I finally think my day is turning up, I lock eyes with the most gorgeous man ever to cross my path. Normally this wouldn't be a bad thing, but after my horrid morning, I've no desire to be social. Wow, he really is something else. Broad shoulders, unruly brown hair, eyes so blue they glisten as they squint narrowly at me. He's the kind of man who depletes the oxygen from my lungs. A look of recognition registers in his perfect gaze, but it fades away quickly as he flashes me a wicked smile. I narrow my eyes and take him in. Hmm, his eyes do look vaguely familiar, but I can't place where I've seen him. He tilts his head at me and his eyebrows rise.

Great, just what I need. Another drunk man hitting on me. Shaking my head, I turn back to what's really important. My Bellini.

No matter what anyone says, you can't get a Bellini like this anywhere outside of Italy. White peach nectar, prosecco . . .

Divine.

The glass glistens as streams of sunlight reflect off the condensation. One sip should take the edge off. I shuffle forward and reach my hand out to grab the cocktail. The crisp refreshing drink does nothing to calm the ache in my heart. It only numbs the pain as it makes its way down my throat.

The aromatic bubbles are a comfort to me, a warm blanket covering my emotions. I want to drown in the oblivion it can provide. But then I would be a pathetic drunk.

So instead of behaving in an uncouth manner, I place the flute down and take in my surroundings. The high ceilings of the converted castle are the perfect location to live in my fantasy world. To forget the past. To forget the heartbreak waiting for me back home. This is my current sanctuary, and nestled amongst the flourishing olive groves and rolling hills, I can lose myself for days.

Stealing a glance across the bar that was once the kitchen at the Castello Del Nero, I take him in one more time.

Tall. Lean. Ruggedly handsome.

My eyes trail further down his face to find a perfectly scuffed five o'clock shadow obscuring a chiseled jaw.

He shifts in his seat to rise. *Oh dear God. Please don't come over.* After the British man in the suit two nights ago, I can't deal with another hot stranger right now.

I turn my head back so I'm not caught staring. My hand is heavy as I lift my glass once more to my mouth. From my peripheral vision, I see that his eyes are locked on me. Quickly I return my focus to the glass in my hand, losing myself within the confines of my mind is easy.

I hear a rustle and feel a presence beside me. Trying to appear uninterested in the company that has joined me, I take another swig of my drink just as he slides onto the old wooden bench and stretches out his long legs. He crosses his ankles as he reclines. *Great, he's getting comfy.*

"Come here often?" His American accent catches me off guard. It's smooth and rich and evokes feelings of home, *comfort.* He smiles at me. Full lips. *How had I missed those in my earlier perusal?* He has the type of smile that makes butterflies take flight. His steel blue eyes linger over me, slowly, trailing over my long, toned legs, up my torso, and finally to my eyes. My body shivers involuntarily.

He smirks. *Shit.* That smirk could be deadly. It should come with a warning note. *Will cause recipient to be rendered useless.*

Feeling uncomfortable from the attention, I gaze down at my glass and break the connection. Maybe if I ignore him he will leave me to my solitude.

"I'm Chase. Chase Porter." *No such luck.* His tanned hand stretches out toward mine. Lifting my eyes, I meet his gaze. I sit useless, openly gawking at him. My fingers continue to rim the glass, not reaching up to his.

"And you are?" A grin curls up the side of his face.

"Leaving." I push back, and the chair screeches across the floor. His head cocks to the side at my answer and then the most beautiful chuckle leaves his perfectly shaped mouth.

"Oh come on, I won't bite . . . hard." He winks. The son of a bitch winks. I roll my eyes at his lame pick-up line. As hot as he is, can't he come up with something better?

"Does this ever work for you?" I force back my laughter.

"I don't know. Is it working now?"

"Nope." I turn my body slightly towards his.

"Okay, help a guy out. One name. You don't even have to tell me your last name if you don't want to."

"It's Aria." I pause for a second. "Aria Bennett."

His eyes light up like a kid in a candy store, and I know exactly what is coming. It's only a matter of time before the jokes start. Maybe he would be smart enough to just let it go.

"Aria Bennett." He tests the name on his tongue as his

smile broadens. "So, you know your name is Aria Bennett?"

Nope. He isn't smart enough.

"Since I've been referred to by that name for the last twenty-two years, yeah . . . I'm quite aware of the fact that indeed is my name." Contempt drips from my lips.

"And you're aware that you are named after the game *Final Fantasy Three*, right? Were your parents' gamers?"

If I had a dollar for every person who thought they were clever enough to figure this out, like they were the only video game geek to get the reference. If only that was the case, though. If only they had named me after her. If only they had named me out of love.

"No. Actually, they had no idea. They hated it once they found out. They even wanted me to legally change my name."

I'll never forget the day they found out. It was also the first day I met Parker. I came home from school so excited and ran into the house beaming with the news.

I went straight to my mom and jumped on her lap to hug her. I remember how she pulled away from me with disdain. My mother was not openly affectionate with me. To be honest, I was more like a thorn in her side than a daughter she loved. I'm able to see that now, but at six years old I was oblivious until that day.

"Mom, Mom! Thank you, thank you!" I beamed.

"What are you going on about, Aria?" she questioned as she tried to detangle herself from my tiny arms. "And make it fast." She gave me a frosty look as she spoke.

"The kids told me at school. I'm from a video game! That's so cool, Mom!"

"Aria, please don't ramble. You know how much I despise

that."

"You named me after the video game Final Fantasy." I beamed up at her proudly. Our eyes met, but hers weren't smiling back at me. Wanting to show her how much I loved what she had done, I buried myself further into the nook of her neck and hugged her tightly. I felt her body tensing underneath me. I could feel her long, sun-kissed hair scratch at me as she pulled farther away.

"I have no idea what you're going on about, Aria." Her mouth was tight as she pronounced my name. A fine line formed in her brow. Her nose scrunched.

She rose and picked up a glass tumbler filled with clear liquid from the bar on the other side of the room. "I have more important things to do than understand that girl," she mumbled to herself, just loudly enough for me to make out the words as she walked out of the room. My chest constricted, and I ran upstairs to hide in my closet. That was how at six years old my life was changed forever with one simple sentence.

I hid in my closet crying. My soft sobs could barely be heard, but I didn't let it stop my emotions from flowing out of me like a rushing tide. There are moments that change your life. I had no idea this would be one of them. I had no clue that at six years old my life would forever be changed. That the moment the door opened, I would be changed. That three words would change my life.

"Please, don't cry." That's all it took.

Three simple words had the power to make me breathe again. I knew there was something special about Parker. The boy standing in front of me looked down on me with a calming look as he spoke. "Please, don't cry." His words floated around me like the first rays of sunshine after a gloomy day. "I'm Parker," he *continued. He had the eyes of an angel, an angel who actually noticed me. His shaggy blond hair fell across his brow as his blue eyes twinkled at me. Soft whimpers continued to leave my tiny body.*

"Shh. Please, don't cry." I nodded up at him as my lips trembled to fight back the sobs.

"How about a little smile then, so I know you're feeling better? Okay?" And I did. I lifted my eyes to look into the crystal blue oceans that had saved me.

"Park? Who are you talking to?" Owen, my older brother, asked him as he looked around to make out who was here. "Is Ari in there? Ari are you okay?" His voice was laced with concern.

"She's fine. She was just looking for something," Parker said to Owen. He stepped out of the closet and intercepted Owen so I wouldn't be seen. He turned back toward me. Our eyes locked one more time. He winked, and my heart melted.

Oh, the irony that she had unknowingly named me after a video game character. Joke was on me, though. I was devastated when she said she wanted to change my name. Completely destroyed. After Parker eventually told Owen what happened, he stepped in like the overprotective brother he always was. He let me believe the dream. He and Park let me pretend I was special.

The gravelly voice of the handsome stranger awakens me from my daydream, and I notice he's still standing before me and speaking.

"Really? You're shitting me? Princess Aria Bennett." A smile tugs at his lips, and if it weren't so perfect, I would want to smack it right off his smug face.

"She's actually a priestess, and we spell it differently. Mine has two n's," I huff.

"Same difference."

My breath quickens as my anger rises. "Well, on that note, I'd like to say it was a pleasure to meet you, but, well . . . not so much." I shift from my spot, but as I'm about to stand, I feel the touch of his hand graze my arm. It stops me dead in my tracks. The heat that radiates from him sends a chill down my spine.

"Aw, come on. I was just playing. So, you live in New York City?" The muscles in my back become rigid. *How the hell did he know that?*

"Accent," he states obviously reading my confusion from my body language. "What brings you here to Italy, Aria?"

And there it is, the question I dread brings me out of my haze, but I can't handle answering it. My stomach knots. *What brings you here?*

I'm running away from my life, leaving it all behind, blind to where I'll end up.

I've left everyone and everything I love to search for the meaning of it all.

My eyes move away from him so he won't notice that I'm teetering on losing it. He must sense my change of mood as he hands me the drink menu. "You're almost done with your drink. Let me get you another one. What are you having?"

I don't know if I should humor him or just cut my losses and walk away. I could always drink alone in my room, but that would be pathetic, and I'm not pathetic.

Taking the menu from his hand, I peruse my choices. Through heavy lashes, I glance back up at him. His blue eyes meet mine, the corners crinkling ever so slightly as he narrows them, and then blinks rapidly to right himself. Something is off with him. With my interest now piqued, I try my best to smile and lighten the mood, so I can figure him out.

"Okay, I guess. I'll have another Bellini, actually make it a Kir Royale. Thank you." I nibble on my lip.

"It's my pleasure, Aria," he says, looking behind me at the waiter.

"*La signora avrà un Kir Royale. Un altro per me.*"

"You speak Italian?" My eyes widen at the discovery. It's shocking that there is no hint of an American accent when he speaks.

"Yeah, I'm here a lot for work, so it really comes in handy." He shrugs like it's no big deal.

"And what is it you do?" What could this ridiculous specimen of a man do other than sit around and be pretty? Model maybe?

"A little bit of this, a little bit of that." His forehead creases.

"Vague much?"

His eyebrows raise, and he chuckles at my response. "I guess you could say I'm a photographer and a bit of self-proclaimed poet. I'm an artisan, really."

"A modern day Renaissance man," I say under my breath causing his lip to quirk up.

"Yeah. I dabble in all forms, from the written word to working with acrylics, to embellishing my photos. My real passion is photography, though. That's how I make my living. But enough about me. What do you do?"

Ah, photographer, poet, ridiculously handsome. That totally makes sense. Of course, he's the perfect man. Lost in my thoughts over how 'perfect' he is, I realize he has asked me a question.

Oh shit! What did he ask me again? *Job? Right?* "Well, I'm

kind of on a sabbatical right now. I . . ." I breathe out, trying to find the right words to describe my current situation. "I just graduated, and I'm supposed to work for my father, but I didn't start. I-I came here instead. Honestly, I'm not sure it's the right fit. I just don't know." I'm shocked by the honesty of my answer to this stranger. For some reason though, it's easy to talk to him. His gaze is locked on mine, and he nods with apparent understanding before he speaks.

"Why isn't it the right fit?"

"There's not enough time in the day to get into that right now."

"I'm intrigued." His right eyebrow lifts.

"Honestly, it's not that interesting, I'm just finally starting to loosen up and don't want to talk about work," I groan out.

"Now that I totally understand. To not talking about work." He lifts up his glass and I clink my almost empty champagne flute with his, then take the last sip.

"So is that your favorite drink?"

"A Bellini?" I ask while lifting my now empty drink to him for emphasis. "Yep. You?"

"Me? No Bellini for me. I love a good full-bodied cabernet."

"Snob."

"Says the girl who loves champagne cocktails."

"Whatever, you're such an ass." He erupts into another fit of laughter, and I follow suit. An hour later and a few drinks down, I find myself back in my bed with a healthy buzz and a lot more knowledge about Chase Porter. We parted with a simple good-bye but I did tell him where and when I would be having breakfast tomorrow morning. I wonder if our paths will cross again. A part of me hopes they do.

CHAPTER FIVE

Thirty days since I spoke to Parker

L AST NIGHT TURNED out better than I imagined. Maybe this is a good idea. Yeah, going to Italy was the right idea. Parker was right. I wish he were here, but I know I need to do this on my own. I need to get my life back on track and figure out who I am. Losing Parker is a huge catalyst in the downfall of my life, but it's only one of many. For as long as I can remember, I've been a little bit lost.

It all started when I was a little girl. My mother always resented me, so I never felt I had a place where I belonged. Owen was her prize. Her prince. I stop myself mid-thought. No, these demons are too old to be unburied. I tunnel my face deeper into the blanket, let out a little scream, and purge the sad and hurtful emotions I'm holding from the memory of Owen and my mother. No, they will not ruin this for me. I already have so many obstacles in my way.

After a few more breaths, I roll out from the safety of bed and welcome the day. The morning sunlight streams in through the large windows overlooking the lush hills in the distance. The grass casts a soft shimmer as light reflects off the morning dew. I stare at the swirls of color as they dance on the horizon. The view is haunting, and the longer I sit and stare, I recall my actions that brought me here. Their burden weighs heavily on me. My emotions are conflicting and, as much as I want to let go and move on, as much as I know I need to—

My stubborn brain won't let me heal.

After showering and slipping on a pale green sundress, I make my way downstairs to the hotel restaurant. It's the only place to grab breakfast in this hotel other than room service, which I'm not doing today. A friendly smile greets me as I'm escorted to a table on the terrace. A scattering of white clouds acts as a canopy above me, allowing the morning sunshine to flow through and bathe the ground in an iridescent glow. If I thought the view from my room was beautiful, then this was spectacular. Breathtaking.

I lean back into my chair and close my eyes. The rays from above warm my face as I breathe the crisp morning air perfumed with the smell of coffee, sugar, and the natural fragrance of the flower blossoms in the middle of the table.

"Good morning, *bella signora*," a deep, raspy voice says from behind me. Chills run down my spine as I turn to my visitor. He's even more attractive today than yesterday.

"Good morning, Chase."

His gaze takes all of me in as he locks on to my eyes, then works his way across my collarbone, over my torso and down to my crossed legs. I can feel heat spread over my cheeks, and I will myself not to blush. Of all times to be affected by someone. Well, this is not the opportune moment. I'm supposed to be soul searching, not being distracted by a gorgeous man.

"Mind if I join you?" he asks. But before I can open my mouth to respond, he's already taking a seat next to me. He turns to the waiter still standing by my table, and in perfect Italian orders us two cappuccinos . . . or at least that's what I think he says.

"So, do you have plans today?" He smiles at me, and I swear it's so perfect it's as though the earth stopped spinning on its axis.

"Um, no." I know where this is going, and secretly in the back crevices of my mind, I'm slightly giddy about not spending the day alone.

"Great. So here's what we'll do, Princess." He smirks, and my breath catches.

Seriously . . . Princess! "Don't call me Princess." I pin him with my eyes as I speak.

His lips turn up. Great, he's amused. "Okay, fine I'll call you . . . Sunshine." He winks.

He goddamn winked again. Ass. What the hell is up with that wink? Is that his move? "Don't call me Sunshine either," I bite back.

"Well, I'm going to have to call you something." This guy was grading on my last nerve, no matter how cute he was.

"How about using my name . . . Aria. Try it out. It's not that hard." Sarcasm drips like bitter juice off my words.

"Yeah, so that's not going to happen. Pick which one you like better."

"Oh. For the love of God! Fine. Whatever. Call me whatever you want to call me," I huff as I throw up my arms in defeat.

"So, Sunshine—yeah, I like that—here's what we're going to do. I agreed to shoot the hotel when they found out I was a photographer. So as a thank you, they scheduled me a one-on-one cooking class with a chef here on the far end of the property. Why don't you join me? It will be really fun. You'll love it. She's not one of those uptight chefs, either. It's actually the owner's grandmother. She lives on the property about a mile up the road in the stone house you probably saw when you pulled up to the hotel. You will love Nonna Agetha."

"Nonna Agetha?" I tilt my head to the left. I'm interested.

"Yep, she's not a traditionally taught chef, but she's very well-known and revered in these parts. So, what do you think, Sunshine? Want to go on a little adventure with me?"

I think about his words. Should I go? I've no other plans, and this is what I'm here for. I say the only words I can at a time like this. "Sure, why the hell not? Take me on an adventure."

"Okay. Let's drink these cappuccinos, then go over to where they keep the bikes and head out."

"Don't you need to shoot?"

"I prefer to shoot at first light or at dusk, so I'll take some of the pictures later."

"Well, I can't ride a bike in this." I fold my arms across my chest in defiance.

"Sure, you can."

My eyes grow wide at his words. "But—" I try to object before he cuts me off.

"Live outside your comfort zone. Do you want to live a dictated life or do you want to travel in your own direction?"

His words ring truth for me. I needed to hear them at this moment. This is why I'm here . . . to travel in my own direction, to find myself just like Parker had said.

"Okay."

I look down. Flat ballet slippers and a sundress. My outfit

replicates a photo of a girl riding a bike in France I'd once seen. He's right. It would be perfect.

After we're done with our cappuccinos, we walk down the stairs and around the building. Lying next to the stone wall of the castle are two old-fashioned bicycles. Yellow, rusted, weathered . . . typical, but perfect. As I sit down, a sharp gust of wind picks up and throws my sun-kissed golden locks across my face.

Snap

Snap

I look up to find Chase's camera aimed at me.

"What are you doing?" I eye him with confusion and a little annoyance.

"I had to capture you. You look beautiful and free."

The sincerity in his voice knocks the wind out of me. I thank God that my wispy locks cover my face that I'm sure is now crimson red. He thinks I'm beautiful. *Nope, shake it off. No distractions . . . you are not here for that.'*

We ride toward the house in the distance in comfortable silence, taking in the views and breathing in all that nature has to offer. The closer we get, the more in awe I am of the architecture before me. This house must be hundreds of years old. It resembles an old carriage house, and I wonder if it had once been part of the original property of the Castello del Nero.

We hop off the bikes and head inside. A whiff of flour hits my nose, tickling it. I turn my head, and the moment I spot Nonna Agetha, I understood why she's referred to as 'Nonna.' Her warm olive skin is wrinkled and weathered with age and experience. Her hair is a mottled grey. Dull and cut short to frame her face. She's everything a Nonna should be.

"*Ciao, un piacere conoscerla*," she says.

"*Ciao, un piacere conoscerla*," Chase replies, then turns to me and smiles as he repeats the words in English for my benefit. "It's a pleasure to meet you."

I smile brightly at her and repeat the words "*Ciao, un piacere conoscerla*." They come out choppy, making Chase smile at me. Comforting me.

As Nonna starts to speak and tell us, or mostly Chase, the history of the estate that was built in the twelfth century, I can't stop my lips from turning up even further. Her broken English and accent make me feel safe, and strangely enough . . . loved. It feels like I belong with her, as if she's my family. It's a wonderful feeling, one I haven't felt in a long time. Joy radiates from her as she pours us each a glass of orange juice and proceeds to describe what we will be learning to cook today.

"We will begin with a traditional ragu. We will simmer—" The word comes out sounding more like shimmer, but I understand what she means. As we braise the meat, I sweat the vegetables in another pan. Onions and fresh garlic, the aroma is heavenly. She moves on to teach us how to hand roll gnocchi. I can imagine Parker loving this. He loves to cook, and he would love Nonna. The smile bleeds off my face. God, I miss him.

Why does this keep happening? My emotions catch like a brush fire, burning up every semblance of happiness I've gained. Why can I not for one second begin to breathe and move on? Just when I think I am, I'm robbed again.

"*Bella*, what is wrong."

"Nothing."

Her tiny hands pass me a lemon. "You know what Nonna always says?"

I shake my head.

"When life gives you lemons . . .make limoncello." And she's right. I can't let every moment of happiness I've had thus far in Italy crumble.

My hands continue to knead the dough. I look up and find her warm eyes smiling back at me. There's understanding in them. She has lost something too. She knows. I try my best to smile back. It's fake, but at least I try.

At that moment, Chase decides to walk over from his station to investigate. We begin to knead together and listen to instructions on the proper technique to make the pastry fluffy and airy.

"I have something very important to talk to you about." My stomach plummets and my pulse accelerates faster than its normal clip. "I tried, but you're just not a Sunshine. Sorry, Princess it is." I let go of the breath I'm holding while I shake my head at him. The corners of his mouth turn up as his eyes gleam. The ass really had me scared, so I throw flour at him, which causes him to break into a hearty laugh. The sound becomes contagious, and I begin to laugh as well.

"So, what brings you all alone to Italy?" Chase inquires as we dust the dough with flour.

"I—well." His forehead furrows as I stammer.

"It's okay, I won't judge." His eyes are soft and kind, and for that reason I trust him.

"I made a mistake back home," I say on a whisper, hoping he doesn't press me. I'm not ready to tell. Truth is I'm not sure I ever will be.

"It's okay to make mistakes. It's how you fix them that defines you."

"My mistake was kind of a big one," I mutter. I chew on the inside of my cheek.

"There's no mistake too big not to fix."

"This one might be." He takes in my words and smiles warmly.

"So, where in Italy are you planning to go?" he says, effectively changes the subject. I let out an audible sigh. Relief.

"Well, I'm kind of wandering aimlessly. No plans, no set destination."

"You're seeing the world, and you don't even have a compass?" He chuckles. "That should be interesting."

"Well, I have an idea. I once planned a trip like this . . . but it didn't work out."

"Plans are meant to be broken. Sometimes that's what's intended. You need to live in the moment and live the life you desire. The one waiting for you, not the one dictated for you."

His words bring me back to a conversation I had with Parker only weeks ago.

"I still have yellow pins on the map. One day, Aria, I'm going to all these places. I won't let my life get stale. I won't live a boring life. I'm sure there is more out there than what we know. I want to know more, see more—that's the life I intend to live. Let's do it together. The only thing stopping us is your own fear. You deserve more than this. More than the life you're living."

"Hey, you okay?" Chase asks as he studies my face. I wonder if he can see how broken I am.

"Sorry, just got lost in my thoughts." I force a smile.

"It happens." His eyes narrow, and he appears far away, lost in his own moment as well. His head moves back and forth as he rights himself, awakening from his daydream. "So, tell me a little about yourself . . .Princess Aria Bennett."

"You will never let me live that down, will you?"

"Nope."

"Okay, hmm . . . Let's see. I recently graduated from NYU." He nods and his lips part into a big smile.

"Oh cool, great school. What did you study?"

"I majored in marketing, with a minor in business." His right eyebrow lifts at my revelation.

"Interesting . . . you never did tell me what it is you actually do for work?" God, I hate that question. I hate talking about my family. Especially about the job that awaits me. Vague is always the best answer.

"Currently?" I ask.

"No, in the past." He chuckles. "Yes, currently."

"Well, I was about to start working for my father's real estate development company. Then I kind of lost it and left." His mouth opens and then closes. I can sense he has more to ask, but I turn quickly to Nonna and ask her what's next. She proceeds to teach us the skills to make homemade biscotti.

After all the food is prepared, we sit at an old farm table set in the middle of the twelfth century kitchen and eat. The meal is by far one of the best I've ever had, each bite more decadent than the last. We eat everything that was prepared— sans Chase's biscotti, which was burned horribly. Hours pass as we drink wine and laugh. The old woman tells us stories of growing up on the property, harvesting grapes, and making wine. She tells us about her mother and her mother's mother and how she came from a long line of wonderfully, strong women. Empowered women. It's inspiring to hear, and makes me realize that Parker was right. There is so much more to my life than filling in for Owen with my dad.

After a wonderful day, we say goodbye to Nonna and step

out through the stone door and are greeted by a beautiful sunset. The red and purple burst through the clouds and create a watercolor effect across the horizon. It reminds me of the impressionist painting *On the High Seas* by Claude Monet—a kaleidoscope of colors so dreamlike I fear I'm not awake. Chase reaches around his neck and pulls off his camera. He starts snapping pictures in rapid succession.

Snap

Snap

His gaze drifts to the horizon as he stares at the bright fields of yellow in the distance. "Come on. I don't want to miss this shot."

We hurry back to the bikes and are on our way. The wind teases my hair, whipping it around as we start pedaling. When we arrive at our destination hundreds upon hundreds of giant sunflowers greet us. Yellow fields stretch as far as the eye can see.

We venture into the field, all while Chase continues to snap pictures and capture their beauty and splendor. I take him in, all of him. He's beautiful, and if this were a different time and place, I would consider the option of flirting with him. But that's not something I can do right now. I'm not ready for that. Not when my heart still belongs to Parker.

As my hair flutters in the wind, I become aware that I'm now the focus of Chase's inspiration. He continues to photograph me, and I try not to smile too broadly. I try to maintain my air of indifference.

I fail miserably.

Smiling broadly, I see glimpses of the person I could be.

"How long do you plan to stay in Tuscany?" he asks me.

"I'm thinking one more day. Until tomorrow, maybe? I'm

taking a day trip into Florence. When I landed at the airport, I came straight to the hotel and didn't get a chance to see anything. So I'm going to go back into town to take in the sites and from there, I'm going to head to Rome. How about you?"

"I'm actually heading to Rome, as well. This is my last night in Tuscany. I'm heading out tomorrow morning." *Of course he is.*

"You're going to Rome, too? That's so strange. Isn't it?"

"Um, I guess. I was supposed to go straight to Rome, but my shoot was put off a day, so I decided to come here and kill some time instead." He winks, and I study his face for a minute. There's something so familiar about him. Catching me studying him, he lifts an eyebrow. "What?"

"Nothing. Where are you staying?"

"Hotel De Russie," he says, and I break out in laughter.

"Of course you are. Why *wouldn't* you be staying at the same hotel as me?"

"Guess fate keeps bringing us together. There aren't many hotels that have the small, intimate feel and all the luxuries I've become acquainted to."

"I'll have to take your word for it. Never been. But my friend Parker told me that's where I need to stay, and he's kind of an expert on hotels and traveling. Personally, I'm starting to think he gets a kickback as all the hotels he advised me to stay at are owned by the same company." Chase's face scrunches up. Maybe I should stop talking about another guy. He seems pissed . . . or upset.

"Your friend is very smart," he mutters as he peers out into the distance.

"Yeah . . . he is."

"We should meet in Rome," Chase suggests, turning his

gaze back on me.

"I think I would like that." The funny thing is, I mean it. It would be nice to know there is a familiar face in a foreign city.

"Okay, great. What time did you say you arrived?"

"I didn't." His eyes widen until I bat my lashes at him. "I'll be there around noon." And now it's my turn to wink.

"So, how about we meet for a Bellini in the hotel bar, let's say five p.m. Then we can head out and grab a bite in the piazza. That will give you plenty of time to freshen up."

I nod in agreement.

"Should we exchange numbers, just in case something comes up?"

"My phone doesn't work here. Why don't you leave a message with the front desk if something happens?" His eyes narrow at my suggestion, his nose crinkling ever so slightly.

"Come on, the sun is about to completely disappear. I have a few more images to take and then we can go home. Do you want to grab a bite?"

"You know what, I'm kind of beat. I'm just going to head back and order room service."

"That's probably a good idea. I need to be up early to head out."

When we make it back to the hotel, Chase lightly takes my hand, which sends goosebumps down my arm. Electricity courses between us as he leads us to the patio overlooking the property. The sun begins its final descent behind the hills of Chianti. Streaks of color trail in its wake until shadows take over. Soft laughter filters through the air on the patio as we sit quietly, searching for something to say. In the quiet, my mind begins to wander, and I wonder what it would have been like to sit here with Parker rather than Chase. The thought breaks me. The laceration forms.

I feel each inch as it grows in my soul until I'm completely severed.

"I have to go," I blink back the tears threatening to fall.

"It was really great to meet you, Aria. I look forward to seeing you in Rome."

"Thanks for everything. Today was just what I needed."

"Until Rome." He leans in and places a light kiss first on one cheek, then on the other. "When in Rome . . ." He chuckles.

"We aren't in Rome yet."

"My bad. Until next time then, Princess."

CHAPTER SIX

Thirty-one days since I spoke to Parker

I N THE MORNING, underneath the early morning sun, I see the Florence Cathedral standing amongst the timeless architecture. The terracotta-tiled dome stands tall over the city. Next, I find myself in the heart of the city admiring the fountain of Neptune, a masterpiece only an angel could have made. A marble sculpture so inspiring it makes me wonder how anyone could create such beauty and how I've never appreciated the craft before. Although my time is limited in Florence, I'm able to see the Galleria dell'Accademia, which houses works such as Michelangelo's *David* and then I head over to the Uffizi Gallery to see Botticelli's *The Birth of Venus*.

As my trip to Florence comes to an end, I find myself eating biscotti, a new favorite of mine, in the Via della Spada. The shops, the art, and the food—I love it. Most especially, I love the culture and the people. It's just as lovely as Parker said it would be. Has it really been thirty-one days since I last spoke to him?

When I return to the hotel, I pick up the pen from the desk and the postcard I bought in town.

> *Dear Park,*
>
> *You were right. Tuscany is magnificent. It's truly spectacular. I'm lighter here. I actually met a photographer when I was at the bar. He convinced me to attend a cooking class with him. The cutest Italian grandma, Nonna Agetha, taught it. How funny that she asks everyone to call her that. She was warm and welcoming and I immediately felt like she was family. It felt good, really good. I miss that feeling. I haven't felt that way since our fight. Being in Tuscany has really been amazing and makes me realize you were on to something when you said I needed this. Okay, I have to finish packing . . . next stop Rome. I just want to tell you I'm trying and please don't hate me. Please forgive me.*
>
> *Ari*

I can't take my eyes off my watch as the time passes, minute after minute. There's no way I'll make this train. It's scheduled to leave in five minutes, and I still haven't made it to the station. As the seconds tick by, we finally arrive at Firenze Santa Maria Novella. The structure is impressive, like everything else in Florence. The design is a contrast with the nearby gothic appearance of the church of Santa Maria Novella. This building is a more modernistic design. When I walk inside, I notice a metal and glass roof with large skylights. The skylights span the entire length of the ceiling and give a feeling of openness.

My gaze scans the space and takes in the trains still present within the structure. My hands fist . . . *Shit*. I've missed my train. Pulling out the train schedule to check if the next one is to Rome, I sigh. It won't come for another hour. With time to kill, I start to walk through the station looking to find a vacant spot. I sit on the floor away from the crowd, lean against a pillar, and remove my e-reader from my purse.

I quickly become lost in my book, and after a while, I check the time. *Goddamn it, I almost did it again.* Only four minutes until the next train leaves. The station is now super packed. I weave my way through the crowd. If I miss this train, I will scream. And possibly cry. I pick up my pace, my luggage trailing behind me. Finally I jump aboard just as the conductor speaks and the train starts to move. Glancing around and then at my ticket, I realize I'm in the wrong car. Can this day get any worse? I try to move toward the correct car, but there is absolutely no room to move and no place to sit.

The only location I can stand in is right in front of the bathroom, and dear lord it smells bad. *Yes, it just got worse.* My stomach turns and bile rises. My legs shake beneath me as the train bumps along its path. This has got to be what Hell feels like.

I don't arrive in Rome until a little after four in the afternoon, which doesn't give me much time to freshen up and meet Chase in the hotel. A drink is definitely in order after my journey, which had become a comedy of errors. All in all, I made it there safely, but damn, I needed a cocktail. Since my time is scarce, I throw on a pair of white skinny jeans and a chambray shirt over a tank. I've learned that it's best to layer, even if it's summer. Restaurants are chilly, as are the stores, and the temperature can dip at night. My options are limited. I only packed for a weekend trip in a carry-on, for God's sake. Being a fashionista isn't in the cards for this adventure.

I walk into the bar and let my eyes scan the room. *Guess he's late.* I settle myself onto a stool to wait for the bartender to approach. My eyes land on a beautiful long mane of platinum blonde hair, but not out-of-a-bottle platinum. More like the perfect shade of a Swedish model. She throws her head back in a laugh, and I can see her hand run down an arm in front of her. As I watch her, she leans to the left to get the bartender's attention, and I get a perfect view of her companion.

There he is. The only sense of normalcy I've had since my life fell apart, my little glimmer of hope for a light evening . . .ruined.

Scenarios start to play out in my brain. He hasn't noticed me yet, too wrapped up in the goddess standing in front of him, and to be honest I don't blame him. The closer I walk toward them, the more beautiful she becomes. As she leans across the bar, I can see she isn't leaving anything to the imagination. Her full, perfect breasts peek out seductively from the short spaghetti strap dress she's in.

Maybe . . .

She's his sister?

His cousin?

His wife?

Holy shit, he has a wife, and I didn't know. My brain goes into overdrive. My movements have completely stopped. I'm stuck, frozen in place. *Move Goddamn it.* But all the synapses in my brain are rendered useless.

I think I'm going to be sick. *Oh Goddamn it, Aria.* What the hell are you doing?

You're just friends with him.

You're not attracted to him.

You're here to find yourself something different to do.

Not fall in love.

Fuck! Who said anything about love?

I have to either move my stupid feet and say hi, or I need to turn around and walk away, but I refuse to be the schmuck standing with my mouth gaping, eyes big like a dear in headlights.

My feet make the choice for me as they continue their path. My mind quickly catches up. Even though we're just friends, I'm not going to let him off that easy. If he's married, he should have told me. If he isn't, what the hell is he doing inviting another girl to our date . . . I mean drinks . . . I mean, *shit*, I don't know what I mean. With each step, I know what I want. I want to hear from him that he's a lying, cheating . . .

Oh shit, he sees me. I'm not ready to confront him. I haven't figured out what to say to him yet.

Shit. He's coming over . . .

This is getting worse and worse because I'm pretty sure my mouth is now hanging agape.

"Hey, Princess, you're a bit early."

"And here I thought this is the time we agreed upon. Funny, I also don't remember you saying I was the second appointment for the day . . . or am I just the tag along? Oh, and one more thing: stop calling me *Princess*."

"I missed your smart mouth."

"Oh, save it. Well, I'll be going now. I hate to intrude on whatever you've got going on over there."

"You're cute when you're jealous."

"I'm certainly not jealous. What in the world would I be jealous about? We aren't romantically involved. I just thought it would be fun to see the sights with someone else. You know what, forget it. Go have fun with your—"

"She's just a model I know." *Geez, that makes me feel so much better. Kill me now.* I can't stop my face from going slack and my cheeks from turning a shade of crimson I'm certain is only present in Hell—where I want to send him right now.

"What I mean is I was meeting with her to see if she's able to work on my next project, but now that's a moot point."

"Why's that?"

"My vision has gone in a new direction. I won't be needing a model after all." He lifts his left brow, making his eyes appear larger. They twinkle at me as if I'm supposed to be privy to his new 'direction,' which I'm obviously not since he doesn't elaborate.

"Um, okay."

"I'll tell you my vision later."

"Cryptic much?"

"You have no idea." And there it is—his signature smirk followed by the wink I'd started to miss in his absence.

Going to hell. Get your head in the game and stop fantasizing about his smirk and wink.

"Earth to Ari."

"Can you not call me, Ari, please? Aria is fine. Just not Ari."

"Oh, sorry. I just—" He stops himself and shifts his weight from one foot to the other as he thinks for a moment. "So, how about I lose the model and we go see Rome?" The pitch of his voice rises with hope.

"Sounds perfect," He stares at me with his eyes gleaming

brightly.

"Okay, give me a second." Then he turns and walks off.

I venture over to the bar but I don't have time to sit down before he returns.

"Wow, that was fast."

"I don't want to miss a second of my time with you." Somehow I go from wanting to murder him to wanting to melt into a puddle and swoon. I shake my head and roll my eyes.

"Flattery will get you everywhere. Next gelato is on me." I smile, and I'm met with his. His earth-shattering smile.

Dear lord, if he keeps doing that I might combust right here in the hotel bar. *Head in the game, Ari. Ari* . . . no one has called me that since the last time Parker did. That's his nickname for me. I bite my cheek at the memory, and as if Chase can discern that I need a life raft, he throws one at me, in the way of a perfect segue.

"The next gelato is on you? Well, let's get me some, woman. But first let's stop at the Trevi Fountain." He beats his hand across his chest, making some ridiculous sound, and it's just what I need.

"Lead the way." I giggle.

"Throw a penny in the fountain and wish to return to Rome," Chase says, and I look up at him, perplexed.

"Isn't that cheating? Shouldn't it be a secret what I wish?"

"I guess you can be greedy and throw two in, but whatever," he chides.

"It's cheating. Maybe I don't want to come back? Ever think of that?" I tease back.

"Is that true?" He gives me a look like I killed his puppy.

"No." My eyes roll.

I position myself and throw the penny into the beautiful cascading pools that Neptune, God of the Sea, the mermen, and seahorses preside over.

"Stop!" he orders. "You're doing it all wrong."

"Oh my God, Chase. There's a right way to throw a coin?"

"Why, yes. Actually, there is." My eyes enlarge at this discovery.

"Wait, really? This I got to hear."

"Okay. The belief is if you throw a coin using your right hand over the left shoulder, you will be assured a return trip to the Eternal City of Rome. That's the way it's done."

"That's the most ridiculous thing I've ever heard. I'll throw it however I want." I stick my tongue out at him. I'm acting like I'm five years old, but it's okay because this banter makes me feel young and carefree, and I like it.

"Why do you have to be such a pain in the ass, Princess?" he says as I toss the penny in. My aim is so bad it actually bounces off the lip of the fountain wall, which then causes it to fly back at us, landing at my foot.

"Guess the fountain decided for you. You're not welcome back in Rome." He laughs. *Ass.*

"That's bullshit. Where to next?" I say in a huff.

"Well, you still owe me some gelato."

"Good plan. I could go for something sweet."

"There is a great little place by the Fontana della Barcaccia."

"Fine, lead the way." He shakes his head, takes my hand, and pulls me in the correct direction.

Five minutes later, Chase pulls me into a small boutique.

It's a mish mash of gifts for children and adults. The perfect souvenir shop. I move about the store and peer over at Chase who's trying on straw fedoras. I can see him taking in his appearance in the mirror. His lip twitches, and a dimple forms.

"Looking good, Chase." My voice cracks trying to hold back the laughter that wants to erupt.

"Right? Totally my look." It really is his look, but making fun of him is so much more fun.

"Yeah, I think it would look perfect on you paired with that sarong over there?" I point to the hangers that hold an array of colored and beaded dresses. I'm unsuccessful at holding back my amusement, and my lips turn up.

"Oh, shut it, Princess. I know I look good." He waves me off and reaches for another hat. This one has a neon pink ribbon, and I burst into a fit of hysterics as he begins to model his new look. He continues to rummage through the bin and then his eyes widen and I wonder what has him so perplexed. When he pulls out a pair of lace bunny ears, I understand completely.

"Why would anyone buy these? They're ridiculous," he says as he places them down and walks over to the other side of the store. I know that they're the perfect purchase. Chase is going to die when he sees it. I bite back a smile and walk over to the counter to buy them before he notices. *This is going to be fun.*

A little while later after hitting up a few more gift shops, we finally make it to the gelato stand. We have a perfect view of the Fontana and the Spanish Steps. My eye catches on the shape of the Fontana. It resembles a sinking ship, and it fascinates me. I remember an old legend Parker once told me when we discussed traveling to Rome. It stated that the ship was carried all the way to this exact spot during a massive flood. As

I recall this old folktale, I can't help but think of the parallels with my own life. I too have been swept to Rome during a storm.

"Since I doubt you ever had gelato as a kid, what was your favorite ice cream?" As I try to recall what my favorite flavor was, a memory stops me dead in my tracks.

Owen and I were at the beach, the water stretched out for miles. We had spent countless days there that summer, Owen, Park and myself. Today was different, though. Parker was out with his family, and it was just the two of us. We were bored and had ridden our bikes there to pass the time. There was something frightening and ominous about the ocean on that particular day. There was nothing on the horizon, just blank, empty space. Endless ripples of uninhabited water. I should have known. But at twelve, I thought I was a good swimmer. I thought I was invincible.

There was no lifeguard patrolling that part of the beach. It was privately owned and was practically empty. A family playing Frisbee was our only company for a mile up the beach. There was not even a warning flag to enter at your own risk. Owen said we shouldn't go swimming. He thought the undertow seemed strong. I sat restlessly, the water beckon to me. It spoke to me, and I answered.

Within a few minutes, I realized I'd made a huge mistake. I started to choke on the water first. My arms fatigued quickly as I pushed against the tide. I remember screaming Owen's name. I remember the frantic feeling of becoming weightless. I remember the world becoming darker. I remember staring up to the sky one last time and seeing the clouds above me as my vision started to become speckled. Later, I was told I had passed out.

I found out Owen jumped in after me, and much later, I found out what pain really was. I found out what it meant to lose a part of yourself. When another swimmer jumped in to help, Owen passed me off to him. I learned that as the stranger was saving me, no one was left to save Owen.

I learned what hate was . . . because I hated myself.

The worst day of my life. The day we buried Owen.

I watched as my older brother was placed into a wooden box for all of eternity. My heart was hollow. One minute, I was admiring the beauty of the ocean, the next it was stealing something so precious from me. No words could ever describe the anguish I felt. It was my fault. He was in the water because of me. I hadn't spoken since he drowned five days ago. Not one word. What was the point? What could I say? Nothing would bring him back. Nothing would wake me from this nightmare.

"Ari? Can you hear me, Ari?" Parker lifted the blanket from my head.

"I think you need to come out. Can you do that for me?" As the blanket was pulled fully off of me, our eyes met. His were red-rimmed and swollen. His teeth gently bit at his lip.

"Come here," he said as he lifted me by my arms and pulled me into his embrace. In his arms, I finally let go. My body was wracked by sobs.

Owen was dead.

Owen was dead.

The words replayed. I'm lost. I can't find my way.

It was my fault. It was entirely my fault.

If I hadn't gone swimming. If I was a better swimmer. If I'd only listened.

I felt him wrap me tighter in his arms.

They held me.

They comforted me.

They guided me.

He was my gravity. He brought me back to him. His arms brought me home. He tethered my soul to his and grounded me. As I lay in Parker's arms, he brought me back to myself. He held me until all the tears in my body dried up. I rubbed the tears from my eyes, and breathed a choked sigh. "You're okay, Ari. You'll be okay. What can I do to make you happy, to make you smile?" And then he repeated what he'd said the first day I met him. "I could get you ice cream?" Our eyes met, and I finally spoke.

"Okay."

"Okay? You want ice cream? I'll get you some. What's your favorite?"

"Cookies and cream." Moments later I was happily eating ice cream in bed.

I shook myself from the memory. I file away my sadness and finally answer. "I always loved cookies and cream. I'm not much of an ice cream eater anymore. But now . . . with this gelato—" My tongue darts forward and licks the smooth hazelnut gelato that threatens to spill down the cone. Chase lets out a ragged breath. His pupils begin to dilate as he watches me with . . . desire. His reaction makes me feel something other than sadness. His reaction makes me feel something I haven't felt in days—playful. I'll take that over sad any day, and I decide to go with it.

"What are you doing, Aria?" His voice is raspy.

"Who, me?" I smirk, and he smiles at the look I'm giving him.

"You know what they say about playing with fire?"

"I just like to lick it." As the suggestive words leave my lips, I can't suppress the giggle that teeters on the brink of erupting.

"I've got something you can lick." My eyes grow as wide as feasibly possible, and I swat at him, but he dodges me and dashes toward the Spanish Steps behind the Fontana. Dropping my remaining gelato in the nearest garbage, I take off after him, weaving in and out of the crowd that's formed around the fountain. I can see its cascading water as I make my climb.

My lungs burn as I try to catch up to him. *God, how many steps are there?* The crowd muffles the sound of my feet hitting the pavement. As I reach the top of the Spanish Steps, my body lurches forward in a series of desperate exhales. My shallow breaths come out in gasps while my heart beats erratically. The gelato I had before this silly climb to the top was not a great idea as my stomach wants to revolt against the sugary thick cream. With effort, I might make it to my destination before my feet give way under my own weight. And I thought I was in good shape. What a joke! Better start back up with the yoga.

Then I eye the scenery before us. My eyes skate across the distance, and I see everything. The view from the top of the steps is awe-inspiring.

"Beautiful, right?"

"It's magnificent!" I marvel at the beauty.

"Yeah, it is." But he isn't looking at the view or the distance. He is looking at me.

We stare at each other, panting heavily, our gazes locked. Then Chase coughs once and breaks the connection.

"So, Aria, what's the plan from here? Where you going? What's your destination?" I bite my bottom lip as my eyes wander across the distant scenery, looking out into the great unknown.

"I've no idea. I'm searching for something, I'm just not sure where to find that something yet."

"I'm a pretty good detective. Do you have any clues to give me?"

"I have this silly idea that I need to go somewhere, and maybe once I'm there I'll find myself."

"I'll get you there. Wherever *there* might be."

"How do you know?"

"Will you trust me? I know everything." He winks.

Reaching into my souvenir bag, I don the children's bunny ear headband I bought at the souvenir store. When I bought it, I really had no intention of ever wearing it. I thought it would be funny to watch Chase stare at me like I was insane. But seeing him saunter through the streets of Rome with such self-assurance, I can't help but make an ass of myself.

"What the hell are you doing?" His eyes flicker with amusement, and he bursts into laughter. Seeing him so entertained makes me bring my hand up to my mouth to stifle my own laughter, but I fail miserably and burst out in my own fit of giggles.

"What?" I mock playfully. Chase shakes his head as his thunderous laugh rings through the air.

We continue to stroll through Rome, Chase with his head held high, me wearing my bunny ears. We really are quite the pair. I believe my companion secretly loves it. I can see the pride in his eyes as I openly embarrass myself. It's as if he knows this is out of character for me, and he loves it. As we make our way further into the city, I notice how vibrant and full of life it is. The picturesque streets are a living, breathing work of art. We lose ourselves among the interweaving lanes of the historic center. As we make our way along a cobblestone path to enter the piazza, I take in Chase. His gait is graceful, his swagger confident. He carries himself with a calmness I envy. His hair is ruffled, and his face looks like he hasn't had time to shave for days. He turns his head to look over his shoulder and waves his hand to hurry me up.

As we navigate our way, I fall in love with Italy all over again. Rome is a complete contrast of Tuscany. No rolling hills spanning in the distance, just cobblestone and history—hundreds and hundreds of years of history. Each building is remarkable. When we finally make it to our next destination, I'm speechless. The Colosseum. To think so many died here. So many gladiators lost their lives during the time of the Roman Empire, and in such a barbaric way. So many lives were changed because of this structure. It's dark and ominous, and evokes a feeling of dread, a foregone conclusion to all those who enter. Death is all around, its murky imprint left for ages as a reminder of the past.

We make our way inside, and I walk further into the pit. Looking down, I study the dirt and imagine the death. Had they known that this was the end for them? Does anyone really know when the end is near? My eyes well up at the thought. Chase's voice is soft as he lulls me out of my dark thoughts.

"What's going on in that head of yours, Princess?"

"Do you ever wonder why? What's the reason for all this . . .?" I move my arms about. "What's the reason for all this death?"

"Sometimes there's no reason. You just have to have faith that everything will right itself in due time."

"How can you say that? So much evil happens. So many bad things that shouldn't."

"The water will rise, the tides will come, but eventually it will recede. Life is a cycle. Things happen for a reason."

"How do you live like that? My mind won't let me."

"Just keep telling yourself there is a truth intended for you. Don't let life become routine. That's not the life intended for you."

"How do you know?"

"Didn't I already tell you? I know everything."

I bend at my knees to scoop some dirt into my hand. It sifts through my fingers like the sands of time, reminding me of history. The history here and my history back home. I stare as time slowly passes through my fingers.

Snap

Snap

I place my hand back on the ground to give me leverage to stand back up when Chase speaks.

"Hey, don't move, okay?"

I suddenly have an immense desire to do just the opposite of what he says. So, what do I do? I pose . . . bunny ears and all.

I turn and glower at him as he snaps another series of pictures. My lips pout and my chin is lowered.

"You should be a model." And with that I roll my eyes, and my lips part as a small smile forms.

"Oh, God," I groan. "Do these lines ever work?"

Lifting the camera again, he snaps a few more shots. "Yeah, they kind of do, actually." He smirks.

That smirk right there?

Yup . . . hook, line, and sinker. His lines work. So what do I do? I throw the bunny ear headband at him. *Real mature, Aria.* My reaction seems to amuse him tremendously, but then his eyes narrow and grow more serious.

"What's wrong?"

"I was just wondering, would you like to spend the day with me tomorrow?

I bow my head and think for a moment. Today has been a good day, a really good day. What harm would it be to spend one more day with him? "Okay. I would love to." His lips part into a big grin at my response.

"Great. Let's head back to the hotel. I have a few shots I need to hit up tonight. We can meet first thing in the morning. Say, eight?"

"Sure. That works. Any idea what you want to do?"

"It's a surprise."

"I hate surprises," I scowl.

"You'll like this one. Promise."

CHAPTER SEVEN

Thirty-two days since I spoke to Parker

"**N**O WAY! YOU must be insane if you think I'm waiting in this line. Holy hell, Chase, it wraps around for like a mile." My eyes widen as I peer over Chase's shoulder to see just how far it goes.

"No fear. You really think I would make you do that?" When I didn't answer right away, he busts out laughing. "Yeah, I just might. Come on. I booked us a tour."

He grabs my hand and ushers me down a long cobblestone street and away from the crowd. As we get closer to the structure, I point in front of me.

"Oh my God! Are we really going? I've always wanted to see the Vatican."

"I knew you'd love it." The early morning sun flashes against his steely blue eyes, making them twinkle. "Come on. We need to hurry. The tour starts in fifteen minutes. If we miss it, it's back to the end of the line." he gestures behind us, and I shudder. *That would totally suck.* We make our way into St.

Peter's Square, and my breath leaves my body as I take in the architecture before me. St. Peter's Basilica stands proud as the most prominent building in Vatican City. I want to peek inside and see the treasures that lay within, but I feel Chase's hand tighten and pull me faster.

"I promise we can check it out afterward. But we're really running late, and I had to call in some major favors to get us on a small VIP tour today." My pace picks up and by the time we reach the side entrance to the Vatican museum I'm huffing from the exertion.

Chase speaks in Italian to the Swiss Guard watching over the door. We're let inside and run straight into a small group of about six individuals. Three couples, with us in attendance, now four couples. *Not that we're a couple.* My faces blushes at the thought.

An elderly man with gray hair and tiny bifocals hands Chase two sets of earphones and starts showing us down a long, dimly lit corridor that leads into the museum. It smells of old mothballs and reminds me of the odor in the section of the library that houses the first editions.

"Make sure you pay very close attention. I would hate for you to miss any of the important historical information." His eyebrows twitch slightly, and he bites his lip to stifle a laugh. I have no clue what's amusing him, so I place my earphones in my ears and follow the group through a set of doors that leads into a courtyard. As we walk further, I turn up the sound on the listening device they provided to hear the tour and catch the word Belvedere. Ahh, we're in the Belvedere courtyard. As we step closer to a large fountain that looks a lot like a giant green pinecone, I realize what is so funny. The tour guide has begun to speak, and I have no flipping clue what he's saying.

Pulling my earphones out, I turn to Chase, who's now in full hysterics.

"Mature, Chase. Real mature."

"I never claimed to be, Princess." Damn smirk. Works every time.

"So, you mind explaining what's going on?" My hands gesture to the guide.

"Yeah. Well, apparently the only tour I could get was in Finnish."

"In Finnish?"

"Yes, Finnish. Like from Finland." Placing my hand to my eyes, all I can do is just shake my head and laugh as well. Of course, the one place I'm dying to visit, and I won't understand a word.

"How am I supposed to understand?"

"I'll give you the tour."

"You know the history of the Vatican?"

"Sure do." My head shakes back and forth at the smug look on his face when he speaks, but no matter how arrogant he looks, I keep smiling.

"Very well, have at it." I gesture to the green statue in front of me.

"This is actually a pinecone." At that I actually snort. "No, seriously, Princess. The statue is of a pinecone. No big mystery or deep meaning."

"Well, that was pretty anticlimactic."

"Right?" He nods as he pulls me toward the group that has started walking to another statue in the courtyard.

"Let me guess, this statue is a globe?" I take in the bronze statue in front of me that resembles a ball.

"Actually, this one I know. This is *Sphere Within Sphere.*

Pretty cool, right?"

"Yeah, totally." As we continue to walk and enter the museum, neither of us speaks, and the group is completely silent as they take in everything they are hearing . . . in Finnish.

"This is boring," Chase whines, and I swat at him.

"Shh. I'm pretty sure it's sacrilegious to call the Vatican boring. I think you just bought yourself a one-way ticket to Hell."

"I'm pretty sure I secured my spot years ago." He gives me a lopsided smile, and all I can do is roll my eyes at him.

"Well, if you're so bored, let's talk about something."

"Great idea, let's play twenty questions." He turns and stands directly in front of me. I groan in response.

"Oh, come on. No. What are you five?" My voice sounds nasally and makes me cringe.

"I'll start," he offers as he ignores my objections. "Hmm. If you had to cook dinner for me, what would you serve?"

"Wait, really? That's your question?" To evade hearing the answer to my question, I move to the right of him and then further into the room and stand directly in front of a marble pillar. He quickens his pace and catches up to me. *So much for avoiding the question.*

"Well, I did skip breakfast, so yeah. That's my question."

"I wouldn't."

"That's not an answer. Try again." Knowing he won't stop pestering me until I answer, I think of all the foods I know how to prepare.

"Fine. Hmm, okay. I would make you lobster risotto. Your turn."

"I would cook you French toast."

"The question was for dinner."

"What can I say? I like eating breakfast for dinner." We step in front of a giant Roman sculpture. The intricate nature of each line and detail is incredible, but when I look up above me, my mouth drops open.

"This is fantastic."

"Isn't it? These paintings were painted by Domenico Torti and Ludwig Seitz," he says while he points up to the ceiling.

"Wow, Chase, I'm impressed. You really do know your stuff!"

"I have my moments. Next question . . . who's the one person you hate in your family?" My eyes dart to him, and I blink a few times.

"You can't ask that. That's the most ridiculous question I've ever heard!" What am I supposed to answer . . . everyone?

"Fine, fine. Here, this one's easier. What is your biggest dream in life?"

"Much easier, Chase." Sarcasm spills off my words.

"This one shouldn't be that hard. Everyone has dreams."

"I—I honestly don't know. I guess this."

"This?"

"Doing my own thing, being able to experience life on my own terms . . . living."

"That's a pretty great dream, Princess. It's mine too, actually. Now it's your turn to ask a question."

"Do you keep secrets?" I'm not sure where that came from, but as soon as the words bust out of my mouth, I regret them. I guess I need to know if I'm the only one living a lie. His eyes narrow, and I notice the Adam's apple in his throat bobbing up and down.

"Yes."

"Care to elaborate."

"No, then it wouldn't be a secret. Well, since we *are* at the Vatican. Next question. Do you pray?" He asks.

"Not anymore." And with that, I step past him and rejoin the group ahead, marveling at a statue of a woman holding a sheaf of wheat.

"That's the *Tyche of Antioch*," I hear from behind me. Turning around, I meet Chase's gaze.

"I'm impressed."

"Come on, let's ditch the group and check out the Sistine Chapel."

"We can't do that, can we?"

"I won't tell if you don't." I nod at him, but I don't dare voice my agreement. I need all the help I can get when entering the pearly gates. I'm not pissing anyone off in the Vatican.

As we walk inside and my eyes linger on the images blanketing us from above, tears prick at my eyes. There it is *The Creation of Adam* by Michelangelo. The image of the near-touching hands of God and Adam rocks me to the core.

"They say that the implication of his position is said to mean that if we truly want something, we have to be willing to move toward it." My chest heaves with the impact of the images and Chase's words. This is life and all its meaning. *This is why I'm here.*

"Thank you, Chase. Today—well, today was really beyond words. Thank you for giving that to me." I didn't speak for a moment. His brows knit together causing a little line to form between them.

"I want to ask you something. It's going to sound a little weird, but can you bear with me and keep an open mind?"

"I can try." My hands cross over my chest, almost in a protective manner.

"I've traveled more than most have, Aria. I've seen some incredibly life-changing things and . . . well, after hearing your dreams, I want to share that experience with you. I want you to come with me."

"What?" My eyes widen more than I think possible.

"I want you to travel with me on my next shoot. You've inspired a vision, and I want to see where it goes. I also think you need this, and to be honest, I'm not ready for our time together to be over."

"I can't." *I shouldn't.*

"Why? Do you have someplace to be?" I think about his question. I should go back home. I should go see Parker. But it's too much. I'm not ready to go. I'm not strong enough to deal with him yet, to deal with the pain I caused him.

"I—I don't know you," I stutter.

"Take a chance. Do this with me. What do you have to lose?"

Accompany him on a photo shoot?

Travel with him? Take a chance with him? No. I'm not ready to take a chance on anyone. When I don't speak, he continues to press on.

"Oh, come on. You are planning on seeing Italy, right?

"Yeah."

"You could do this alone, but it would be a lot more fun with me. So come on, be crazy for once in your life. Be crazy with me."

"I . . . I . . ."

"Have you ever felt like your life was passing you by and you didn't know how to push pause and take the time to appreciate it? I'm giving you that chance. Each one of us is meant to have a journey to find our truth. Maybe this will be your journey." His gaze locks onto mine. "Come with me?" I want to, I really do . . . but I can't.

"I'm sorry, Chase, but no. I can't." He tilts his head toward me and nods.

"I knew it was a long shot, but the idea crept in my head, and it would have been amazing."

"I'm sorry. I bet you wish you kept the model?"

"Not at all. Never. You inspired the idea, for you. Wouldn't work for anyone else. I'll just come up with another idea. No worries, okay?"

"Okay."

"So, what do you want to do for the rest of the day? What do you want to see?"

"Funny, I haven't thought about it."

"How about we have no plan? How about we let the nature, the scenery tell us what to do? We go where we feel we should."

"That sounds like a good plan."

"First stop: dinner. I haven't eaten anything since—well I guess I haven't had anything since yesterday, and I don't count the gelato."

"What should we eat?"

"I have a genius idea. We're in Italy, let's grab pizza."

"That's genius. Pizza it is."

We make our way to the Piazza Navona. The grand centerpiece is a large fountain featuring images of the four river gods—Nile, Ganges, Danube, and Plat. Surrounding it are numerous restaurants and cafes. After a brisk walk around the square, we choose a small restaurant that offers everything, including pizza. This restaurant has the best view of the water illuminating the square which appears magical against the darkness of night. From our seats, we can see numerous artists setting up and musicians starting to play. It's divine.

We sit, and a pretty waitress comes over batting her big brown eyes at Chase. She places one hand on his bicep, and ice fills my veins. My visceral reaction is jealousy. This feeling creeping inside of me comes as a surprise. Why do I keep feeling like this? How can I be jealous? But it doesn't matter, because I am. I'm jealous of this woman. I'm jealous that he might want her, and I'm jealous that she has the courage to go after what she wants. I'm not that fearless. I never have been. All those years I loved Parker from afar, but once he rejected me, I never dared try again.

The waitress leans over suggestively to hand him two menus, and I shoot daggers at her. Chase waves the menus off and proceeds to order in Italian. I'm not sure what he orders, but it seems lengthy, and I think I hear the word *pizza*. She continues to swoon at his every word, her smile huge. He doesn't even notice her advances, merely continues to stare at me from across the table as he orders. When she finally walks away, a small dimple forms in his cheek, and the corners of his eyes crinkle.

"What are you looking at?" I ask him nervously. My hands tap in my lap.

"Just you. There seems to be a lot hiding behind those gorgeous brown eyes." I sit frozen, my face warming, and I'm sure he can't miss the blush that must be apparent on my face. His lip ticks upward, his steel eyes glimmering. "I'm from the city," he says, and my eyes dart up to his, my forehead puckering with confusion.

"I thought you might be more willing to open up if I told you a bit about myself first." He grins. "I'm an only child. I picked up my first camera when I was in high school, haven't put it down since. I was your typical 'hipster,'" he air quotes. "I wrote poetry, snapped pictures . . . I was very existential in my youth."

"How come I believe you still are?" My eyebrow rises, and he smiles back.

"I guess only time will tell. After college, I traveled. I traveled a lot. I was kind of an adrenaline junkie. Skydiving, rock climbing, cliff diving, mountain climbing. You name it, I did it, and I brought my camera everywhere I went. I started to blog my adventures, and then I started an Instagram page and began posting my locations. As the time passed, I became more and more sought after, and now I make a living doing what I always dreamed."

"That's incredible! I only wish that was my life." That's all it will ever be, though. A wish. The air in the room grows heavy around me. I want to crawl into a hole as he speaks, bury my head in the sand, and not see the jealousy coursing through my veins. It would be amazing to do what I love . . . be happy. I'm not sure how to be happy anymore.

"It can be. It's like I said before. I don't know you well, but I can tell you're lost. It's like you've been told what to do your entire life, and you can't decide which way to go at the fork in the road—left or right. Do what others want or what you want. This, Aria, this is your first day trying to choose which direction you should go."

"I don't want to work for my dad," I blurt out of nowhere, and I'm starting to think there is something wrong with me and my mood swings. I've no idea why I said something so random. *I'm totally losing it.* Chase doesn't miss a beat.

"What made you decide to go into the family business?"

he asks.

"Well, I don't actually work for him yet. I was set to start."

"That's right, sabbatical. If you don't want to then why are you?"

"I have no clue."

"Come on there's got to be a reason."

"I never felt I had a choice. Twenty-two and I already have a corner office with my name on the door. For the last ten years, I thought it was all I wanted. I can't remember what I wanted before then. I can't remember what my dreams were before I started living the reality that was meant for someone else. It didn't matter what I dreamed of. I never had a choice. It was made for me. One day my life changed, and I needed to succeed, if not for me then for him."

I felt I needed to succeed to atone for Owen's death. It would never happen, but for some reason I thought it would make it better. Maybe my mother would treat me nicer if I was more like him, and in turn maybe my father would notice me. My mother was never nice to me, but after Owen died, something in her broke. I would have done anything for her approval growing up, even if it meant living a life I hated. It made no difference to her, and it certainly didn't make my dad see me. No matter how much I pretended, Owen was still gone. He's still gone.

"For whom, Aria?" he asks as if the source of my pain matters to him.

"My brother, Owen. He was being groomed to take over. But with Owen gone . . ." I stare blankly into the distance, fighting back the memory threatening to drown me.

"What happened?" I turn my gaze back to him. He has himself raised up on an elbow, his head tilted, his brow raised with concern.

"I . . . can we not talk about this actually?"

"I'm sorry. I didn't mean to pry."

At that moment, the waitress decides to bring over the wine that Chase must have requested when he ordered in Italian earlier. I welcome the interruption. *Much needed wine.* As she walks away, Chase's attention lands back on me. He picks up his glass, and his eyes lock on mine.

"Cheers to the ones who cross our paths, the journeys we take, and cheers to the people who come into our lives, even if only for a brief moment to teach us something about ourselves."

"Yeah. Still existential." Chase throws back his head and lets out a boisterous laugh. It's infectious, and I quickly join in. A few minutes pass, and our waitress returns with a pizza pie. This time she isn't smiling, obviously giving up on her attempts. I reach across the table, and my fingertips meet Chase's as I grab for a slice. He lifts an eyebrow as I take a bite and swallow.

"So, what do you think of the pizza?

"Oh, it's so good. I love it. It's different from the pizza we get back home, isn't it?"

"It's funny. As a New Yorker I think our pizza is the best, but this . . . this is in a category of its own. There's absolutely no comparison."

When we finally leave the restaurant, the area surrounding us is vibrant and full of life. Together, we walk back to the hotel, leaving each other in the lobby with a soft kiss on each cheek.

When in Rome and what not.

My limbs flail in the bed. I just can't get comfortable, no matter the position. It feels like a freight train filled with questions and ideas is plowing through my brain, but it's so disjointed it has no direction. Chase's words replay over and over again.

"Have you ever felt like your life was passing you by and you didn't know how to push pause and take the time to appreciate it? I'm giving you that chance. Each one of us is meant to have a journey to find our truth. Maybe this will be your journey."

Maybe he's right. Why else am I here? To find me, to take a journey. To discover parts of myself I couldn't find under the painful memories in New York.

Back home there was so much pressure to be someone else. To try to please so many people. This was the plan all along. Travel and find myself. Granted, Parker was supposed to be with me. Could I go with Chase? Do I trust him? The answer is yes. For some reason, even after only a few days with Chase, I trust him completely. Could I? Isn't this the exact reason I came here? He's offering me all I ever dreamed of.

No, I can't. Who travels with a stranger they barely know? But it's like I do know him. Even though we have only known each other for four days, I feel like I can trust him. I mean, is it that much different than what most college grads do when they decide to backpack through Europe? So many of my friends met random people and then they traveled together. This really was no different, and it's not as though we would be sharing a space. Hotels have plenty of privacy. *Right?*

CHAPTER EIGHT

Thirty-three days since I spoke to Parker

TODAY STARTS DIFFERENTLY than every other day since I arrived in Europe. It's a welcome reprieve from the forlorn feeling I've known so well for the last week. Last night was quite the epiphany. Deciding to surprise Chase has invigorated me, and although my heart is still heavy, and I miss Parker tremendously, I woke up today with a feeling of butterflies in my stomach from the excitement. I come instantly awake rather than hiding under the covers like the previous days. I actually feel alert despite the fact that the clock reads only seven forty-five. The dazzling rays of morning sunlight welcome me. They speak of the excitement of a new day beginning. It feels like the first bloom in May after months of April rain.

I walk briskly around my room collecting clothes from my suitcase that I haven't bothered to unpack. That now seems like a smart idea, seeing as I'm actually leaving Rome. I wonder what we'll see today?

The Vatican again? We never did go back to St. Peter's Basilica. We've already seen the Trevi Fountain and Spanish Steps. I wonder if we'll return to either one? The penny I threw didn't actually land inside, so I could make a wish today. I was in too much of a rush to catch up with Chase to stop and try again.

It doesn't take me long to get ready. My clothing options are slim. *Maybe I should go shopping?* I chuckle to myself at the idea of Chase cooped up in a clothing store. He doesn't seem the type. He's more of a free spirit. Parker is a healthy mix of both. He might be a world traveler like Chase, but he's okay in a designer store as well. I miss him. I miss picking up the phone and talking to him. Since that isn't an option, I head over to the desk in my room and look through the drawers until I find what I'm looking for. *Bingo!* Another postcard.

> *Dear Park,*
>
> *So I have something insane and so not like me at all to tell you. Remember the photographer I met in Tuscany? Well, I arranged for us to meet in Rome. Totally out of character. I'm listening to what you said and I can admit you were right. I did need to change things. I need to step outside my comfort level, so I am. He asked me to go on this shoot with him, and although I said no, I've decided to surprise him and go. But do you want to know the really crazy thing? I'm excited! I can't remember the last time I felt this way. I have no clue where we're going or how we're getting there, but that's okay.*
>
> *Miss you!*
> *Ari*

After I place the card on the desk, the hotel phone rings. It's Chase telling me to meet him downstairs to head out for our last day together. *Little does he know.* Picking up the card, I slide it in my purse and grab my carry-on bag. Looking around the room one more time, I smile to myself. *I guess the journey starts here.*

I turn the corner to enter the lobby, my hair blowing back as I take long strides. Little flutters of excitement begin to bubble in my belly. My impatience to speak with Chase makes me flustered. I see him from across the room. His long, trim body leaning against the wall, his right foot crossed in front of the left. He's dressed casually in a white T-shirt and gray cargo shorts, with a straw fedora on his head. I raise my eyebrows as I size him up. He looks gorgeous. Chase's gaze is focused on the floor, but as he lifts his chin, his eyes widen. He looks at my suitcase, seemingly perplexed. His pupils dilate ever so slightly and his mouth curves into a smile.

"What do you have there, Princess?" The hair on the back of my neck tingles with anticipation.

"I . . . I changed my mind. I . . . I'm coming with you." My heart stirs in my chest. Shit, did I really just agree to travel with this man? Breathe, Aria.

"What do you mean?"

"I tossed and turned all night. I kept thinking *what am I trying to learn? What am I trying to accomplish?* And then it hit me. *This.* This is what I'm supposed to do. Step out of my bubble and do the unthinkable. That's why I'm here. So . . . umm . . . can I come with you?"

"Nothing would make me happier," he exclaims. His eyes widen so much I can't help but get excited, too.

"This is kind of crazy." *No different than backpacking.* "So, where and when do we start?"

"We'll start where all stories start. The beginning."

"The beginning? What does that even mean?"

"Do you trust me?" I nod, and he takes the bag from my hand. "Good, because this is going to be one hell of an adventure. But first, let's give your bag to the porter and try your luck at the Trevi Fountain again." He gives me a lopsided grin, and I know he's right. This is going to be one hell of an adventure.

―――――――

Hours later, my feet ache from another long trek around Rome. This time when we went to the Trevi Fountain, my coin found its proper destination. Standing in the correct position and making a silent wish to one day return to this very spot, I tossed it over my shoulder. As it sailed into the water, I knew I would be back. After we browsed through a few shops and had a leisurely lunch, we mailed off my postcard. Then Chase and I walked back to the hotel and hopped in the hotel's courtesy car to make it to our final destination in Rome . . . wherever that might be. Chase was vague.

Our cab pulls up to the marina. The water glistens like tiny crystals being hit by light at the perfect angle. It's remarkable. The sun sits high in the sky, and through the car window, I imagine the beams hitting my face, my body soaking up the warmth. I wonder if we'll have a late lunch or a cocktail here before heading on our way. We step out of the vehicle, and the heat hits me instantly. It's exactly as I envisioned. The breeze is light but enough to send my hair swirling around my shoulders.

"We grabbing a drink here before we head off?"

"Something like that."

"I don't see any cafes. Where are we grabbing one?"

"Right this way." He guides me closer to the water . . . to a sleek two-mast sailboat that looks like it needs a crew of six. A light mist gathers on my brow. No, surely we aren't going on this striking, white polished sailboat? As we continue closer toward the dock, my feet refuse to move forward. My breath has become ragged.

"Are we—what are we doing here?" My ears start ringing. It's as though the ground is giving way under my feet. I'm having a panic attack.

"Hey . . . Aria what's wrong?" Concern is etched on his face.

"You should have told me. I didn't have time to prepare." I run my fingers back and forth against my pants. My fingertips heat from the friction.

"Prepare for what?" His head tilts to get a better look at me.

"The boat, the water. Are we going on there?" I'm biting my fingernails as I speak.

"Are you afraid of the water? Can you not swim?" He doesn't understand the full implication of his questions. The full story of my past.

"I can swim, it's just . . . well, sometimes . . ." The world starts to close in on me. My breathing comes out ragged, and I will myself to calm. What should I say to him? How can I get him to understand? I need Parker. Parker always knows what to say. I continue to breathe heavily as I try to figure out the best way to tell him about a part of me I want no one to know.

Chase reaches out his hand, and his soft fingers make contact with my chin—lifting my face up, forcing my eyes to meet his. My lip trembles as I simply stare at him, lost in his gaze I'm able to relax. His finger loops around a tendril of hair.

"Will you tell me what's wrong, Princess?" Can I tell him the truth? Do I trust him enough? I'm going on this trip, and that's a huge step for me. Am I strong enough to do this as well? Searching within myself, I will the strength to move forward. Inhale. This is a defining moment for me, a leap of faith to let him in. Exhale.

"My brother, he drowned. He drowned in the ocean and I haven't really been in since. I've been in the water, pools and what not, but I just haven't wanted to go in the ocean. I just . . . seeing it and knowing we would be on the water, it threw me for a loop. I'll be okay. It was like the first time I went in a pool afterward, but then Parker—" Saying his name makes the tears start to flow.

"My friend Parker, he helped me." I look into Chase's eyes as tears stream down my cheeks. His eyes are fixed on me, but appear to not see me at all. Hollow. They match how I feel, sad and lost.

"I'll help you, Aria. Let me help you." He nods and stares off for a minute before he continues to talk. He seems to choose his words with careful precision. "What does Aria say in the game? 'Promise me you will banish the darkness,' right? I promise I'll help keep the darkness out. Okay?" His words sear me. They are so sure, filled with so much promise. They are absolute, and I believe him.

He takes my hand in his, and then pulls me to him. I'm engulfed in his warm embrace. "There's no time like the present to change your future, Aria." Slowly, my tears dry up, and for the first time in over a week, I feel safe. I barely know Chase, but surprisingly this man makes me open up in ways only Parker had been able to. In a matter of days, I've told him so much, from the important to the most mundane. But even after all that, I realize I've felt the safest in his arms, as though he would protect me. I pull back finally, and his gaze penetrates me. Unnerves me. I wonder if he feels it, too.

"We all have different journeys to fulfillment. Maybe this will be yours. Come with me? I got you." And I take the leap of faith. I reach out my hand, loop our fingers back together, and we start to walk. Getting closer and closer to the dock my heartbeat accelerates, but every time it does, Chase lightly squeezes my hand.

A gentle reminder that he's with me.

That he has me.

We kick our shoes off and climb aboard. The boat lurches forward, and I lose my footing and fall into Chase's arms. My slender hand grips his waist for dear life as I struggle to correct my footing. Each ripple of his perfectly defined chest is not lost on me.

"Copping a feel, Princess?" he teases, and I laugh. Chase has this way of making me feel just a little bit better. Not fully, but enough to make me believe there's hope for this trip even after a rough start.

Shaking my head at his joke, I step aside and walk past him. As I make my way toward the middle of the boat, my eyes dart around to get my bearings, slowly taking in the surroundings that will be my means of transportation for the next few days.

"So where's the captain?"

"You're looking at him."

"You've got to be kidding me. There has to be someone else helping."

"Sorry, Princess, I'm all you get." I try to come up with something to say, some argument to tell him this is crazy, but I've been rendered completely speechless. No words seem able to leave my mouth. Nothing. I stand in front of him openly gaping.

"Relax, I'm just messing with you. Luciano will be on board to help me."

"Who the hell is Luciano?"

"He's an old friend. His family owns the company that chartered the boat to me. Any time I sail Amalfi, he comes with me. Honestly, you won't even notice him. He's like a sailing ninja."

"That's not comforting, at all."

"Just trust me will ya?" He says this as if it's the simplest thing in the world. And it might be, but I still don't think I can do this.

"I don't think I can do this. No, I know I can't do this. In the past—"

"Stop. Stop, Aria. Your story is not yet written. Don't let your past dictate your next move. Live every day with intention. And today you intend to do something new. You intend to face your fear. This boat is safe. I've been sailing boats this size since I was a kid, so has Luciano. You will be okay."

"Promise?" I choke out. His eyes lock on mine. Not a hint of humor. His irises have grown and darkened, making his usual steel blue appear black.

"I promise, and I'll never break a promise to you, okay?" His unwavering gaze penetrates, makes me believe.

"Okay." He smiles at my answer, and my heart warms. "Um, Chase. Is there a bathroom on this thing?"

"You're on a boat now. If you have to pee, you have to say

'I have to hit the head.' Got it?"

My eyes roll blatantly at him.

"Aye Aye, Captain."

"Don't get smart with me, or I'll make you walk the plank."

"For someone so cute, you have the cheesiest lines I've ever heard." My words leave my mouth faster than my brain works, and I immediately clamp my hand over my mouth. *Shit.* He'll never let me live that down.

"So . . . you think I'm cute?"

"Oh, good God, Chase. You know you're cute, so shut up."

"Well, you are not cute." My eyes widen at his words. It's like a sucker punch to my gut, and I didn't understand why. *Who cares what he thinks of me?*

"You're gorgeous, Princess." My heart skips a beat, and I just stare at him, because once again he'd rendered me speechless. *Who cares what he thinks of me? Answer . . . me.*

I stand motionless, and his eyebrow arches suggestively at me. "So . . . you want to get out of here and start an amazing adventure together?"

"Why not? What do I have to lose?" *What do I have to lose?* No one would miss me, anyway. "Yeah, let's do this. What do you need me to do?" From across the front of the boat—the bow, Chase called it—I spot an older man with olive skin and salt and pepper hair. He's not at all how I imagined Luciano, so I wonder who he is. But as Chase points to the man across the ship and he gives a wave in my direction, I realize it's the sailing ninja himself.

"Okay, I'm going to talk to Luciano. You stay here. We're going to sail to the island of Ponza. It should take us an about an hour. Can I get you something from the galley?"

"The what?" My eyes go round, and I imagine the confusion is evident on my face.

"Kitchen. Would you like something from the kitchen?" His lips start to pull up, forming a sexy crooked smile.

"No, thank you. I'll just sit here and enjoy the view."

In what seems no time, the sun is setting, and we begin to sail toward our next destination. Colors streak across the horizon like vibrant ribbons dancing in the night. The ocean breeze hits my face as we coast across the distance. The air tastes salty on my tongue. My posture tenses as I see how vast the ocean is and fear shoots through me.

"Are you okay?" I hear Chase say and I peer up at him. His face is laced with concern.

"Yeah," I swallow. "I guess I'm a bit nervous."

"You know what I find helps?" I shake my head at him and he gives me a comforting smile.

"I find that if you're afraid of something, the best way to conquer your fear is to face it head on." As he speaks, he motions with his hand for me to come to where he stands behind the wheel.

"What?" *Surely he doesn't mean for me to sail?*

"Do you want to try?" My eyes widen in disbelief and I shake my head adamantly. "Come here. Don't be scared." I hesitate for a moment, before finally making my approach. "I want to show you how to sail." He begins to back away from the large steering wheel and with shaking steps I take his spot. The wind whips across my face as my fingers graze the stainless steel. With a tight grip, I hold the boat steady. My knuckles begin to turn white from the exertion. Chase steps closer into my body, his back grazing my exposed skin as his fingers gently caress my hands. It feels like there's a swarm of bees flying in my stomach as he touches me, small goose bumps break out across my skin.

"Not so tight." His words tickle the back of my neck. "Point the boat into the wind." I turn my head over my shoulder and shoot him a questioning look. "Turn the boat to the *port side* . . . left. Like this," he says as he helps me steer. My grip relaxes as Chase helps guide me. Together we sail into the distance. The ocean, the waves crashing across the helm . . . and then it all begins to melt away. All the tension in my muscles dissipates as I breathe in and start to relax.

"Next time I'll teach you how to hoist the sails," Chase says as we continue to coast across the water. After a few minutes my legs begin to fatigue from standing and I make my way back on my perch to admire the sunset. I lose myself yet again into the bewitching colors drifting across the sky.

"Aria?"

I turn to him, and my hair whips across my face.

Snap

Snap

"Perfect. You really are a natural." Shivers run down my body as the wind picks up. I clench my arms around myself, running my hands up and down to make myself warm.

"You're cold. Why don't you run below and grab a sweater?"

"I will in a minute. I just want to see this sunset. It's really beautiful."

"Yeah, it is," Chase, says, but he's not looking at the sky. He's looking at me. I can feel his gaze on my skin. Chase thinks I'm beautiful, and I realize I want him to. Does that make me a horrible person? *Yes, it does*. I'm not ready for that. Not after what I did to Parker. He was always there for me, and for what? So I could crush him. I think of all the things Parker helped me with over the years. All the times he stepped forward and was there for me no matter where he was.

"Hey, Park. Can you talk?"

"Yeah, I'm just with Everest in our dorm. Hold one second while I step out of the room." Of course, he was with Everest. Every time I called he was with him, getting into some sort of trouble. Off on some crazy stunt. I rarely got him on the phone without Everest interrupting to steal him away.

I heard, *"Okay,"* then a low mutter, *"Dude. I'll be right back."* Then I heard the words, *"The girls are waiting,"* from a voice I could only assume was Everest. My stomach knotted, and I wished I hadn't heard that. I wished I could rewind time and never have called. Knowing Parker was going out with girls was too much for me to handle right now. I heard a rustling sound and then a door shut. Thank God, at least I didn't have to ask my embarrassing question in front of his friend.

"What's going on, baby girl? You okay?"

"Oh, yeah. It's nothing like that. Umm, this is kind of embarrassing, actually."

"Ari . . . seriously, I've seen you at your worst. Just spit it out."

"Canyougotopromwithme?"

"Try saying it a tad bit slower and enunciate your words."

"Argh! You're being a dick. Forget it." I went to hang up on him, but his voice through the earpiece made me stop

"Oh stop, Ari. I was just playing."

"Fine, will you go to prom with me?"

"No one asked you?"

"You don't have to rub it in."

"Isn't there anyone you like who you want to ask?" I died

right then and there. Of course there was someone I liked who I wanted to ask . . . and I just had. But he didn't see it. Because he was too busy meeting girls and partying with 'Everest.' What kind of stupid fucking name was that, anyway? Mortified, I pulled the phone away from my mouth so he wouldn't hear my gasp. Calming myself, I let my voice dip to a low whisper.

"No, I don't have anyone."

"Well, you always have me, baby girl, and I would love to take you to your prom. Just give me the details, and I'll book a flight."

"Thanks, Park."

"Anything for you."

I breathe audibly.

No matter what, no matter how much his friend always tried to come between us, Parker put me first when it was important. I owe it to him to concentrate on myself now. To learn to be happy, to not be distracted by a guy, no matter how beautiful he is.

A few hours later, lights begin to twinkle in the distance. They grow brighter and more prominent the closer we get.

"You ready to see what you're capable of?" Chase asks.

"What do you have in mind?" My stomach shifts uneasily and I wrap my arms around my stomach as I wait for his answer.

"While we're in Ponza, we're hiking to the top of that hill." He points toward the horizon to a dark, shadowy shape. I look at him in complete wonder as his words really sink in, my face contorts into what must be an expression of shock.

"*Hill?* That's a fucking mountain!" This man has got to be out of his mind.

"Princess. That ain't no mountain. I should know. I climb mountains." My head cocks to the side, and I look up at him. He snickers to himself and my reaction seems to amuse him.

"No way."

"You afraid?" His pupils flare, and I groan loudly.

"Fine. Show me this hill." I throw my hands up in defeat.

"Atta girl!"

As he steers the sailboat closer to the dock, I get ready to jump off and help pull us closer. Two men are already there, waiting for us to near.

"No worries. Luciano has this. I radioed ahead to get clearance to dock here overnight."

"Oh, okay. Should I get my bag?"

"Why would you do that?"

"Umm, to sleep." I stare at him. This is such an obvious notion. I don't understand his confusion.

"Where do you think we're sleeping, Princess?" he asks with what appears to be a smug look on his face.

"On the island, obviously." Chase busts out laughing. "Wait, Chase. We're sleeping on the island, right?"

"If by sleeping on the island, you mean sleeping in this boat . . . then yes, we're sleeping on the island."

"You cannot be serious!" He stops laughing and concentrates on docking the boat.

"Totally serious. Now pick your mouth up from off the floor and watch what Luciano does. That way, the next time we go sailing, we won't need his ugly mug." Luciano flips him off, and Chase erupts into another fit of laughter.

"Wait, but there are no beds. Are there beds?"

"Of course there are beds. It's time I take you to see the boat."

"Yeah, I would have to agree with you." As he steers the boat, Luciano rushes past me to grab the rope and toss it ashore. The men who work at the marina make quick work of lashing it to a cleat and pulling us taut. Chase stands up and stretches his arms into the air. His shirt rises ever so slightly, giving me a view of his perfect V. As the drool collects in my mouth, he catches me gawking and smirks. He turns to walk away, then turns back again, still smiling. "You coming?"

"Uhh," is all I get out before I curl my tongue back in my mouth and run to catch up to him.

"So, this is an Oyster 475. She's actually the best in her class for size and stability," he says as he softly caresses the stainless steel handle on the door leading down into the cabin.

"Well, that's comforting. But it doesn't mean I want to sleep down there."

"Oh, come on, Aria, Where's your sense of adventure?" he turns the handle and opens the door leading to the steps.

"I'm adventurous. I'm here, aren't I?"

"Would you have come if you knew you were sleeping on a boat?"

"Well, no." I shrug as if the answer to such a silly question is obvious.

"And why is that?"

"I barely know you, Chase Porter. How can you expect me to sleep on a boat with you and some guy named Luciano?"

"Princess . . ." he taunts me.

"Don't 'Princess' me right now. I'm not sleeping in the same room as you."

"First off . . . cabin."

"Oh, God—" I grumble.

"Secondly, there are multiple 'cabins' down there. Follow me. I should have done this before we set off. Let me show you what this baby has to offer."

We stride down the stairs leading into the bow of the ship. Each step downward is tentative. I try to balance my footing as the boat sways with the rolling of the sea beneath us.

"So, this way is the pilot's cabin, and over here is the forward double."

We walk through a large area with walls finished in white and sky blue furniture with maple accents.

"This is the salon. There are books on the bookshelf over there if you need something to read and board games, as well." Across the salon, I notice a glass armoire. Squinting my eyes, I notice it carries multiple bottles with every hue of amber liquid in them. My mom would be a kid in a candy store. With a shake of my head, I catch up to Chase, who's now a few steps ahead. As we continue our tour, we enter a narrow corridor.

"This is the galley, and in the back . . . that's the owner's cabin."

"Is that where you'll sleep?" I whisper, biting my lip.

"Well, normally yes, I do sleep there, but since you are the guest. I figured I would let you have that cabin."

"Really?" I exhale loudly, relief flooding me. His smile broadens at my reaction.

"You will be the most comfortable there as Luciano tends to favor staying in the double forward."

"Thanks for being so considerate, Chase. I really appreciate it."

After he shows me to my cabin, where he'd already placed

my bag, we walk through the galley once more, and he pops open the fridge. My lips turn in a smile up as he pulls out a tray of *charcuterie* and a bottle of Rosé.

"How did you have time to get that?"

"Whenever I charter a boat from Luciano, he stocks it with all my favorites. While we were in the Côtes de Provence a few years back we stumbled upon the Château Saint-Maur Rosé. It wasn't expensive, and we found it to be the perfect pairing for so many—"

"Cut the shit." My eyes boldly met his, daring him to lie.

"Okay, okay. A girl I once dated liked it, so we now stock the boat with it."

"You never cease to amaze me, Chase Porter. Was this bottle here for the model you were expecting? Am I about to drink some other girl's wine?" He looks rather amused by me.

"Don't be silly." He grins.

"Well, am I?" His mouth widens considerably as he seems to consider what to say next. His eye looks up to the right as if he's trying to come up with a plausible lie to tell me.

"Technically yes, but it's not what you think." *Wow! But at least he decided to not lie.*

"I don't think anything. All I think is I need a change, and you're giving me one. I'm not reading more into it than that."

"Well, in that case." He smiles and grabs my hand, and my hand being the traitor it is, is happy to be in his.

"Just stop talking, Chase, and let's go have that wine already."

"A girl after my own heart."

"Where are the glasses?"

"Top right cubby. It's a bit tricky, as it's locked shut so everything won't bounce and break if we hit a big wave. Here, let me." Placing the bottle and food down on the counter, he leans across me to reach into the cabinet above me. He's close enough for me to feel the warmth that's emanating from his body. My whole body shivers at his proximity. It's unnerving how my body reacts to him. The boat rolls to the left, and his warm hand surrounds my waist, keeping me steady, while his other reaches to grab the glasses. He removes his hand and moves it to entwine our fingers.

I'm a live wire.

Electricity courses through my body.

His steel eyes find mine as he dips his head dangerously close to mine. His breath is so close I can almost taste him. For a moment I think he might kiss me. I think I might let him, but then I would hate myself, and I can't do that. I can't cross that line. Not now, not ever. I jerk my head away, move toward the bottle, and grab it.

"Here, you take the food. I'll get the drinks."

By the time we make it back on deck, the sun has fully set over the pastel houses and rolling hills in the distance. In our position on the dock, we're surrounded by dozens of tiny fishing boats. The lights twinkling off the water cast a glow. To the starboard side of the boat all I see is the vast ocean expanding into the horizon, cloaking the distance in darkness.

He pours the wine in the glasses, and I take a sip. It tastes like a pretty bouquet. White peach and apricots. It's light and refreshing. Plus, it's doing a remarkable job of soothing the tension that has been growing inside me over my conflicting feelings for Chase. It couldn't come at a better time as I'm still imagining how his lips would have felt if he kissed me. The only thing I can come up with is . . .

Divine.

"So, what exactly is all this stuff?" I point to the tray of food in front of me.

"Just a little something I whipped up," he says casually.

"When you say whipped up you mean took out of the fridge, right?"

"Yes, obviously. You saw me at the cooking class. You don't want me preparing your food."

"What did you pull out for me?"

Chase bursts out laughing, and all I can do is giggle in return and shake my head.

"Not real mature, are we?"

"Where's the fun in that?" He leans toward the plate and starts pointing.

"This here is Serrano ham, and here is a Prosciutto, and to be honest I have no idea what these are, so we'll just call them . . . other hams."

"Everything looks delicious. And the wine, even if it was for another girl is fabulous." I smile at him and wink. Then I grab my glass and take another sip.

Hours have passed. I blink my eyes, and I catch myself trying to hold back a large yawn. We have finished the bottle and polished off the "hams," but the best part of the evening is that we have done nothing more than sit and talk. Chase tells me story after story and I listen. He speaks of numerous adventures and with each tale he tells, I grow to like him more and more. I love how he gets animated when he's excited. How his eyes light up as he remembers each story. The small dimple that appears when he laughs. He's stunning.

And I'm scared of my feelings for him.

The moon illuminates the water, casting shadows across

the distance. In this moment, I feel the ghosts I harbor deep within me begin to recede.

In this moment, I feel alive.

Exhale

CHAPTER NINE

Thirty-four days since I spoke to Parker

Six days since I met Chase

"WAKE UP. IT'S time to go." *What time is it?* It's got to be way too early in the morning for him to be this chipper. *Can he just go away?*

"Go where? Are you kidding me? It's eight in the morning," I groan from under my pillow.

"Yep, and we have places to go."

"Where could we possibly need to go at eight in the morning?" I snap. I don't even attempt to hold in my anger at being woken at this ungodly hour.

"Damn, Princess, you're cranky when you wake up." I might have to beat this man if he doesn't shut up.

"Less talking, more coffee. If you want me to talk to you, I need coffee, and I need it stat. Actually, I needed it five minutes ago."

"Well, then, you are going to love me. Open your eyes,"

he says as I sigh dramatically. Pulling his arm out from behind him, he presents a steaming cup of coffee. The robust aroma infiltrates my senses. His smile is huge and playful.

"See, now you like me." I grab it from him, not giving him time to change his mind. The rich taste floods my mouth, and my body warms.

"So, where are we going?" I inquire.

"Oh, now you want to talk." He pretends to be annoyed, rolling his eyes and shrugging his shoulders theatrically.

"Well, now I have coffee. So hop to it."

"Do you remember what I said we would do once in Ponza?"

"Oh my God, you can't be serious. I thought you were joking. I'm not climbing that mountain."

"Come on, it will be fun. I even packed a serious picnic. You should be excited." A wide grin spreads across his face.

"Fine, fine. Let me get dressed."

His eyebrows arch as he runs his eyes up the bed.

"You naked under there, Princess?"

I answer his question with a pillow to the head.

The early morning sunshine beams in through the windows in the hull. Taking brisk steps, I make my way to the galley and find Luciano. Although he has been a constant fixture since yesterday afternoon, he has yet to sit down and talk to us, rather ducking out every chance he got.

"Morning, Luciano," I say as I walk to the coffee pot and pour myself another cup. "What time are we heading out?"

"Good morning, Aria. Pleasure to see you this morning. I

won't be joining you two, as I have to head into town and pick up more food to stock the boat. But I do hope you enjoy this wonderful island. It's quite spectacular."

"That's a shame, but maybe you can meet up with us for dinner?"

"We shall see. Thank you for considering me."

As I set my cup on the counter, Chase strolls in. His smile is crooked and his eyes sparkle extra bright when he takes me in. He's dressed in a white V-neck T-shirt, cargo shorts, and Converse sneaks. I stare at his defined arm when he stretches for his camera from the countertop and loops the strap around his neck. He looks up through long lashes and beams at me.

I can no longer see straight, he's that beautiful. As he runs his hand through his short, tousled hair, my knees go weak. I can't think these thoughts. They only lead to trouble. He's just a guy, a guy I'm on a boat with, spending the day with alone . . .

Head in the game. He's just some guy. No way am I going there, not with him. Not with anyone. *Not after what I did to Parker.*

An hour passes as I leisurely drink multiple cups of coffee and eat oatmeal for breakfast. Luciano has already left the boat for the day, and I'm ready to go, as well, antsy to have some space from Chase. Every time I move, there he is. Our arms bump, his finger grazes mine. I'm constantly trying to avoid his touch, yet I can't help myself from seeking it out. I'm a dog in heat, and I don't like that one bit.

Stepping off the boat is interesting and I'm not at all prepared for. Apparently, if you have your sea legs on board, you will have them on land, too. My stomach turns as the pavement beneath my feet dips and spins around me, but it's all in my mind. Nothing is spinning. Nothing is weaving but me.

My stomach turns as nausea fights its way up. I swear my face is green. What does one do when they can barely stand? They wrap their arms around Chase Porter's torso and hold on for dear life.

"Whoa there, tiger, I got you!"

"I don't feel so hot, Chase," I groan.

"Just keep your eyes on the horizon and take deep calming breaths."

"Shouldn't this only be happening *on* the boat?" I ask through a deep inhale.

"Typically, people do feel sick when the boat is on the open sea. But the ride from Rome was only an hour, and you were above deck. Since we're on a sailboat, the moments were more defined so you got your sea legs right away. That's good for when you're on a boat. Not so good when you're off."

"Is it weird that I wish I was back on the boat?" I pout and look up at him with big eyes. His response is to squeeze me tighter into his body. Then I feel the whisper of his lips on my hair.

Soft.

Delicate.

Heavenly.

My insides warm.

"Come on, this way." Chase guides us through the marina and onto the cobblestone streets with little stores overlooking the cove.

"You know what will make you feel better?"

"Getting back on the boat?" I offer a wan smile and try to be funny, but it only makes my stomach turn more.

"No, some soda and maybe a slice of pizza."

"We just ate a few hours ago." The thought of food is

enough to have me running to the nearest garbage can. My hand runs instinctively across my belly to soothe it.

"You ate oatmeal. That's not a meal. That was a snack. Come on. Let's get you a bite. There's a pizza place that's amazing just up the road."

As he leads me further into town, a thought creeps into my mind. God, I'm comfortable in his arms. It's insane how perfectly I fit. Am I a horrible person for thinking about this? I'm here being comforted by Chase, but who's back home comforting Parker?

"There it is! Trust me, you will love it."

"It's a hole in the wall?"

"Yeah, isn't it great?" he says as I peer at the structure before me. My eyes grow in disbelief. I'm not sure what I expected from my first pizza place on an isolated island off the coast of Italy, but what I got is not it. First off, it's just a hole in the wall, and I don't mean that figuratively. It actually *is* a hole in the wall of a stone building. And behind the nicely cut out hole is a kitchen you cannot enter. There's nowhere to sit other than a well-worn bench to the left of the stone front. If I thought the ambiance was a reflection of how the pizza must taste, boy was I wrong. I take my first bite, and there's a symphony of flavors playing in my mouth. Each taste is more succulent than the last. It's truly the best pizza I've ever consumed. Turning to Chase I say, "Ten stars. No other place will ever be this good."

"Challenge accepted."

"Chase, there's no challenge. This is the best pizza I've ever eaten."

"See, right there is a challenge. Because if I'm greeted with a smile like that every time you taste something as divine as that pizza, I'll search the world to top it."

My cheeks flush.

I melt.

Chase Porter isn't fighting fair.

After we finish our snack, I have to admit Chase is right. The soda and the pizza really did the trick. Although my legs are still wobbly, I no longer feel ill.

"Was I right, or was I right?" I turn my head toward Chase and begrudgingly nod.

"Yes, oh smart one. Believe it or not, and it pains me to say, you were right. The pizza hit the spot."

"Since you're feeling better, how about we walk through town? Give yourself a little more time to adjust, and then we take ourselves up that hill. Once we get to the top, we can bust open this backpack of treats." He pats the bag on his back then pulls it toward his middle, unzips it, and pulls out his camera.

"Sounds like a plan."

After about thirty minutes, we start walking up a steep road leading past the outskirts of the town. Chase points up ahead where a tiny gravel path can be seen.

"See right there? That's the path to the top. You ready for this?" He grins.

"Ready as I'll ever be."

Within a few minutes, we're on the path, and it's not as easy as before. It isn't a bumpy path per se, but I have to pay close attention to my steps as the rocks give way a little with each step. I look over to find Chase snapping his camera at the horizon. I have no clue what he's taking pictures of, but I'm curious to find out.

"What kind of camera do you shoot with?"

"What is this, twenty questions?" He winks. "It's a Nikon D50 and a Canon Rebel T2i, They're not the fanciest cameras, and my lens is kind of banged up, but it adds to my style."

"Your style?" I mock.

"Yes, Princess. I have a style. Most photographers do."

"And what, pray tell, is this *style* of yours?" I ask while air quoting.

"I underexpose my camera while I'm shooting."

"That's it? That's your big style?"

"There's more."

"Such as . . ."

"If I told you, I would have to kill you."

"Fine. Be like that. I don't want to know your badass style, anyway. What will you do with the picture before you develop it?

"Edit."

"Any more info?"

"I use Lightroom and Photoshop."

"You're such a pain in my ass."

"Come on, I'll show you." He grabs my hand and pulls me with him off the path. The swift action sends chills rushing down my spine.

"So, proper exposure is one of the trickiest things to get right in photography. Are you paying attention?"

"Yup, exposure." I exhale as his fingers skim mine.

"Then I use a technique called bracketing."

"Umm, what?" My eyes flutter shut with the feel of his hands on mine. My heart pounds.

"Focus, Aria. Bracketing is taking multiple photos of the same thing. Same conditions each time, just different exposures. But you want to know a little secret?" I snap my eyes back open when I realize he just asked me a question.

"Sure."

"The greatest thing about photography, all rules can be broken. I say the most important thing is this and someone says it's that, but really it's all you. You have to wake up your senses. See the world around you. Look through the lens. What do you see?" Seriously? I don't know what the heck I see.

"Umm . . ." *That was the best I had? Umm?*

"Look at the flower. Now put your hand—here, let me help you."

He steps behind me and brings his head alongside mine, so close I feel the tiny tickle of his breath across my chin. His arms wrap around me, and he grips the lens and turns it ever so slightly. Bringing the camera back up to his line of sight, he turns it again counter clockwise, and then deposits the camera back in my hands. I lift it to look again, and this time the image is clear and crisp.

"Carefully focus in on the dew collecting on the petal. Place your hands on the lens, and simply twist the focus ring."

My breath hitches as I peer through the lens and see the flower yet again, with new eyes.

"It's magnificent."

"Now turn the lens a little bit more. See that right there? See the butterfly wings flapping against the petal of the flower? That right there . . . that's nature. Everything you will ever need to know you can learn from that. There's no pretending. That's beauty. That's life, Aria. That's everything." His words are profound and speak to something within me. They unravel me.

As we make our way further upward, the stone path becomes more and more weathered. It starts to feel untouched by man. Moss grows over the rocks, making it hard to walk, let alone climb. A bleak feeling tugs inside me. I can't do this. My heart pounds in my chest as we reach closer and closer to the top, to the end of our journey. Adrenaline courses through my veins, but I can't will my legs to move.

"I can't do this," I huff on a labored breath.

"No saying can't. There're no limitations in life, just limitations you place on yourself. You can do this. We're almost there. Only a few more steps. Forty-five seconds max. You can do anything for forty-five seconds."

"What if I fail?" I ask, but my question means so much more.

"Failure isn't the end. It's actually the beginning of your next try."

I continue to shake my head no. I'm almost delirious from exhaustion and nerves.

"You have to take a chance. The biggest risk you can take in life is not taking a chance at failing. You're strong, Aria. Dig deeper. You can do this. Find the beauty in the pain. The pain we feel helps mold us into the person we are meant to be." I want to throw a rock at him and all his self-help bullshit right now, but deep down I know he's right.

Drawing in a deep breath, I let my shoulders slump forward and let go of all my resistance.

Chase builds me up as I make forward progress. He replaces the void and fear inside me with hope, and he holds my hands as I cross over the boundaries I placed on myself.

I drop to my knees. My shaky hands run through my hair. *I did it.*

I turn toward Chase, and my eyes mist. I'm overwhelmed by the emotions swirling inside me.

"One day you will look back on this moment as the time you realized your life had changed." *Dear God, I hope so.*

"I want to capture this moment and hold on to this feeling forever."

"You should. Store it away and whenever you feel down, remember what you accomplished here. Moments like this pass, Aria. They pass as quickly as sand through an hourglass. Instead, embrace each precise second and cherish it forever." As I listen to his words, I rub my hands through the earth around me. Sand falls through the cracks of my fingers. The sadness I've been harboring flows through my veins, pulsing, searching for release. My feelings are divided between moving forward and staying tethered to the past. To Parker.

Breathy gasps leave my mouth. Confusion clouds my judgment. I rub my face to keep my mind clear. To enjoy this moment. To not falter. My dirt-covered hands are probably leaving streaks on my cheek. Tears fill my palms. I hear the snap of a camera, but I don't care. Everything I've been holding on to for the last few days comes pouring out of me.

A dam breaks.

A levee bursts.

And the flow has begun.

Chase pulls me into his arms

He comforts me, protects me. I'm ripped apart. I let it all seep out—the loss of Owen, of my childhood, of Parker.

He holds me with firm arms and doesn't ask any more questions. Never inquiring about what caused me to break apart, just continues to embrace me until my body stops shuddering and I'm empty. Until I cry so hard I laugh from the release. From the dizzying feeling of letting go.

As I pull away, Chase pinches his nose and his teeth gnaw on his lower lip.

"You okay?" His smile is hesitant but comforting, and I laugh.

"Sorry about that. I'm okay."

"It happens. The first time I climbed I had a similar reaction. It wasn't the largest mountain, but I reached the top, and the endorphins pumped through me. My eyes opened, and I saw the world in a different way, and I lost it. Cathartic release and all." He swipes a tear from under my right eye, and then he reaches for the camera around his neck.

"Don't move, okay?"

Snap

Snap

Snap

"What are you doing?"

"I've never seen you look so magnificent. You look almost ethereal." My heart thumps in my chest, and I look down to get my bearings.

Snap

Snap

"Hey, Princess. Let me look at your face. Wow, you really do look like an angel up there. It's insane. Like you're perched above the earth looking down. Don't move. I almost got the shot." His words make my soul take flight. At that moment, kneeling on the edge of the mountain, I'm weightless.

Free.

His hands find mine, and he pulls me up.

"Stand here, will you?" I scramble to my feet and make my way back beside him. I square my shoulders and turn my chin upward to the sky. My eyes flutter closed, and I nod.

Snap

Snap

I reopen them and turn to meet his gaze.

"I'm glad I'm here with you." I offer a smile. "Thank you

for making me do this."

"It's my pleasure."

"Why are you doing all of this for me?"

"I want to help you."

"But why?"

"Does there need to be a reason for me to want to help?"

"I'm not used to people being so selfless."

"I'm not completely selfless. You inspire me, and inspiration is imperative for a photographer."

"I'm not sure how I inspire you, but thanks—"

"Everything looks more brilliant with you in my life."

"Why? I'm nothing special, just ordinary old me."

"There's nothing ordinary about you, Princess. You are splashes of vibrant color on a monotone palate." My body heats as his gaze meets mine. I look away and out over the landscape of Ponza.

"When I look at the world like this, I wonder why? I look around, and I just want to know how I can live a more exceptional life. How can I make my life matter? God, Chase, I have no clue who I am. I don't even know why I'm here in Italy, in Ponza with you? I've no idea who I should be. I'm trying to find out . . . but I'm just so confused."

"There are no answers for those types of questions. I don't honestly know why things happen in life. I don't know why obstacles are placed in front of us. What I do know is that you have to persevere, take what life hands you, and believe there is a greater outcome."

"You keep saying stuff like that, but what the hell does that mean?"

"It means believe in more, Aria. The future is unseen. Right now, you barely exist. You need to learn how to live.

There's so much more intended for you."

"And how do you propose I do that?"

"Live in the moment."

"Yes, but how do I learn to live?"

"You throw yourself into the maddening unknown. Hell, we'll jump headfirst together." He grins and lifts me into his arms. "Let's learn to fly."

"Put me down." I laugh, kicking my legs until he lowers me back down.

"Seriously though, Aria. You'll figure out your path."

"Do you have a road map? Brilliant idea, maybe you can even tell me where this road leads?"

"Aria Bennett, you really are a sweet breath of air among all the crap." He throws back his head and chuckles. His laugh is deep and warm, and makes me feel all types of crazy things.

"Will this 'road' at least be easy?"

"Great things never start out easy." His eyes soften. Grow tender.

"What are you, like a life coach?" His expression stills at my question, and then he nods.

"Yes, I do like to help people."

"Do you think you're going to help me?" I watch his face closely for his answer.

"I'd like to." And he does. It's written perfectly across the lines forming on his flawless face.

"Do you have any glue?" I tease, hoping to lighten the mood.

"What?" His eyebrows rise, causing a frown to set in his features.

"That might be an easier way for you to help put me back together." I smirk.

He laughs, and it's the most beautiful sound I've ever heard.

"Seriously, Chase, I'm not a pet project for you to fix. You can't just take glue and put me back together."

"I can't guarantee it, but I can sure have fun trying. Okay, enough of this profound shit. Want to eat?" He cocks an eyebrow at me.

"Sure, I would love to. I'm starved."

"Come over here," I make my way to him. From where we are now perched it's as if we're sitting on the edge of the world. No one around but us, no sounds but nature.

"Look what I have here. Prosciutto, cherry tomatoes, mozzarella and lots of ice cold—okay, warm wine." He laughs.

"Oh my God, you walked all the way up here with all that in your backpack?"

"It's nothing. Seriously, I climbed Makalu, Everest and Mount Kilimanjaro. Walking up this hill with a little food is like walking down the road for me.

"You don't have to be such a show-off." I roll my eyes at him.

He smirks, and all is right in my world.

"This is wonderful, Chase, and absolutely perfect."

"These are the moments, this view . . . look around you. You just have to be happy in the moment." His chest rises and falls with his breathing. Standing here, I understand why Chase loves this place so much. I understand why people go out of their way to discover it. We sit down in silence, and this time it's peaceful rather than jarring. I stare out into the distance and admire the flat clouds blanketing the sun from above. Everyday concerns blow away with each peaceful gust of wind.

Time stands still as we sit here. Minutes pass, but they are irrelevant. Time is irrelevant. All that matters is the right here, the right now.

"How about you take a few pictures. Here, try." He holds the camera out to me. His gaze locks on mine for what seems like an eternity. My breathing becomes ragged, and I run my fingers through my hair, pulling at my scalp. My vision drifts away from him, and I look up at the sky.

"I don't know what I'm doing."

It was a simple statement for the moment but held more meaning. He nods in understanding. This is why it's easy to be with Chase. He understands me. He knows just what to say to make me laugh, to calm me.

"Let me help you. Point the camera on what you want to focus on, like I showed you when we were climbing up here. Once you picked an image turn the focusing ring. When it starts to highlight and sharpen, you capture the image. There is no right or wrong. That's the beauty of art. Just take pictures, and together we'll see what we can make of it."

"Okay." I pull the camera toward me and focus it like he told me. I focus out into the distance.

"So, you've been shooting all your life, but you never told me what made you pick up a camera."

"I was very rebellious growing up. I used to get in all sorts of trouble. One time I got caught shoplifting from a grocery store near our apartment. My parents were shocked. It wasn't like we needed the money. Quite the contrary, actually. They sent me to a psychologist. I was always very artistic, always had an eye for beauty. When the therapist suggested I pick up a hobby—that I needed an outlet for my rebellion—they bought me a camera. My first. They encouraged me to always have it on me. I shot everything. Everyone. I went to college and tried to hone my craft, but truth be told, halfway through freshman year, I couldn't stand being in one place. I felt locked up, so I left. Dropped out."

"What did you do? What did your parents say?"

"At first my parents were pissed. Royally pissed. But in the end, they let me. Money was never an issue. I had my trust that kicked in when I turned eighteen. I didn't really need their permission." He raises his hands and runs them through his hair as he speaks.

"Where did you go?"

"I think the better question is where didn't I go. I went everywhere. I learned how to climb. I traveled the world, and I shot pictures of everything. I realized that the life they wanted for me wasn't what was intended for me. Traveling and sharing the beauty, that's what my life was meant to be."

"Wow, Chase. That's amazing."

"Thanks." I stare at him as he answers. He seems proud, and it makes me wish I could do something I loved that would make me feel proud, too.

"Will you do me a favor and stand perfectly still?"

"Why?"

"Will you just trust me already? You're going to like this." He laughs, and then his expression grows more serious.

He places the camera in the crook of my neck. My fingers begin to tremble as his breath tickles my neck. It's like a soft whisper. My lips part. His heart beats against my back. The steady cadence only makes mine pick up. *What is he doing?*

Snap

Snap

"What are you doing?"

"Taking a picture, of course."

"I can hear you taking a picture, but why and of what?" I attempt to keep my head perfectly still so I don't bump the camera sitting in the groove between my neck and my right shoulder.

"The view from up top, and I'm taking it this way—" He stops and seems to be thinking through his answer, but all he gives me is a simple, "Because I can."

"You're taking it from my neck, because you can?"

"Yup, from your neck . . . because I can." I furrow my brows. Sometimes he's so weird. But he makes me feel things I haven't felt in a long time.

He makes me believe in more.

He makes me believe in hope.

When he's around a calm falls over me. He gives me peace.

Lord.

This man . . . he's dangerous to me.

He makes me feel alive.

As if reading my thoughts again, he pulls away, and our eyes lock. The camera dislodges from my neck. Our breaths come in tandem. Our faces are so close I can smell the light peppermint from the gum he's chewing. His hand pulls a strand of hair that has fallen forward. As he twists it in his fingertips, his pupils dilate, and he leans forward. His lips begin to descend toward mine. But all I see is Parker. He surrounds me. His words fill me.

"Chase, I can't. There's someone—" I stutter, but stop myself before I say any more. His head jerks back. My words seem to slice through him. His eyes flash. Sadness radiates off him. I don't know why I said that. But being with him—although it feels right—feels as though I'm hurting Parker. As much as I want to move on, Parker is rooted in my memory.

Chase's eyes have darkened at my words. His face has turned pale. I swear I even feel frost blowing through him. A moment later, a pained look that I can't comprehend crosses his face. Anguish? His eyes appear to glass as he steps away from me, leaving me chilled from his absence. It makes no sense. He barely knows me. Why is he so hurt?

The silence stretches as the seconds pass. He squints, and his lips purse. His whole attention is focused on me. His mouth opens to speak, but hangs open as if searching for the right words to say. Nothing comes out. He just shakes his head, turns and kneels on the dirt. I see him refocus his camera and begin to shoot again. *What just happened?* This is more than rejection. The thought makes my legs tremble, and I'm not sure how to fix it or fix him. My heart sinks knowing that I might have hurt him.

About thirty minutes later, Chase walks back to where I'm sitting on the grass. His face is still tight. Looking at him makes my heart wrench. It was never my intention to hurt him. I need to talk to him, I need to explain why I pulled away.

"Chase." My voice is low. When he doesn't turn, I wonder if he can hear me.

"Chase, can I talk to you for a second?" I twist the small gold band around my right ring finger.

"Yeah." He turns toward me, his bottom lip caught between his teeth.

"I just wanted to—"

"No need. I was wrong to do that." I step closer, his face near mine. His deep breaths gently tickle my cheek.

"It's not that I don't want to. I just—"

"It's really not a big deal." He turns and squats. He lifts his camera to his eye, but I can't miss the hurt and sadness still present in his gaze. I inhale and breathe through the pain of knowing I put that sadness there.

Toxic.

I cross my arms in front of my body.

Always toxic.

Staring across the distance, I see a damask rose. *A touch of pink. A splash of white.* Words I wrote so long ago to describe a similar flower. Feels like just yesterday when I used to write poetry.

What the hell is this?" she asked in slurred words. "My castle in the sky." Her voice was taunting. The words came out lazy and jumbled, blending together. Her speech is obviously impaired as she crumpled the paper I spent hours working on. The paper that held a piece of my bleeding soul. She threw it into the trash and stumbled out of the room. Retrieving it, I held it in my little fingers as I heard a knock at the door and the sound of the door opening. Delia my housekeeper greeted the guest and I heard the familiar sound of Park's voice as he thanked her and entered the room.

"What you got there, baby girl?"

"Nothing." My lip quivers as I stepped back to put some distance between his question and me.

"Let me see." His hand reached out, and I crossed my arms in defiance.

"No."

"Come on, Ari. You have no secrets from me, right?" I let out a sigh and handed him the paper. As he unwadded the ball that my mom had formed, the noise scratched at my ears. The sound was almost deafening as I waited for his response.

"Did you write this?" He cupped my face in his hands. *"Don't ever stop. Okay, Ari?"*

"Okay, Parker."

Lifting my long waves up into a knot, I secure it on top of my head, and then tuck the loose strands behind my ears. A breeze tickles my neck, making my whole body shudder.

"Hey," I hear from behind me. Sighing deeply, I turn my body to face him, and my arms fall to my side when I see a smile line his face. Whatever was eating at him before has passed. I can't stand having any distance between us, and I'm ecstatic to see he has let it go.

As the day draws to a close, I notice Chase glance down at his watch.

"It's time, Aria. We're heading to the island of Ischia tonight so we can make port. Luciano is expecting us before sundown. We really need to head back."

As we make our way back down the mountain, I watch as the sun meets the horizon, bright vibrant colors spreading across the ocean in front of us.

Dear Park,

What an adventure my life has turned into. You'd be so proud. Not only did I take your advice, but also I do believe I've excelled at it. Today was extraordinary. For the first time in forever, I didn't let my fear take over. Today I climbed to the top of a mountain. Or, as Chase called it, a large hill. It was a mountain in my mind, and I conquered it. I can't tell you the feelings I had when I made it to the top. I felt like I could conquer the world! I owe that to you and Chase. You'd like Chase. He really has opened my eyes. He makes me see that I can hope for more. He kind of reminds me of you.

Miss you more than you know,
Ari.

I lay the postcard down and look over the words I wrote. "You'd be so proud." He would be, and it reminds me of the last time I did something to make Parker proud of me.

"I'm so proud of you, Ari." Joy radiated off me as my face lit up brighter than the rising sun seeing Parker standing there. He stepped closer and placed one hand on my back. His finger began to trace circles. My lashes fluttered as I looked into his crystal blue eyes, hoping to find what I was looking for. Praying his eyes reflected what I felt. Love. But all I saw was friendship. I felt my shoulders tighten at the revelation.

"Owen would be really proud of you, too," he said as he handed me back the diploma. My eyes softened. "You think?"

"I know."

The memory brings about feelings I've held back for a long time. Confusion filters through me, but I shake it away as I realize that something seemingly impossible has occurred. I went on this trip for Parker, but now I want to do this for myself. I realize how much Chase has impacted my life in such a short time. It's been so gradual, I hardly realized the difference until now. But reading back my words, one thing has become apparent.

Chase Porter is breathing new life into me.

CHAPTER TEN

Thirty-five days since I spoke to Parker
Seven days since I met Chase

YESTERDAY WAS A turning point for me. Standing on the summit of the mountain opened my eyes to everything Parker had been trying to say to me all those days ago. As much as I wish he were here with me, deep down I know this journey can only be taken with Chase. There's something about him that's comforting, refreshing, and familiar. He reminds me a lot of Parker, just a little more spiritual. He makes me see this huge, magnificent picture that I was blind to before him.

I awaken this morning feeling happy and excited to see where the day will take me. This is a new feeling. My heart pounds with excitement. I can't stop thinking of the way Chase looks at me. The way his hands feel when he touches me, and how special he makes me feel.

Last night we dropped anchor off the island of Ischia. Only a few miles off the coast of Italy, it was a secluded paradise—the secret gem of the Amalfi Coast. Hidden away and only accessible by private boat.

A tiny beam of sunlight peeks in through the portal in my cabin. I smile. A true, honest to God smile. After stretching my arms and yawning to dispel the morning sleep still harboring inside me, I have to 'hit the head' and then freshen up. Looking at myself in the mirror, I stare in horror and laugh. Chase can*not* see me like this. Since when do I care what Chase thinks of how I look? And in that moment, I realize I do care. I care a lot, and although that feeling originally scared me, it doesn't scare me now. It excites me. My cheeks turn a soft shade of crimson. *I have a big crush on Chase Porter.*

I make my way into the salon and find Chase reclined on the white sofa, his head resting against the pillow. His eyes are closed. I cough once to signal my presence, and when his eyes catch mine, they sparkle so brightly they take my breath away.

"Hi." It was almost a whisper.

"Hey, you're up early." His lips part so broadly, it melts me. Good to know I'm not alone in my excitement.

"The sun was streaming in and woke me."

"That will happen. Do you want me to make you some breakfast?"

"You don't have to do that."

"I know I don't have to, but I still want to."

"But your food is poison." I wink.

"I don't think it's too hard to splatter a little Nutella on a piece of toast."

"In that case, I would love some."

"Okay, great. Let's go." He stands and brushes a single kiss against my forehead, then takes my hand in his and leads me into the galley. Goosebumps form across my arms, my body responding immediately to the gentle kiss and my hand being enclosed in his.

I watch from the table as Chase prepares my breakfast. His long, lean body works in precision as if he's creating a masterpiece. As I sit there and stare, I'm hungry— ravenous—but not for food. In such a short period of time I went from wanting to keep him at a distance to seeking him out every day constantly. I hunger to know more about him. The need to know everything grows immensely inside me. Every time we speak, I feel as though he's helping me not only unlock another piece of the puzzle of who he is, but also of who I am and who I want to be. My eyes trail his movements. I once thought that guilt would consume me for having these feelings. That I shouldn't want him. But that's not how I feel at all.

He leans forward, and I suck in air as his finger lifts to swipe away Nutella that has collected on my lip. His hand slowly falls away from my face and I watch as his fingers trace his lips. My breathing stops.

"You're delicious." His gaze rakes my body and smolders like two burning embers.

My body heats.

My heart pounds.

I want to lunge for him.

I want to kiss him.

He looks at me, and everything becomes clear. The curtain has been lifted. He wants this as badly as I do.

So why don't I jump into his arms and make him consume me? Because I don't deserve this. I don't deserve him. If I let him in . . . I'll crush him.

Just like I did Parker.

No. I won't go there again. I can't hurt anyone else. This

is the only way.

Nothing can happen.

I tell myself this, but not one part of me believes it.

We step out on deck, and the morning air is chilly on my skin. My arms instinctively wrap around myself and are then replaced by two strong and firm ones. I peer up to find Chase looking down at me. His arms enclose me.

"Want me to grab you a sweater?" I shake my head.

"I'll be okay, plus I have you to keep me warm." My eyebrow rises suggestively. *Where the hell did that come from?*

"That you do. That you do." His hands slide up and down my arms, causing the friction to warm my body further. My breaths of the cool air become short and shallow. I will myself to calm at his close proximity. My visceral reaction tells me to run. Run far and run fast. Instead, I continue to breathe through the panic.

"What's the plan today?" I ask as his soft fingers make circles across my forearm.

"I made arrangements to go to a local vineyard, followed by the best lunch you will ever eat. You ready to see this island?"

"Sounds fun. Thanks for doing all this. For planning everything."

"It's really my pleasure." His eyes focus on the water, and I watch him. Take him in. He's so beautiful it makes me lose focus on everything but him. What's really beautiful about Chase is not just his looks but also everything else that makes up the man who stands before me. As if he senses me staring, he turns his head and smiles down at me. A knowing smile. A smirk. Then he turns back and continues to stare into the dark abyss gently lapping below us, once more consumed by his own thoughts.

We arrive at the private vineyard a little after eleven. Stepping out of the cab, I walk toward the wrought iron gates.

"A bit early to drink." I look up at Chase, and with a tip of his head, he motions for me to enter the courtyard.

"Never too early to get a bit frisky." He offers me a devastating smile. Even the white of his teeth dazzles me. I'm sure he can hear my sudden intake of breath as a devilish look creeps into his eyes. Something is brewing between us. I sense it in every look, in every touch, and I no longer know if I have the strength to stop it.

"Want to sit down over here?" He points to a table overlooking the vines. Tilting my head up, I peer at him and nod then turn away, taking in my surroundings. Lush green, rolling hills, and olive groves fan the property. It stretches out like a quilt of green and gold, a pattern so intricate and beautiful it takes my breath away. The sun is radiant in the distance. The perfect backdrop to an afternoon drink. Just then, a woman with wavy red hair strides through the courtyard toward us. Her fiery locks float in the wind. When she arrives at our table, she gives us a casual nod and pours two glasses of a light wine. I lift the glass to my mouth for a sip. It's fruity and refreshing. The smell is heavenly.

Chase leans back into his chair, sipping the liquid contentedly. I turn my attention back to the sommelier that's offering us an explanation of the wine we are tasting in broken English. She rustles her hands through the unusual layers of her dress. Blood red tulle flaps lightly against neon yellow silk. "I shall get some light snacks. If you need anything, I'm Pia."

"Thank you, Pia. This is Chase, and I'm Aria."

"How beautiful, Aria. It's very fitting." She makes a slight gesture toward me before placing the bottle down on the table.

"Yes, it is," Chase, agrees as his eyes find mine. I raise my brow at him in question.

"Your name—Aria—in Italian, means air. Look at you. You're like a beautiful, refreshing breeze that I know will pass shortly." *If he only knew how accurate his words were.*

As we sit in the vineyard sipping glasses of Pinot Grigio, Chase decides it's a perfect time to play our game again, offering up twenty questions. I wasn't aware this was 'our game,' but I go with it since I love the idea of finding out everything about him.

"Favorite movie?" Chase asks first, kicking off the game.

"*Heathers?*" I reply.

"I can see that. You are totally the type." His eyes gleam with mischief.

"Are you saying I'm crazy?" My eyes narrow, but I can't stop my lips from betraying me and turning up into a smile.

"No, just the dark, brooding type." He laughs.

"Whatever. I'm so not. What about you? Let me guess. *The Godfather?*"

"Think I'm that predicable? For your information my favorite is *Field Of Dreams*."

"Of course it is. I forgot you're existential and shit. Okay. My turn. Favorite singer?" I stick out my neck and mock him.

"Ol' Blue Eyes."

"God, really? Who are you, a seventy-year-old man?"

"Princess, I can promise you I'm not." His eyes light up as he raises an eyebrow at me. I shake my head and roll my eyes. "Okay, there, killer. Next."

"No, you go first."

"Fine. Adele."

"Hmmm. First Date?"

I'm frozen in place knowing I need to answer, but a memory flashes through my mind from a few years back.

If crying were a job, I would win the award for best employee after I sat on the front steps of my house with tears streaming down my face.

"Hi, baby girl." If I could die of mortification that would be the moment when it happened. Of course, he was there.

"What are you doing here?" I choked through my sobs.

"I called the house to see if you were home, and your mom said you were sitting outside. What happened?" I peeked up at him. My hair covered most of my face, but his soft fingers pushed the stray, limp strands back.

"I don't want to talk about it."

"Oh, come on. You know you can tell me anything." His hand cupped my face, and I relaxed into him.

"He never showed," I whispered, my eyes locked on his.

"Who?"

"Dave. At school he said he would come over to watch a movie. He never showed," I stammered.

"Shhh, Shhh. You're okay. I'm here now. I got you." And I knew he did. He always did. "You're too young to date anyway. God, Ari. You're only fourteen."

"I'm not a kid, okay?" I snapped at him. God, why couldn't

he see that? If only he did, I wouldn't be here crying. He wouldn't be comforting me about another guy. I would be his. But that wasn't in the cards for us. I blinked my eyes a few times to stop more tears from falling.

"I know, I know. Shit, Ari, you got to stop crying. You're killing me, and now I'm going to have to kill him. What's his last name?" I pulled away from him and crossed my arms at my chest.

"You will do no such thing, Park. God, I would die of embarrassment. Please don't do anything. I don't want anyone at school to know."

"I don't know, Ari. I kind of think I have to. One day I'll see Owen up above, and he might not let me enter the pearly gates if I don't kill this douche bag." I laugh.

"There she is. There's my favorite girl." He smiled broadly. "Good to have you back, baby girl. Get up. Let's go watch this movie you were supposed to see."

I shake my head as I pull myself out of my memories.

"Umm. No, too embarrassing to admit. Next."

"Okay, fine. First time?" He crosses one leg over the other and reclines back, waiting for my response.

"I'm so not telling you that." I shake my head adamantly.

"You suck."

"You wish," I joke back, but he's no longer laughing. His pupils have dilated, and his breathing has become shallow. "Fine twenty. Another glass—" I stutter, and he lets out a soft laugh, never breaking our connection. "Your turn in the hot seat," I lift the almost empty glass to my mouth to conceal the sheepish smile playing on my lips.

"Ask me anything you want." He straightens his shoulders

and cracks his knuckles preparing himself. He's such an ass.

"Okay. First time?" I say, raising an eyebrow.

"Sixteen." He looks proud as I murmur 'player' under my breath.

"Don't hate the player, hate the game." He's such a dork. "Since you won't tell me your first time, how about your craziest sex location?" My whole face warms.

"Cab," I mutter under my breath.

"No shit, Princess. I didn't see that coming. Your turn."

I eye him with a calculated expression, and then ask, "Ever had a torrid love affair?"

"A few times."

"Last one?" I try to keep my response composed and indifferent.

"Last summer." My heartbeat accelerates with his answer. *Last summer?*

"Name?"

"Maria." Oh God, she's Italian. She's probably gorgeous with olive skin and green eyes and had—*Why do I even care?* Because I do, and that in itself is troubling and should send up red flags that I'm out of my depth.

Hours later, and with a healthy buzz, we find ourselves in a white terra cotta building set above the rest of the city. The restaurant sits atop a bluff with a view of the blue sea breaking against the jagged rocks below. The panoramic view of the harbor is breathtaking.

The family run establishment is well known for its delicious local recipes and welcoming environment. It has a peaceful feel and gives me a sense of tranquility when I walk in and take a seat at a table nestled in the corner overlooking the ocean. Although Chase says it typically draws in a larger crowd, it's quiet this time of day.

Suddenly from out of nowhere, the waiter theatrically appears with a steaming platter of prawns sautéed with garlic, parsley, and a dash of fiery pepperoncino. We are served as our glass flutes are filled with Prosecco. As the next dish arrives, so does the entertainment. From across the room the entire staff is now walking toward us. They circle around the table. Each is holding a different instrument, and all are encouraging us to sing along. After the amount of sparkling wine I've consumed, I'm happy to oblige.

I jump to my feet and onto my chair and swing my hands in the air to the Italian music serenading us. Chase walks around the table to me, places his hand under my arms, and lifts me from the seat. Our bodies sway together, our chests touching as he brings me to dance with him. Our bodies rhythmically move to the music. Our hips brush as his arms enclose me in his. I feel the warmth of his body. His fingers lift my chin, turning my face toward his.

I lose myself in his steely eyes as he stares at me intently with desire.

My immediate reaction is a loss of all thought and necessity. A strange feeling weaves its way through me as he continues to move closer.

Need.

I need his touch.

I need his lips.

Most importantly, I need him.

If he doesn't touch me, I might explode.

Drunk off emotion and desire, I thread my hands around his neck.

His lips hover over mine. His breath lightly brushes against my mouth. I close the distance. Pressing my lips firmly against his, I place the softest kiss.

"What the hell was that?" He smirks.

"You looked like you wanted a kiss," I whisper. Now I'm unsure whether I made the right decision.

"That wasn't a kiss. There wasn't even a spark." My eyes widen at his words, then begin to mist. I'm so embarrassed. I can't be rejected again. My heart can't handle it. My brain begins searching for the memory buried so deep.

A painful memory. It rushes at me. Sadness engulfs me.

Parker. I loved him, wanted him. And he rejected me.

I leaned forward and placed my lips gently on his. Softly coaxing his open, I feel his lips feathering across my own until he jerks away.

"What are you doing, Ari?"

"I just thought—"

"I can't, Ari. You're Owen's kid sister. I just can't."

Slowly the fog lifts. I look up before a tear can be shed.

"You don't want a kiss?" I stumble over my words, trying not to break down. I can't take another rejection. His gaze locks on me. I feel as if he's looking into my soul.

"No, Princess. I do want a kiss, and not just a kiss that has a spark. I want a kiss that will light the night on fire," he says in a gravelly voice filled with desire. He leans down, placing a soft kiss on my lips. He nips on my lower lip, causing my mouth to part, then his tongue sweeps against mine. Electric currents shoot down my body, and I tremble. "How was that for a spark?" he asks. Our mouths are still touching. His breath tickles my lips.

"It was perfect." As the words leave my mouth he grabs me by the back of my head, presses us even closer together, and kisses me again. He kisses me with a passion I didn't even know was possible. We move together in perfect sync as our lips touch. His fingers trail through my hair, pulling gently. Each caress of his soft lips makes me warm on the inside.

Each touch of his lips makes me feel whole. Like the pieces of me that are broken aren't that bad.

This kiss terrifies me. My need for him scares the shit out of me, but as he continues his assault on me, my worries fade away.

Because when I'm with him . . .

I forget anyone else exists.

I forget that the world exists.

I forget that I exist.

"You banish the darkness," I whisper.

He pulls back. His eyes bore into me, and I lose myself in his gaze once more.

CHAPTER ELEVEN

Thirty-six days since I spoke to Parker
Eight days since I met Chase

WAKE TO A sweet aroma filling the boat. When I find Chase, his eyes sparkle when he smiles at me from across the galley. His long strides eat up the distance as he makes his way to directly in front of me, then leans down to place a soft kiss on my lips. My cheeks warm.

"Morning." He kisses me again. My lips turn up against his, and my cheeks heat with what must be a crimson blush.

"Morning."

"What should we do today?" His voice sounds husky.

"Anything," I whisper against his mouth as I lean in and kiss him again. Now that I've had a taste, I hunger for him and can't get enough.

"Anything? Is that so?" A huge grin spreads across his face.

"Oh, shut it." Giggles begin to escape but are quickly cut off by him descending yet again. His mouth moves leisurely, savoring every delicious taste. He catches my bottom lip in his and sucks before pulling away and leaving me breathless. A whimper escapes my mouth as he pulls his body from mine and reaches for a coffee cup.

"Here, sit. I was just making you breakfast."

"I could get used to this."

"Good, that was the plan."

"What are you making? What was the wonderful smell that woke me up?"

"French toast. It smells ridiculous, right?"

"I'm so confused. You went from not cooking to making French toast?"

"It might smell good, but it could suck for all you know."

"Like anything you do could suck?" He raises his eyebrows. "Knock it off, Chase," I laugh at him before he can even speak.

"It will be ready in about five minutes, so I guess only time will tell."

"How did you even learn to make French toast?"

"Google."

"There's Internet on this boat?"

"You've been on this boat for days. How did you not know that?"

"I, um. I haven't checked."

"Wow, I can't believe that. I do so much of my business on Instagram, I couldn't imagine not checking."

"You'd be surprised how easy it is when you have no one waiting to hear from you." Silence descends upon us like the mist on a hazy day.

It stretches between sips of coffee, until it's almost deafening.

"What about your parents?"

I reach across the table and pour myself another cup. "When will breakfast be ready?"

"Why do you do that?" He asks, as I add sugar to my cup.

"Do what?"

"Change the topic when I mention your family?"

"Because they aren't good people."

"They can't be too awful if they created you."

"They're assholes. She's an alcoholic, and he's an enabler. He's a handsome man who doesn't give two shits about anyone but himself and his precious empire, and she's a beautiful woman who used to be a model, but now is a shell. Years of drinking have robbed her of her beauty, but if you ask her, I robbed her."

"Do you think she will ever get better?"

"Yeah, she will get better. Every month when she goes to her spa, she gets better. But then she comes back and bam, she hits the bottle again. In truth, she will be a drunk until she dies."

"And your dad?"

"He's almost worse than her. She drinks and lashes out, but he just forgets I'm there."

"How do you cope with that?"

Tears.

Lots and lots of tears

Parker.

"It's all your fault. You should be dead. You're not Owen. Owen was everything and you? You're nothing," she shrieked.

Tears streamed down my face as her drunken breath slapped at my cheeks. I didn't know what to say to make her understand. *To make her forgive me, so I just cried out,* "*I'm sorry. I'm so sorry.*"

"*You're sorry? You're sorry? It's too late for sorry. He was my baby. And now he's nothing, and I'm left with you. She stormed out of the room, and I picked up the house phone.*

"*Can I come over?*"

"*You don't ever need to ask.*" *Sobs wracked my body*

"*Are you okay, Ari?*"

"*No, but I will be once I come over.*" *Once I run from this hell.*

"My friend, he helped me." Feeling the familiar tightening of my chest when I think of Parker, I steadied my breath and took a sip of my coffee. "How about some grub?"

I change the topic, and this time he lets me.

A few minutes later, I lower my cup to the table and peer over at Chase. He's lost in his own thoughts. The timer on the oven comes to life, awakening us from the fog. Chase hops up, slides the kitchen gloves on his hands, and removes the tray.

"Grab us two plates?" he asks, motioning over to the cabinets.

"Isn't Luciano going to join us?"

"He's already off the boat running errands." He places the tray down and turns back toward me.

"For a boat so small, I've yet to see him more than five minutes. What's up with that?"

"I might have asked him to give us some space." I feel like my eyes pop out of my head with what he just said.

"Why would you do that, Chase? Oh my God. He must think I'm the biggest bitch."

"No, trust me, he doesn't. You were just so nervous about

being on the boat with two men, I thought this would be easier."

"No ulterior motives?" My eyes squint at him as he leans forward. Our lips touch again. The touch of his mouth brings on a smile.

"Believe it or not, no. No ulterior motives in this case." I pull back and stare deeply into his eyes. I believe him. I just don't know what that means for us.

"How do you see this playing out?"

"Like all good stories do. The climax has to come to the forefront."

"I like who I am when I'm around you, Chase."

"I like who you are all the time." Warmth flushes across my face.

Enamored.

Happy.

Before Chase, my walls were built high. No one but Parker had ever broken through. *Not so much anymore.* Can Chase Porter see the cracks he's causing?

That he has rocked me to my core?

"Good?" he asks as I take a bite of my French toast.

"Absolutely, positively, delicious!"

"Only the best for you, Princess." He winks.

After I'm done eating, I step away from the table and place my dishes in the sink.

"What time are we heading out?" I ask over my shoulder.

"We should probably leave for Capri after lunch. That way we can see some sights and have dinner there."

"Sounds great. I just want to head into town today and mail a postcard."

"Do you want me to come with?" He steps up behind me,

placing his plate in the sink. I can feel his warmth emanate off his body.

"You can come, but if you're busy, I'm fine going alone."

"I would love to come." Relief rushes over me, and I grin.

"Great. I'll just freshen up."

"I'll be up on deck. Find me when you're ready to go."

I walk to my cabin and sift through my bag for my lip-gloss. My fingers come across my phone.

I promised I would check in with Sophie. Now is as good a time as ever.

After powering up the phone, I wait for it to find a signal. As soon as it connects, it instantly starts beeping, and I groan. Text after text comes in.

Sophie: Did you make it?

Dad: Is there a reason you are not in your office?

Sophie: Please respond

I look at the time stamp and it was from my first day. I could only imagine how many more texts there were from her

Mom: You are a disappointment

One a.m. New York time. Obviously, she was drunk. I couldn't deal with my mom, but the right thing to do was let my dad know I wasn't coming in before I continue to read any more texts.

Me: Dad, I need some time to decide if working for you is the right fit for me. I'm sorry I'm such a disappointment to you and Mom, but I need to do what's best for me.

Parker would be proud, and that makes me smile.

Sophie: Okay, I'm freaking out.

Sophie: I called the hotel you mentioned in Tuscany, so I know you checked in. No thanks to you.

Sophie: Okay, seriously! It's been days. You promised.

Oh, shit. I really need to let her know I'm okay. I quickly type out a message and hit send.

Me: *Hi Soph, I'm fine. I'm so sorry for making you worry. It's actually been quite an adventure. I know you don't agree, but this was the right decision. Love you, will check back soon.*

I switch my phone back off and pull out the postcard I wrote earlier this morning.

> **Hey Park,**
>
> **It's hard to admit this to you, but we have always been honest with each other, even when it hurt. I met someone. Yeah, I know you know this and I know you know we are traveling together, but I think this could be more. I wish you were here to talk things out with me the way you always do. I guess I will just have to trust that over the years some of your genius has rubbed off on me.**
>
> **Love and miss you,**
> **Ari**

I hold my breath. Excitement courses through me as I take in my surroundings. The Blue Grotto. The infamous cave looms in front of me.

"What are we doing here?" I say in awe as Chase's arms wrap around me from behind.

"Want to take a dip?" His mouth tickles the back of my neck. I feel the warmth from his lips as he speaks.

"What?" I say, perplexed. He couldn't possibly have said

what I think he did.

"Take a dip. Go for a swim. Get in the water."

"I know what you mean. Stop fooling around. We aren't going in, obviously. Is it even allowed? Plus, I'm not wearing a bathing suit." I thank my lucky stars that I can clearly see the sign banning entry on top of the cliff.

"If you mean is it illegal and dangerous? Then, yes. It closed hours ago. But come on, it will be fun. Plus, you can always go naked. I don't have a suit on, either." I feel the curve of a smile form against my skin.

"I—" My heart starts to pound. Invisible walls start closing in. I can't get in the water. I can't.

"What's wrong?"

"I . . . I don't know. I don't think I can, Chase. I . . . I haven't been in the ocean since Owen's death." My shoulders collapse forward. A lone tear trails down my cheek.

"Oh, God, I'm so sorry. I— Shit. I fucked up." He steps out from behind me. His face is ashen. Ragged breaths escape his lungs.

"I'll be with you. I won't let anything happen to you. We'll do this together. What can I do to help you?"

"God, I don't know what to do."

"Do you think it will make you feel better to talk about him, about what happened?"

I feel as if I'm about to be sick. I don't want to go back. I don't want to remember.

"It might help you heal if you talk about it," he replies in a gentle voice.

I'm floating in a sea of despair and I'm about to drown.

I'm completely overwhelmed by fear. My eyes are blinded by the tears pouring out as the grief surges through me every time I try to breathe. The emptiness in my heart from reliving this memory threatens to suffocate me. I shake as I look at the water. My teeth rattle in my mouth.

"Shh, don't hide from your fears. Conquer them. Be present, be here. We can do this together." I stare at him through swollen eyes. Where had I heard that before?

"What did you just say?"

"You can't hide from your fears, Princess. You can't stop living."

"I stopped living years ago. I've barely existed since Owen passed. I fucked up. It was my fuck-up that killed him. I hurt everyone around me."

"No matter what happened, you can change things. Live, fuck up. The only thing that's important is that you learned from those mistakes and continue to move forward."

The painful memories of Owen's death hum within me. I want to scream that I'm not ready for this. Soon, the white noise fades as Chase holds me close. He looks at me, and our eyes meet, and I'm rendered speechless.

He silences my world. The craziness in my brain stops.

Peace.

"Lean on me, okay? Once we get in the water, I got you. I won't let you go."

"This isn't easy for me."

"I know."

"I'm not used to feeling this lost. I don't want to need anyone. But I need you. That used to scare me. But well, I'm not afraid of that anymore. I know you won't let anything happen to me." His eyes light up brighter as I speak. His lip turns upward.

"You'll do this with me?" he asks.

"Just give me a minute, okay?" I inhale deeply and hold the breath in my lungs.

"Breathe," he commands in a playful voice.

"It hurts to breathe," I whisper back without letting out the breath I'm holding.

"Take it one step at a time. Just inhale." My chest rises as I suck in the salty air. "Exhale." And I do.

"Okay, what do I need to do?"

"I'm proud of you."

"Just tell me before I freak out again."

"Since it's late in the afternoon the waves are higher than normal. You'll have to swim underwater right at the mouth of the cave, okay?" My heart rate picks up at his words.

"I have to swim under?"

"Yeah, but I got you." He looks down at me, and I know he does.

A crazy notion filters through me. Trust. Quickly, before I have time to change my mind, I strip off my clothes and stand before him in only my bra and panties. He pulls off his shirt and leaves his shorts on. Holding hands, we step toward the back of the boat, directly in front of the mouth of the Blue Grotto.

"I can't, Chase."

"You can. Repeat after me, I intend to conquer my fears."

"I intend to conquer my fears."

"Okay, on three. One . . . Two . . . Three . . . Jump!" And we do. The wind is knocked out of me as my body connects with the frigid water. It feels like tiny needles as my body adjusts to the sudden drop in temperature. Once the shock wears off, I kick my legs, and we swim toward the opening. The gap to the low mouth of the cave is already small, and with each minute that passes it shrinks further as the tide rises.

"Hold my hand. Swim underwater with me." I follow his lead and make my way into the cave. When I pop up on the other side, a bright azure reflection surrounds us.

"It's beautiful, Chase. How does it look like this?" I'm treading water, my chest bobbing with the ebb and flow of the tide.

"It happens because of the sun. The sunlight enters the cavern through an underwater opening. Then the light reflects off the cavern walls."

"It's unbelievable." My eyes widen in delight.

I look back at the opening where beams of sunlight pass through, illuminating the seawater. It's truly spectacular. I feel my mouth pull up at the corners. I've done it. Once more I pushed passed my resistance and accomplished something I never believed possible.

"Thank you, Chase."

He swims closer, and I wrap my arms around him, allowing him briefly to kick for me. To support my weight. I give him my full trust.

"Thank you," I say against his lips. I offer a series of soft kisses as he treads water.

"Anything for you. Anything." The happiness, like the azure blue water surrounding me, soaks into my soul.

"Aria, we should swim back. The tide is rising fast, and I don't want you to hit your head on the rocks when we leave." I hold his hand as we kick toward the entrance. He smiles and encourages me to dive deep. When I resurface in the open water, a laugh escapes my body. Chase leads me back toward the boat.

We swim a short distance before we reach the ladder. His

arm snakes around my waist, pushing me forward. I grab the railing and turn to face him, my legs wrapping instinctively around him. His hands tighten around me, skimming over my hips. Pressing our bodies together, I entwine my arms around his neck. Hidden emotions bubble to the surface. God, I want him. My lips part, and his mouth rushes to meet mine. His tongue seeks entry and my skin pebbles. A chill runs down my spine. The only sound in my ears is the waves lapping against the boat. My heart pounds so erratically I feel it might burst. Chase nips at my lip and pulls away. A moan escapes me. Kissing Chase is exquisite torture.

"You're driving me insane." The words sound sultry and he laughs. The tone carries over the water. It's a rich harmony to my ears.

"Come on, we have to get dressed or we'll be late."

"Late?" I'm breathless, my words barely audible.

"A surprise." He smirks.

As his mouth moves back over mine, silencing me, I become lost in his trance once more.

Chase Porter has cast a spell on me. He beguiles me, and every time he smiles I go weak in the knees.

Chase clears his throat as I step out of the shower wrapped only in a tiny towel that barely covers me. He slowly drinks me in. His eyes are hungry. They dilate with every inch of my body they linger on. They devour me. I move past him, swaying my hips and making my way into my cabin. He groans behind me, and I chuckle to myself.

After getting ready to leave, I meet up with Chase on the

dock right outside the boat. He's engrossed in a conversation with a beautiful Italian woman. *Who the fuck is he talking to?* He throws back his head in laughter, and anger boils deep inside me. She places her hand on his arm as she joins him in laughter. Hours ago we were kissing, and now he's laughing with some goddess. The corner of my mouth twitches as my lips begin to pucker. I'm jealous.

Insanely jealous.

As I take him in, I feel as though I'm going mad. He looks so handsome in white linen pants, driving loafers, and a baby pink button down. Not many can pull off that color, but against the scruff of his jaw, his hair brushed back and wavy, and his steel eyes that are locked on mine. He's sheer perfection, and I hate him right now. Pulling my shoulders back, I march up to them and don't even pretend to calm myself.

"I'm Aria, and you are?" I say as I push my hand out, my nose scrunching as I speak. *God I sound like a bitch. What the fuck is wrong with me?*

"Aria, this is Maria. Her family owns the dock. She came over to make sure we were settled in okay," he says as an introduction. What the fuck? Maria? Maria? As in torrid love affair, Maria? Why was she standing so close to him, and what in God's name were they laughing about? My mouth tightens, and my anger rises so fast it's like a raging inferno with no extinguisher in sight. *Clearly I'm just the next summer fling.* Maybe I need to leave. *I feel ridiculous standing here as they gaze longingly at each other.* Self-doubt begins to cloud my anger, and I'm not sure what I'm even still doing here. He must feel the heat radiating off my body, or he sees the daggers and flames shooting from my eyes because he places his arm around my back. Slowly stroking. Calming. Putting out the fire.

"Umm," I choke out. "Well, it's a pleasure to meet you." I bite my lower lip into my mouth.

"The pleasure is all mine, Aria. I hope you enjoy your stay on our lovely island, and if you need me, please don't hesitate to call." She beams, oblivious to my attitude and outburst. *Thank God for small favors.* Chase squeezes my side tighter as she makes her way further down the dock to greet other residents staying at port. I look up at him, and our eyes meet. His eyes twinkle down at me in delight. *Shit, he noticed.*

I use my hands to flatten my dress. I need to keep them busy to distract myself from the nerves growing inside me. The delicate eyelet dress ruffles slightly as I run my fingers against my thigh. Chase's eyes roam leisurely, following the path of my hand. Then he runs his gaze up my body. He leans into me, pulls me closer. His lips brush against my ear.

"You look gorgeous, Princess." He places a kiss on my shoulder between each word. I exhale with relief and grin up at him.

"You don't look too shabby yourself," I reply. I'm happy to have my petty behavior go unmentioned.

"Were you jealous?" My gaze falls to the ground.

"No." My voice doesn't sound very convincing.

"It's okay if you were. I would like to think you wouldn't want me talking to another woman. I would be pissed if I saw you talking to another man." He growls, and surprisingly it calms my nerves to know that Chase Porter is just as affected by me as I am by him.

"Okay, A little. But that's your Maria and—"

"First off, you have nothing to worry about, and second, she's not my Maria. She's not my anything."

"Sorry, about that," I murmur under my breath, embarrassed from my previous outburst.

"Good. I'm glad we got that settled, because I've been dying to do this ever since you walked out in that dress." His voice is assertive as he grabs my face. His other hand glides up my back, grasping the back of my neck, bringing my head to his. He plunders my mouth with a rawness I didn't know he was capable of. Yep . . . Chase Porter is affected by me, that's for sure.

He pulls away and grabs my hand in his. Slowly, he escorts me further from the boat. The click of my flip-flops echoes off the wooden planks as I attempt to keep up with his pace. Once we make it out of the Marina di Capri, I'm shocked to see how crowded the island is. As we walk toward the street, it's as though the entire population of the island is blocking our path. We look down on the street from above, trying to discern the best route to cross to where all the restaurants and shops are.

Chase grabs my hand, squeezes lightly and motions to go toward the cab. Neither of us wants to wait another minute to start dinner. We want to return to the boat and quench the lust bubbling up within us. His fingers lace through mine, and he pulls me toward him. His other hand lifts my chin and his lips descend.

"Maybe we should stay on the boat?" I purr.

"We have nothing I want to eat on it."

"Who needs food?" I smile coyly at him.

"As much as I prefer your idea, I need to feed you."

"Why?" my lip pouts as I bat my eyes.

"Because you will need all your energy for what I have in store for you."

After maneuvering our way through the dock, we proceed up the narrow path that leads to the top of the hill. We pass designer shops and little restaurants. On the left of the street there's a quaint trattoria overlooking the ocean. The view is spectacular. The restaurant sits high on the bluff. From our table we have a perfect view of the island's jagged shoreline and an even better view of the blue sky as it's just beginning to meet pink in the far distance, dancing across the horizon. We sit across from each other in a silence. I'm suddenly nervous. I shyly smile at him through my heavy lashes. I'm foolish to be this unnerved, but today has changed everything between us, and I'm not sure where the night will go.

A young woman approaches our table wearing a wide smile and carrying two menus. Her hair is perfectly pulled back and she has a dusting of small freckles across her nose. Chase greets her, momentarily looks over the menu and proceeds to order for us. She nods and walks away. We sit in silence and within minutes she returns but this time with a bottle of wine. Quietly and with perfect precision she pours us each a glass and leaves us. Nervously, my finger rims my glass until I can't stand the silence between us, and I speak.

"What's it like photographing someone new every time?"

"It's like going on a blind date every night."

"That doesn't sound fun."

"Surprisingly, it is. Learning new things, experiencing something for the first time."

"Umm, okay," I say, bringing my attention back to the glass. At that moment the waitress arrives with two large bowls filled with pasta then makes her retreat.

"There's no need to be nervous. Okay, more questions. Ask me anything. That should take the edge off." His eyes twinkle, and I'm shocked to realize just how much he has grown to know me and all my nuances over the last few days. It's almost as if he has known me my whole life. He smirks as I lift the fork filled with penne to my mouth. His eyebrow arches upward.

"Delicious, right?"

"Mmmm." My mouth is still a little full when I mutter out my first question between bites. "What was taking your first picture like?"

"The first time I took a picture, I wasn't a natural."

"I have a hard time believing that."

"I'm pretty perfect, aren't I?" He shrugs, and I shake my head at him.

"Pretty modest." I snort. "Tell me something I should know about you, Chase Porter."

"Like what?"

"Tell me the craziest thing you've ever done"

"That's easy. After I dropped out of college, a buddy and I decided to hike up Upuigma-tepui." My face must look utterly confused, because he proceeds to elaborate. "Venezuela." I nod, and he continues with his story. "It's a relatively isolated and unexplored peak. Basically sandstone flanks rising above the rainforest. Climbing them would be a giant feat. We were so young, only twenty and ill prepared for what lay ahead of us. We knew it would be adventure to get to the top. We just didn't realize how big of one. To say the land was uninhabited was an understatement. There was open grassland, then raging rivers. Jungle so dense we needed to use our machetes to cut through, and that wasn't even the worst of it."

"What was the worst?" My eyes go wide with awe.

"The blood sucking sandflies. Let's just say we barely made it out alive, and when we did my buddy was laid up for days in a hospital to patch the wounds those vampires left behind."

"Wow, Chase. That's intense."

"You have no idea, Princess. You have no idea. But like all things in life, there was a lesson to be learned from this trip."

"And what was that lesson, Chase?" I wait on bated breath for the profound statement I'm certain Chase will deliver.

"Never go climbing in a South American rainforest." He chuckles, and I giggle along with him. "I'm kidding. The lesson I learned was no matter what the odds and challenges you face, all you have to do is set up a new path, and you will find your way home."

"That's remarkable. That's how I want to live."

"Sounds like a plan." He shifts his attention back to me. His blue eyes search mine, probing into my soul.

Forty-five minutes later when we are finished with dinner, we walk through the local shops, weaving through abandoned cobblestone alleys. Every so often, Chase stops to photograph a building. Again as he takes the images, he stops to place the camera in the crook of my neck and fire off another round. I draw in a breath with each pass his fingers make across my shoulder blade. I never know what he's doing, or why he even bothers. But Chase is Chase, and one day he will tell me his vision. As we walk toward the edge of the city, I place my hands on the railing to keep me safe from crashing into the ocean below. A series of clicks from behind has me turning my head over my right shoulder to find Chase now taking shots of me.

"You should see this shot. You're beautiful. You are living, breathing art," he says while he admires his work. "I could photograph you and only you for the rest of my life. Your beauty will always inspire me." My cheeks flush as I look up at him.

"You can make anything look beautiful," I reply.

"Beauty isn't something you can buy or possess. Beauty is something that flows from the soul. True beauty is incomparable and free of all restraints." His voice is filled with conviction, and I'm in awe of his passion.

"You weave poetry when you speak." I turn my attention back to the ocean and catch a glance into the distance. The sky is now on fire. What was once a mixture of blue and pink streaks is now scorching red flames in the distance. It burns bright and ignites reds until it descends into the purple horizon. In the opposite direction of the water, the buildings in the distance appear ominous. The haze of the daybreak now gone. The only light cast upon the ancient structures comes from the small glow reflecting outward from the glass windows. A shadow casts down on the path where we walk.

"It's a bit scary now." My voice is only a whisper.

"I've got you." Chase squeezes my hand, and I know his words mean so much more than he says. "Come on up here." I feel the tickle of his breath against my neck. He hoists me up a narrow set of stairs on the side of the terra cotta building in front of us. My foot catches on the first set of prongs. Steadily, I climb to the top, and the view is magnificent. Lights flicker in the distance, a million majestic diamonds reflecting off the dark abyss of the sky. Gripping his hand a little tighter, a grin spreads across my face.

"It's beautiful." I marvel at the view.

"Uh-huh," he mutters, and I turn my face toward him, scrunching my nose.

"You're not even looking at the view, Chase Porter," I playfully scold.

"The view I have is quite spectacular, too." He smirks as

his eyes twinkle.

"What is that?" My hand points out into the distance, across the island.

"That's Anacapri. I'll take you there tomorrow if we have time."

The air is damp, and the sweet smell of rain infiltrates my nose. I peer up to look for traces of clouds but the darkness that blankets us from above makes it nearly impossible to see anything, let alone the impending rain, which I'm sure will come. Chase draws me into him, his breath tickling my neck as he inhales deeply.

"What are you doing?"

"I'm breathing you in." Puzzled, I look fixedly at him, speechless. My right eyebrow rises in question, waiting for an explanation. "You're my air, Aria." My heartbeat batters inside me as my chest tightens. I remain fixed on him even though cool water begins to streams down my hair and into my eyes. The sky has apparently opened. The hard rain pricks our skin like small needles. Water is collecting around our feet, the puddle filled with a murky liquid. I can feel the soft caress of hands under my knees, and I'm being lifted into Chase's arms. My hands wrap around his neck of their own accord. He begins to carry me toward the nearest wall of the building. We need to find cover from the torrential water, but instead he pushes me up against the wall, rearranging his arms as he slams my body against it. Our mouths collide. His grip tightens around me. He pulls away and places feathery kisses down the damp skin of my neck.

"Please, Chase," I plead with him.

"I don't want you to regret this." There's uncertainty in his voice. I shake my head adamantly back and forth.

"I could never regret you."

Enraptured.

Breathless anticipation.

Our eyes meet, and his gaze burns into me, locking intensely on mine.

Setting me on fire.

"God, you're amazing, Aria. I wish you could see yourself the way I see you. If you did, it would make things so much easier." His words come out slowly through his shallow breaths.

His fingers gently stroke my chin, and my back continues to press up against the wall. I'm eager to feel the soft caress of his mouth. Our mouths smash together again, and this time I don't ever want to let go. My arms enclose his neck tighter, deepening the kiss. His tongue gently licks mine.

Tugging.

Nipping.

A whimper escapes my mouth.

"Please, Chase," I moan.

"Shh. Soon. Soon." He continues his assault on me until I'm begging and panting for release, but he keeps me at bay. Teetering above myself. My heart thumps erratically in my chest, like a freight train going off the track.

"How long did you know you wanted this?" I ask through my labored breath.

"From the very moment I saw you sitting all alone and sad on the veranda, drowning your sorrows in a Bellini."

"Am I just some girl?" I need to know, even if I don't like the answer. I've never felt like this with someone I just met. I need to know if this is one-sided, if I'm just another 'Maria.'

"You are more than just a girl. You are my Aria. You are my air." My heart ceases its pounding. Goosebumps run up my arms. Passion, emotion, they engulf me.

His words break me into a million pieces and then pick me back up and mend me. I have no words. No reaction other than loss of all thought. A strange feeling weaves its way through me.

Urgency. Desperation.

"You banish the darkness, Chase." Chase stares at me intently, with a strange look in his eye. His movements are sudden, as though he's lost all control of himself. He fists my hair in his hands and pulls back, his lips finding my neck. This isn't sweet, this isn't loving. This is a frenzied kiss as if we can't get enough of each other. He owns me, has laid claim to me.

A cool breeze streams in, whipping its way through my hair. My body doesn't cool though, not until his soft hands lift the hem of my dress. Chills run down my back as the pressure of his fingertips increases on my upper thighs tracing patterns on my ivory skin.

Soft fingers trace the edge of my lace panties, delicate feather-like whispers against my skin.

"What are you doing to me, Aria?" he groans. "I feel like you're holding me prisoner. Once I peered into the endless abyss of your eyes, I knew I would drown."

Cold water fills my veins, dousing my body with a chill that, over the years, I've grown to know all too well. My lungs feel like they are filling with water. My breathing grows more and more rapid.

Drowning . . .

Drowning . . .

Drowning . . .

I'm drowning again.

Breaking the surface.

Ripples in the current.

"Stop! Stop, Chase. I can't do this right now!"

"What . . . what's wrong? What happened?" Concern rims his eyes. I must look like a crazed animal, my eyes feral and unfocused.

"I'm so sorry, so sorry," I say as tears spread down my cheek.

"*Shh*, Aria. What's wrong? Please, Princess. Tell me what happened. What did I do?" His touch becomes more hesitant as he watches me warily.

"Drowning. Drowning," I repeat in confusion. "You said you were drowning."

"Shh, breathe. Aria. I'm okay. I'm okay. We are fine. You are fine. No one is drowning."

My breathing regulates as I start to focus. Chase softly lowers me to the ground. I hold on to him for dear life. Reality is setting in.

He holds me for some time bringing me back to my surroundings. His lips lay soft kisses on my hair as he strokes my back, and makes me feel loved. He cherishes me completely, and as I watch him through tear-stained eyes, I know I can one day fall in love with this man.

When we return to the boat, his arms wrap around my back as he lowers us into my bed. Our breathing is tandem. The images before of Owen were so clear, so vivid, but in Chase's arms they fade. He pulls me from the numbness, rescues me from the waters that threaten to drown me.

"Will you please stay? Hold me?"

"Always."

I look up at him with dreamy eyes, half asleep, almost in twilight.

"Thank you, Chase." He stares at me with dark eyes.

"You are a beautiful dream, and I'm afraid to wake." His arms wrap tighter around me as if he really is scared I'll leave. This is my fear, too. That this is just a beautiful dream and when I wake up everything will come crashing down again. That the reality of everything from my past will hit me and I will never be able to awaken from that nightmare. I inhale, and my chest tightens. The weight of all my decisions once again hangs over me.

Dangling. Waiting to drop.

Waiting to cover me once again. Cloak me in darkness.

I exhale and try to push it aside, pretend it's not there. Pretend that if I look up, the parts of me I'm running from won't come crashing down. And then he pulls me tighter and encases me in his warmth, and everything I worry about slips away.

Sometime later, I'm rustled awake by the caress of his body against mine. Quietly, I attempt to slide out of bed when I hear Chase.

"Hey, beautiful. Where do you think you're going?" He wraps his arms around my middle and pulls me back. It's the middle of the night, and I'm able to see the moon casting a shadow against the far wall. I can't make coherent thoughts as I feel his warm hands splay against my ribs. "You're going nowhere. I'm not nearly done holding you yet."

"I have to freshen up, Chase Porter. Will you be done with me soon?" I pretend to chide him, but I can't control the laugh that breaks from my lips.

"Patience." His eyes crinkle as his mouth parts into a grin.

"What are you so happy about?"

His eyes flicker the way they often do when they warm my heart. "You. Always you." Not a second passed before I was flipped back onto the bed. Lips trace a path across my hip bone, small kisses. His tongue presses gently against me, causing heat to rush across my body. My core contracts and my breath becomes erratic as he continues his sweet torture. As I feel myself coming apart on his tongue he pulls away, leaving me vacant and needy. Moving up my body he traces my right breast with his tongue and then the left, lightly nipping on each nipple. Devouring them in his mouth, leaving me desperate for his touch.

Desperate to be filled.

"Please," I whimper. He reaches for the nightstand and pulls out a foil wrapper from the drawer. I feel like I may die from anticipation as I wait. Finally, my hand finds him hard and ready, and I tighten my grip around him, pulling him closer to where I need him most. His lips part against mine, and on the exhale, he pushes into my heat. The warmth of his breath as it lingers on my lips is sweet. His tongue traces the seam of my mouth, seeking entry again. As his movements pick up, I cling to his broad shoulders. My nails scratch down the lines of each defined muscle until I clutch him harder, willing— begging—him to increase his speed.

Faster.

Harder.

Shallow.

Deep.

I become lost in the pleasure, lost in the emotions.

My body starts to contract and pulse around him.

I'm being pulled tight, like a rubber band about to snap.

I explode.

Lights dance in my vision as I return from heaven.

"You steal the breath from my body," I say while gasping for oxygen.

"And you put the air in mine."

I lay wrapped in his arms.

"Are you happy?" And in that very moment, I know the answer to the very bottom of my soul . . . I am.

"What are you thinking about?" I stop and ponder his question before answering truthfully.

"I'm thinking about how much my life has changed since I met you. How this trip has opened my eyes. How I see life in a different way. It's funny how you think the road only goes in one direction, and then you realize it can go a completely different way. You know, my friend, he told me this, but I didn't believe him. I was so stuck on the idea that I need to be someone else for everybody."

He pulls me closer into him, my long, messy locks fanning across his chest.

"Sleep," he whispers, and I do. The steady cadence of his heart lulls me into a deep slumber.

Finally, at peace.

CHAPTER TWELVE

Thirty-seven days since I spoke to Parker
Nine days since I met Chase

THE MORNING SUNLIGHT dances over the lush hills in the distance. Capri. It seems to be everything I dreamed it would be in the early morning glow. A soft shimmer casts over the grass as streams of light reflect off the dew collecting on the leaves.

It's a beautiful view, almost impossible to put into words. I feel peaceful this morning. The wind hits the sails with a soft hiss as I sit on the deck drinking my coffee. I awoke before Chase and quietly escaped the confines of his embrace. As I sit enjoying the waves crashing against the rocks of Capri in the distance, I think of my life back home. The sound of the surf hitting the earth is a stark reminder of the summer it all changed.

For years after the accident, I wore the perfect mask, never showing how the loss of my brother affected me. Never showing how my mom's words hurt me. How they cut me to the bone. After losing Owen, I desperately needed the survival technique Parker taught me.

"Never show her your pain. She thrives on it, baby girl. Look her in the eye with indifference. That's the only way she will stop. Your happiness is the best revenge you can give her. Being yourself is more important than being the person they want you to be. If they can't appreciate who you are, that's their loss. Not yours."

He was right, of course. Parker was always right. Always there to hold my hand and protect me. That's what made this trip so hard. He told me to do this, and I said no. But he was right. *Always right.* I don't belong in a corner office. I belong here, feeling the sun on my face, drifting in the wind. No destination in sight. At peace.

"What are you doing out here all by yourself?" Chase inquires as he places a lazy kiss on my lips. And when he kisses me . . .

He makes me feel whole.

Like the pieces of me that are broken aren't that bad.

"I was just thinking that this is where I'm meant to be right now. That I believe I'm meant to learn something from this trip."

"I agree with you. You know, while I was climbing my first mountain, I learned a few things about myself as well."

"If you don't mind me asking, what did you learn on that first trip?"

"Not at all. I learned what real beauty was. I learned how it felt to be stopped in your tracks and left in awe of the intricate nature of all matters of life. Often, we get so caught up in the destination that we never see the impact the journey has on us. I learned to appreciate my body and to push myself to excel. I learned to push myself past my comfort level because unless we do that, we'll never grow. To fall down and pick myself back up again. All the lessons I learned climbing that first mountain I've now applied to all aspects of my life, but I'll tell you what the most important thing I learned on all my travels was, Aria."

"What's that?"

"To always remember to breathe." I stared at him, stunned. Unable to speak.

Rendered useless. *Again.*

"What do you want to do today?" Chase asks from across the cabin sometime later. He smiles at me, and the way his lip turns up gives him a boyish charm. A dimple appears on his right cheek. On a normal occasion, it's harder to see through his five o'clock shadow, but today it seems extra deep. I grin back mischievously, thinking of how we had spent the last hour after he found me drinking coffee.

"None of that right now." He laughs as I watch him move. Each stride is fluid as he makes his way around the room. He stands with his hands on his hips. His eyes search the room for his discarded clothes from this morning. My face flushes at the memory.

"You want to go to Anacapri?" I shrug and stick my tongue out.

"Sticking your tongue out, are you? I have someplace for you to stick your tongue," he mocks.

"Promises, promises." I rise in one fluid motion. He smothers a groan as I approach him and lift up to my tiptoes to place a kiss on his lips. My naked breasts press again his strong torso.

"Aria," he says in warning.

"What?" I tilt my head and smirk.

"Nope, not happening." I pivot my body away from his as he lightly smacks my backside.

After a frigid shower to wash away my dirty thoughts, I enter the galley to grab a snack. As I lean into the fridge, two strong hands wrap around my middle. A squeak escapes as Chase lifts me into his arms and sits me on the counter.

"You okay, Princess?" He grins mischievously.

"I'm perfect," I allow my fingers to trail down his chest. "There is one problem I might need your help with." I continue to run my hands down the V of his torso, dipping inside the waistband of his jeans.

"And what's that?" His voice is husky. I lean into him, place my lips on his, and bite down softly. His mouth parts, and I become ravenous. I'm on edge from the delicious torture of delayed gratification.

"Luciano?" I moan into his mouth.

"Don't worry," he mumbles between kisses. "He won't return until tonight."

"When did you tell him to stay away?"

"When you were showering. I knew I couldn't resist you for long."

"Just wanted to torture me a little?" Slowly he pushes my panties down my thighs and I push forward toward his hand. Tilting my hips up to meet the warmth of his caress. I'm silently begging, pleading with my body for him to touch me. Soft fingers tease my sensitive skin. They dip inside me and then find the wonderfully sensitive spot buried deep within.

My body starts to quiver as he pushes upward with his fingers massaging me, bringing me so close I'm teetering on the brink of eruption but just as I'm about to explode he pulls back leaving me vacant and greedy for more. Reaching into his jean pocket he grabs a condom then rips it open before he aligns himself against my core.

Our bodies slowly come together and his lips press firmly into mine. His grip tightens around me as his control wavers. He's holding back. Letting me adjust to him. I push forward, taking him deeper, and again our bodies meet as he enters me fully. I exhale, relaxing into him, letting him claim me completely. He thrusts in and out, each stroke lighting a fire. The bond between us grows with each move he makes. My heartbeat pounds as he throbs within me. The surge of release tingling as a shiver claims my whole body until I soar higher than I ever thought possible.

Cleaning up and re-showering is necessary after "breakfast." We decide to spend the day on the other side of the island near the city of Anacapri.

Once at Anacapri, Chase says we should take the chairlift up to Mount Solaro. I'm nervous. The chair lift has me completely on edge. It's nothing more than a chair strapped to a long piece of wire.

"This is insane. I'm not getting on that thing." Chase is not affected at all. He laughs as I refuse to get on, then leans into me and gently takes my hand. His lips places tiny kisses across my knuckles, and I've forgotten what I'm so afraid of.

"Don't live in the past. Don't be stifled by your previous fears. You can do this." This saying sounds so familiar, but I just can't place it. I take a giant gulping breath, and my fears begin to diminish. All the way to the top, I keep peeking at the chair behind me. I'm so completely distracted with the lust bubbling inside me—threatening to explode from me at any second—that I don't even notice we've made it to our destination.

Getting to the top turns out to be an amazing experience. One of the best of my life. One for the books.

The views are more breathtaking than anything I've ever seen. We make our way away from the lift and head to the gardens. There we find a pair of chairs with a view overlooking the sea and the famous Faraglioni rocks, and enjoy the caprese sandwiches and wine we had picked up at the market below.

"So, what did you think?" Chase asks. The rich timbre of his voice makes me want to reconsider not having my way with him right here in public. *What the hell has gotten into me? Chase Porter, that's what.*

"This is amazing. These are the kind of little destinations I need to add to my bucket list."

"You have a bucket list?" His eyebrow arches.

"It's not really a bucket list per se. More a list of places I need to go." My mind begins to flutter with memories of Parker, but I nudge them away. I refuse to allow them to ruin this perfect moment. Chase studies me as if he wants to say something, but nothing comes out. "Do you have a list of places you want to go?" I ask him.

"Hmm, I've been everywhere already. I guess my bucket list would be to take you to some of the scariest places I've been, and make you push yourself past your comfort zone and try something new." His expression is serious. His eyes tell me he isn't lying. This is what he intends to do.

Crazy thing is . . . I want him to.

Chase's fingers stroke my arm as we step into the little souvenir shop in Marina di Capri. As we walk through the doorway, the cool breeze from the air conditioner hits my bare skin and leaves a trail of goose bumps. I withdraw my hand from his and make my way to the far wall. Leaning down, my fingertips trail over the postcards. I pick one up and study the image. It's of the Faraglioni rocks. I swallow hard and let my eyes roam the room to find Chase. He's staring at me. The beginning of a smile tips the corner of his mouth. He must realize he's been caught. I break into a wide grin at the thought. His beautiful eyes are brimmed with humor. Every gray speck sparkles with the light that reflects off them. The postcard grows heavy in my hand, and guilt washes over me. But not the guilt I expected.

This time I didn't just have guilt over Parker. There's a pang in my chest for how Chase would feel if he saw the postcards I sent to Parker. Sometimes, some things are better left unsaid. Chase doesn't know I write to Parker, and Parker doesn't need to know just how quickly I'm falling for someone else.

I recall Parker's postcard from Costa Rica. I couldn't contain my excitement when I found it lying on the marble countertop. My lips split so wide, they actually hurt. But then he crushed me.

> *Dear Ari,*
> *How's your summer been? I'm actually in Costa Rica. Everest was here, so I decided to bail on summer classes and head out and meet him. This place is crazy. You'd hate it. Horseback riding, ziplines. Hell, we even rappelled down a*

waterfall. I thought of you when doing it. I would pay good money to see you do something that crazy. So, I know I said I would be back for your mom's Fourth of July party, but I won't be able to make it. I met a girl. Her name is Melanie, and she goes to school by me. Mel wants to head over to Catarata Llanos de Cortes and then see Arenal Volcano. So I'm going to go with her. I think you'd really like her. Okay, we are leaving soon to go surfing, so I should get going.

Speak soon,
Park

The agonizing feeling was like nothing I'd ever felt before. Ice spread through me. Anger that he was with him. Of course Everest was there. Of course he'd followed him yet again. Rejection quickly following. The last time I saw him, I showed him how I felt. He rejected me. He said it was because of Owen, but deep down I assumed he was a typical guy, and he just wasn't ready. But now I know that wasn't the case at all. He was ready. Just not for me.

Everest probably gave her his stamp of approval, something I'm sure I would never get since I complained so much about him. This was the last time, I told myself. I was done putting my heart on my sleeve for Parker to crush. I needed to move on and concentrate on what really mattered. School, being successful, making Owen proud.

I shudder inwardly at the memory. No, it was better to not send this card. I knew how it felt to know the person you loved had moved on. I put the card down and look back at

Chase. He's still watching me. His eyes widen ever so slightly. The blue pierces me from across the distance that separates us. They flash an emotion, and it looks a lot like concern. Stepping away from the card display, I make my way to join him. His arms capture me to him, and I bury myself in his shoulder.

"Let's get back to the boat." His silky voice sends chills up my spine. I know what he wants, and I want it, too. The anticipation to get back is almost unbearable. Every time his gaze meets mine, my pulse accelerates and shudders with a sense of urgency. I long to be wrapped in his arms, to feel the electricity from his touch. His nearness is overwhelming, and when we finally arrive, he hauls me into his arms, violently as if he wants to consume me. As if he wants to banish any memory of anyone else.

My limbs tremble against him, desperate and needy for release. The mere touch of his fingertips leaves me panting. His mouth covers mine with a hunger I didn't know he was capable of. Demanding me to submit to him and I do. Over and over again.

We spend the rest of the afternoon making love in my cabin. He ravishes me so many times I almost lose count before I finally fall asleep in his arms. I awake alone some time later and my body is sore in the best way possible. Stretching my hands above my head, I look around the room for Chase. I feel the boat moving, hitting the waves, and I realize he's obviously on deck. He and Luciano must have decided to start our course to Positano. I smooth my hair out of my face and put on Chase's discarded shirt and a pair of leggings, then make my way up to the cockpit. I find Chase and Luciano taking turns at the helm. My cheeks warm as I watch him.

A terrifying feeling washes over me . . .

More.
I want more.

CHAPTER THIRTEEN

Ten days since I met Chase.
It feels as though I've known him a lifetime

L AST NIGHT WE made it to Positano much later than we expected. I guess we left later than anticipated. My cheeks heat when I recall our reason for running behind schedule. By the time we arrive, it's too late to get off the boat, so we drop anchor about 300 meters off the coast. Fatigue settles into our bones. We're both exhausted, so we crawl into bed and pass out.

I feel refreshed this morning as I turn down the hallway to find Chase has set up a makeshift picnic on the deck of the boat. Two cappuccinos, some fresh strawberries, and yogurt are set up to eat before we start our day. This man . . . I can no longer deny that he has buried himself deeply in my heart. He makes everything else fade away. We click, he understands me, he wants me, and most importantly, he wants to see me happy. It's an awakening experience to realize that for the first time, a man has connected to me, just for me. He isn't tethered to me by my past, by a friend, or by my brother. He's here for me.

—————

As Chase and Luciano pull the sailboat up to the dock that's only available for drop off, I peer up at Chase with confusion.

"How does this work? I thought you needed two people to sail this bad boy?"

"Since it's technically intended for two, yes, that would be ideal. However, since it has a standard engine, Luciano can use the motor to pull away from the dock."

"Has he ever done that before?"

"Come on, Princess. Now you're just being silly. Of course he has. In order to get a license, you have to be able to perform a man overboard drill."

"A what?"

"Man overboard drill. Basically, I would jump off, and Luciano would have to prove that he can pick my sorry ass up and save me, if it was just him and me on board."

"And could he do it?"

"I'm here, aren't I? If Luciano couldn't do it, I wouldn't be." I shrug and turn my attention back to the dock as we pull closer. Luciano brings us alongside the dock, and Chase grabs my hand to help me off. As we make our way toward the street, the intricate buildings loom above us from the village of Positano. Beautiful houses appear to tumble down the mountainside leading into sea. Sun-kissed peach, pink and multiple terra cotta colors cascade down the mountainside, as they seem to reach for the water below. It's a heavenly enclave set deep within the hills.

We venture upstairs so steep, that I'm not sure how we'll

be able to make it to the top. Of course, that's where Chase is leading us to the very top. To where the view is 'awe-inspiring.' *It better be.* Because as I look up at the sharp lines of what appears to be a vertical cliff, I decide we'll never make it. It's just too damn far, but wow, is it beautiful. The lofty distance before us is filled with terraced rows of lemons and olives, and I can see why he would be inspired. Intermixed within the plush vegetation, sit cliff-side mansions. I imagine a world where we sit among the vines on the patio of one of the houses. We would enjoy the bright morning sky in our very own courtyard. My heart swells with the idea.

Continuing up the pathway, we now have to walk along the road amidst festive locals and excited tourists. The road is also cluttered with fast driving cars, motorcycles, and Vespas. The energy is great, and being among all the people is definitely one of my favorite parts of the trip thus far.

We stop along the way to shop, poke around in a few galleries, and continue to compare and contrast gelato flavors at a few local favorites. We take many photos. Some of me, some by me, but most are taken from the nook of my neck. Whatever he sees from that angle doesn't matter because I love the way it feels when his body is pushed up close to mine. It's intimate and personal.

Sometime later, we finally reach our destination. Il San Pietro Di Positano is a beautiful hotel built into the hillside with an epic view of the Tyrrhenian Sea. It's a multi-sensory experience, filled with delicate colors and scents.

We decide to sit on the terrace and enjoy a cocktail, one of their world famous Bellini's. The terrace is vibrant with color, and we choose a yellow and mosaic bench overlooking the coastline. My hair floats around my shoulders like mist with each pass of the breeze.

"I can't imagine being here with anyone but you."

"Me neither." His voice is calm, and his gaze steady. He seems to grow more serious, and the sunlight in his blue eyes reflects my image back at me.

"Is it weird that I feel this way after such a short time? It's like I've known you my whole life." His eyelids slip down, hooding his eyes.

"No, I feel the same way. Come here," he commands in a hoarse voice as he pulls me into his chest. He grips me tightly as if he's scared to let me go, and somewhere inside me, I hope he won't.

After cocktails, the hotel manager comes to give us a tour of the beach restaurant. The establishment is accessed by a rickety enclosed elevator that runs down through the rock four hundred feet. I look at the elevator and then at Chase, and I can't help myself—I burst out laughing. This man is trying to kill me. He smirks at me. *And he knows it.*

"I know, I know. Comfort zone," I mutter.

As the elevator descends, and we make our way through the rock, I feel a little claustrophobic, but it's over soon, and as the elevator doors open, I'm taken aback. My breath comes out in a rush of surprise. There in front of me, I'm met by the most beautiful private beach I've ever seen.

It's just gorgeous. Under the cerulean blue of an endless Positano sky, I think life can't get much better than this. I turn toward Chase and notice the camera lens staring back at me. I blink my eyes at the sun gleaming down at me from behind Chase and hear the familiar snapping.

"Stop taking pictures of me, Chase. I look like a sweaty mess."

"Inside and out, in every way possible, you could never look like a mess. You're magnificent." My heart swells with a feeling I realize I've never felt before. Complete and utter adoration. It's a different feeling than Parker used to evoke in me. I'll always love Parker but this is unique. He's making me doubt everything I thought I knew. For so long I've felt adrift, but this crazy man makes me feel anchored.

His mouth moves against my shoulder as I lean back in his arms—light, feathery kisses across my bones. This man is pure temptation. I look around the beach and wonder if anyone will notice if I straddle him under the canopy of stars that blankets us from above. *Would* anyone notice? Would anyone stop us? I'm fighting a battle within myself to find restraint as the firework shows begin. The sky lightens in a festival of colors. I haven't seen such colors since my parents' Fourth of July party.

I opened the door to Parker's apartment and let myself in. As I made my way further inside, I spotted Parker in the bathroom, brushing his teeth.

"Running late, are we?" This man was never on time.

"Sorry about that, Ari. Mel just left."

Mel . . . Melanie, the girl he abandoned me for last summer. No such luck ditching me this year. I made it very clear that if he made me go to Mom's party alone, I would beat him within an inch of his life. As I contemplated how close he got to losing a limb, I noticed something across the room that grabbed my attention and made my stomach drop. Boxes. Shit. *Where was he going? I could feel my heart pounding erratically in my chest as I imagined the possibilities. Melanie.*

Making my way to them, I kneeled closer to get a better look.

"Umm—are you moving?"

"No. Why would you think that?" he shouted over the splash of the running water.

"I totally thought you were moving in with Melanie," I say from beneath my breath.

"Oh, God no. Actually, I just broke up with her." My shoulders visibly dropped with relief.

"Why?"

"I realized she wasn't what I wanted."

"Oh? What is it you want?" Please say me. Please.

"Not sure yet. But not her. Maybe just to be single, play the field." It felt as if I'd been sucker punched. It was time to admit Parker would never see me as anything more than a friend. It was time to retire my plans of him having an epiphany that he was madly in love with me and he dreamed of growing old together. No more. This time I meant it. I was moving on.

"So if you aren't moving, what the hell are these?" I pointed to the open boxes on the floor.

He peered his head out the door and followed my gaze. "Everest's shit."

Parker shut the bathroom door, so I took the opportunity to look in some of the boxes. I picked up an interesting stone. The rock appeared to be limestone, but I couldn't be sure without asking Parker, and I knew he wouldn't approve of my snooping. Next, I pulled out a handmade and mostly brass-plated Buddha. Who the fuck was this guy? I knew little to nothing about him. All I knew was he was a thorn in my side since Parker's freshman year of college.

They had been roommates back then, and I had still never met him. He was always traveling, going places, and dragging Parker along. Never around whenever I visited, making Parker miss trips home to travel with him instead. Honestly, I was starting to take it personally. As though he was purposely evading me so he didn't have to hear the hatred I wanted to spew at him. I was sure Parker had told him my thoughts on him. Recently I had not been quiet about my feelings over this friend I had never met. The toilet flushed, and I silently replaced the mini statue.

"So . . . Everest . . . you're storing his stuff here because—?" I couldn't hide the disdain in my voice.

"He's moving in."

"What? Are you serious?" My fingers gripped at the skin on my arm, turning my knuckles white and aggravated.

"Well, not so much moving in as storing his shit here. He travels a lot for work and needs a home base, so I figure it's a win-win. He'll pay half the rent and never steal my food." Typical Parker, always about the food.

"Figures you have some ulterior motive. So, when will I finally get to meet this guy?"

"Oh, you just missed him."

"Seriously? This is ridiculous, already. I really want to meet him! We've been friends for years so how the hell have I not met this guy?"

"We could wait for him to get back, but your mom will freak if you're late. Next time."

"It's almost like you never want me to meet him. Is he hot or something and you're afraid I'll fall madly in love with him?" His eyes became insanely dark. Was he jealous? My hopes began to rise. Little butterflies danced in my stomach.

"God, no," he said, crushing my heart. The feeling cours-

ing through me stung. It hurt worse than ever before because after telling myself I should never hope for anything more than friendship from Parker, I had gone and believed, only to be shot down again.

"It's just that we're in a rush. I promise next time. Okay?" I shrugged.

"Sure. Whatever. I'm never going to meet this guy. It's not even like you told me why the stupid nickname."

"He climbed Everest, That's why. Okay, seriously. We've got to go or we're going to be late."

Pulling Chase's arms tighter around my body, I sink into his embrace and enjoy the explosions of color above us. Everything I need right now is here with me, and I won't allow myself to get lost in my memories.

CHAPTER FOURTEEN

Eleven days since I met Chase
Ten days since my life completely changed

WAKE UP THIS morning and realize that yesterday was the first day I hadn't counted the days since I spoke to Parker. My brain sorts through numbers, and I realize I can't even remember how many days it's been. I feel guilty, but then I feel Chase stir under my body, and I turn my head to burrow myself into his nook. Chase Porter is my salvation. He's opened my eyes to so much in such a short time. It's insane. I can thank him for the rest of my life and it will never be enough. Through him, each day, I'm learning to live in the moment.

"Thanks for making me whole again," I whisper into his bare chest. I place a small kiss over his heart.

"I didn't do anything. You did it all by yourself." He runs his fingers through my locks. The caress is soft, and I wonder if I imagine it. My stomach growls silently, but I don't want him to stop touching me.

I want him to touch me everywhere. The pressure of his

body underneath me lights me on fire. I'm drowning in emotions for this man, but this time I'm not afraid. These feelings are completely unique to anything I've ever felt before. I've never felt so close to anyone. I feel as if his soul has melded to mine.

Throwing my leg over his, I straddle his naked body. His gaze travels over me and searches my eyes. I'm stripped bare emotionally in front of him. Chase's large hand takes hold of my face and lightly strokes my cheek. He traces the contours, then slides further down to my collarbone. His hand continues its exploration until his grip tightens around my waist. Then he brings them around back, trailing soft touches up and down my spine. The man treats me as if I'm a priceless masterpiece. I align myself above him, teasing him.

"I need to grab—" he starts, but I cut him off. I don't want anything between us. I just want to feel him.

"I'm safe. I want to feel all of you," I say. I continue to stroke him against my heat until I can't take much more. He nods in approval, and I lower myself. My body molds to him as his fills mine to completion. Once he's all the way seated inside me, I begin to rock up and down on his thick length. He meets me stroke for stroke. Our rhythm growing more frantic the closer we get. A moan of ecstasy slips through my lips as I climb higher than I think possible. I shatter into a million pieces and then he pulls me toward him, putting me back together with one single kiss.

"We should head back to Positano. I was thinking this time we could go all the way up to the 'Path of the Gods.' It's really the best view of the Amalfi Coast." He reclaims my lips, and then pulls away. "I'm going to hop in the shower."

"Want some company?" I slip my hand up his arm, trying to bring him back to me.

"As much as I want to say yes, I fear if you join me, we'll never leave."

"And that's a problem because?" I playfully drag my fingertips down to reach his hand, but he laughs and shakes me off.

"Because believe it or not, I'm here for work." He pulls out of my grasp and walks to the ottoman sitting at the foot of the bed. He starts to rummage through his backpack on top of it.

"Aw yes, I did almost forget that."

He pulls his camera from his backpack, and then grabs my hand to position me directly in front of the window beside the bed. Gathering a black sheet, he secures it to the wall behind me, hanging it from the edge of the painting fastened to the wall.

"Place your hand under your chin," he directs.

"What are you doing?

"Trust me, will you? The effect will be incredible."

I place my fingers under my chin, allowing them to curl up over my lip. "Do I just sit here like this?"

"Stop talking. This will come out amazing."

My life isn't amazing, nor is it extraordinary. There's nothing particularly special about me, but when I'm with Chase, he makes me feel special—as if I'm so much more. I believe him when he says it will be amazing.

The click of the camera has become a calming sound for me. I've grown so used to Chase snapping shots of me it's now just a soft hum.

After Chase is done getting the perfect shot, he lays the camera on the bedside table and then heads to the bathroom to get ready. Not even a minute passes before I hear his voice over the running water.

"Hey, Princess. Will you grab me a razor? It's in my bag by the wall." I move across the room to open his small carry-on suitcase that for some reason is in this cabin. Somewhere between Capri and Positano, Luciano decided to move things along and have us bunk together. I laughed so hard yesterday when we returned to find his bag placed on my bed. I unzip it and rummage through, but come up empty-handed.

"It's not in there," I shout through the half-open door.

"Oh. It might be in my backpack."

I move back to the ottoman, open the zippered top and start digging around. After an extensive search, my fingers finally find the razor. As I grab it, I come in contact with something that feels a lot like a postcard. Pulling it out to have a better look, everything around me stops. *What the hell?* The words on the paper begin to waver from staring at it so intently. My heart starts to hammer in my chest.

Thump, Thump

Thump, Thump

The sounds around me become a hum as the room begins to spin. My erratic breathing makes me dizzy as the anger rises. The emotions I feel are palpable, like a crimson haze coursing through me. I attempt to calm my body by taking a deep breath. Chase's footsteps echo in the small space.

"Why do you have this?" My eyes still won't leave the card. The words I've written are barely legible through the tears teasing at my lids. I peer up and find Chase staring at me, and his mouth opens and then closes.

"Why the fuck do you have this?" My voice rises with each word that erupts from my mouth.

"I—"

"You what? Fucking speak!"

"I can explain."

"You can explain this? I sent this to my friend Parker. How do you have this postcard?"

Tension radiates off Chase as I hold the postcard in my hand. The postcard of the Brooklyn Bridge. The postcard I sent to Parkers apartment the day I left New York. The postcard he shouldn't have. His blue eyes focus on the nondescript piece of paper that an unobservant onlooker would never know was so important. His brows draw together. A small frown line creases between them.

"Please, Ari. Please let me explain." The nickname slips out, and he clasps his hand over his mouth. *Ari, Ari, Ari.* The name only Parker calls me.

"Don't call me that. Ever!" I say though clenched teeth.

"Please, Aria."

"Who the fuck are you?"

"I can explain, Princess."

"You lost the right to call me Princess when you left a small fact out. Explain. Explain how you have this! Fucking explain! Because I don't understand how you can have this in your possession. How the fuck do you have this, Chase? Who the fuck are you?" I clench my stomach as tears roll from my eyes. I lurch forward, dry heaving. "Who the fuck are you?" I scream as my breathing becomes more erratic.

"Shh, calm down." Sobs wrack my body. "Stay in the present," he says, and Parker's words rush through me. Memories become so vivid I can't push them away as my world crashes around me. Thoughts once lost in my subconscious infiltrate my mind—and that's when I know. I know exactly who he is.

The words he'd spoken so many times finally come into focus, and I realize why they sounded so familiar. Why *he* always seemed so familiar.

"Ari, as my friend Everest always says . . . Stay in the present. Don't live in the past. Be strong. Be you."

My eyes meet his, and realization dawns on him. He knows that I know.

"Let me explain." His eyes slide down and lock on the ground at his feet. His hands reach to his temples, and he begins to scrub at them. I've never seen him look this way. But it doesn't matter. He lied. Everything was a lie. He's a lie.

"You're him?"

"I—"

"Are. You. Him?"

"Yes."

"How could you? I opened up to you. I told you about my parents. Oh my God. I told you about Parker!" I dry heave again, and then his phone goes off. The sound of the vibrating burns at my ears. When he reaches for it I want to smash it, scream, 'How dare you check it! How dare you find me of so little importance that you would dare look!'

Then I notice the look in his eyes, and I realize something is seriously wrong. A shiver runs through me. Chase stands taller, gathering his composure. The change in his voice is evident.

"You need to go home."

"Shut up, I don't need to listen to anything you say. You've been lying to me this whole time. You knew who I was." My rage starts to ignite like a fire burning within me.

"But—"

"But nothing . . . Everest. You lied. There's nothing you can say now that's going to change the fact that you knew exactly who I was when we met." With brisk steps he makes his way to me, reaching out his hand to touch me. I swat it away.

"Do. Not. Touch. Me." I grit out. "Don't come anywhere near me. I never want to see you again."

"Just listen to me, Aria. You need to go home."

"No." I start to turn but his hand stops me, grabbing my forearm to halt my progress.

"Look!" he exclaims as he flips the phone to my face. His expression says my life will forever be changed yet again. My visions blurs as I see the letters that form words that make me finally understand. Tears swell up in my eyes and I shake my head back and forth.

"No! Oh God, NO!"

It's time to stop running. It's time to go. My chest constricts as I choke on my own breath to stifle back a sob. With my head down, I move away from Chase and grab my suitcase and throw it on the bed. The sound echoes in the silence as I continue to bite back the agonizing howl that teeters on the brink of eruption. My shoulder shake from the restraint I'm placing on my body to hold back my emotions. But I refuse to break down in front of him. From my peripheral vision, I see him walk closer to me.

"Please just let me expl—" Tears start to stream down my face as he speaks, but I whip them away. Exhaling, I try my best to place a mask of indifference on my face as I meet his eyes.

"No! You, Chase Porter had a chance to explain the day you tricked me. You're a coward and a liar." Whatever the reason for his lie, whatever the explanation will be, it won't come now. I welcome that disconnect, because I'm not ready to hear it. I'm not ready to deal with any of it. I'm so lost. I'm so confused. I'm so angry with Chase, but I won't let him see any of that. I won't let him comfort me. He lost that right.

"Aria, please- I want to be there for you. Please give me a —"

"No, this is all your fault. I can never trust you again. The Chase I thought I knew is a complete stranger."

"You can trust me, Aria. I know you're upset with me, but if you need—"

"Need? The only thing I need from you . . . is for you to leave me the fuck alone." My voice is laced with disgust, my anger palpable. I turn on my heel, pick up my clothes and start tossing the clothes in the suitcase. "Get the hell out of my room. I never ever want to see you again."

Breathe

CHAPTER FIFTEEN

Now I'm on my way back.

Back on a plane. Back on the run.

But this time I'm running home.

Running away from Chase Porter. Running away from Everest.

I can't even fathom what went down in Positano. My brain can't wrap itself around everything I now know and everything I thought I knew. All the lies built on lies. All the false truths spun.

It was hard to breathe in those first few seconds after understanding flooded my senses. I felt as if my arteries had been severed the moment the truth descended upon me. As if the lifeline that held me together was slowly unraveling, and I was bleeding.

Funny how little had actually changed in the last fifteen days. Fifteen days ago, I left New York hiding from my truth, and now I'm hiding from Chase's truth. Chase—I can't even call him that. Who is he? Is he my Chase or is he Parker's Everest, the Everest I resented. The somewhat mythical creature

Parker made him out to be over the years. The Everest whom I always believed was the hindrance in our relationship. He'd always been there hovering over us, the bane of my existence by the time I graduated from college. The friend of my best friend, a person I'd never met, had never seen, and had such strong feelings of animosity for. Then there was the look in his eyes that seemed so familiar that first day in Tuscany . . .

It was as if my soul had known his before we'd ever met, an instant connection brought on by our mutual love of Parker Stone. But then the truth came out, and maybe I could have forgiven the lies, but only if he didn't know how I felt about him. But he knew, and still he withheld his identity.

After everything unraveled, I was relieved when he told me to leave, and I did just that. I left. I climbed above deck and told Luciano to steer the boat to port. I never turned back, and Chase never tried to stop me. A part of me would like to pretend it's because he knows this is what I need, but how the fuck could he know me when everything we had was based on a lie? Fifteen days have passed, and my heart is empty yet again.

I turn my phone on the moment my feet hit ground and text after text comes through in a wave.

A decision has been made.

You need to come home.

Where the hell are you?

Get your ass home.

The look in Chase's eyes still haunts me, even though I want to hate him. And God, do I want to, but he took a girl with no hope, lifted her up, and taught her to fly. Anger creeps into my blood. He might have taught me to fly, but then he cut my wings. He destroyed me. I made quick work of getting out of Italy, only briefly answering Sophie's text and informing her

I'd find a flight home. I called the airlines and booked myself on the first flight out from Naples. A complete fog hung over me. I'm even unsure how I managed to find a cab, how I managed to grab my belongings—how I managed to get away.

I take the lone available seat on the plane, it's definitely not the fancy cocoon that comforted me on the arrival here. This time I'm next to an elderly lady with short wisps of white hair. Small bifocals rest on her weathered and wrinkled face.

"Would you like a peppermint?" I turn to her, perplexed as to whom she's speaking.

"Yes, you, sweetie. Would you like a peppermint?" My eyes mist. This complete stranger is the final catalyst to my breakdown. She doesn't know me, she doesn't know what I need, but the kind nature of her face is enough to bring me to my knees. "What's the matter, sweetie?" There's no questioning the concern and sincerity in her voice. Tears stream down my face, and I notice her prune-like hands reach into her purse and pull out a tissue. I'm coming undone thirty-nine thousand feet in the air.

"Whatever it is, it can't be that bad," she says, but she has no way of knowing what awaits me when I arrive home. "Would you like to talk about it?" Then just like that, the floodgates burst. All of it.

Everything I've done pours out. Everything I've said. It all comes out in heavy tears and choked sobs. As if I'm purging the memory of a bad dream. A nightmare. One that's far from over. As I cry, the memory playing through my brain paralyzes me. It grips my throat until I can no longer breathe. White spots dance in my vision as it completely engulfs me.

"Hey, baby girl, what are you doing?" Parker rounded the

198

corner into my bedroom. Frustrated, I stared blankly at a pile of clothes on my bed.

"I have nothing to wear." My hands ran through my hair as my eyes glared at the mountain of my belongings.

"Funny, because it looks like you have a shit ton of choices."

"Nothing in this pile works," I huffed as I tossed more clothes onto the bed. Parker lifted a black lace top. He arched an eyebrow.

"How about this?"

I snatched the top from his hand. "You are absolutely no help, Parker," I barked, throwing it in the hamper.

"What are you freaking out about anyway?" He pushed the clothes out of the way and sat on the edge of the bed.

I waved my hands in the air. "You're making a mess! Don't you have somewhere else to be? Off playing with Everest somewhere?" I grit out as I bent over and picked up the blouses that had fallen to the floor.

"Ari, this whole fucking bed is a mess. And no, he's somewhere between China and Pakistan right now, climbing K2." A boyish grin grew on his face. "So why don't you breathe and tell me what's really got you so hot and bothered."

"Work, Park, work! I'm supposed to start tomorrow."

"Then don't."

"That's not really an option."

"Who says it's not? Seriously, Ari." Parker reached for my hand, and I pulled my gaze away from his. "Who says you need to start tomorrow? Is this even what you want? Do you even know what you want?"

"I want this," I barely whispered. I didn't know whether I was trying to convince him or myself. I pulled my hand away and stood. "It's all I've ever wanted." But saying those words *made my chest feel as if it was caving in.*

"Since when? Or is this something you think you want? What would you be doing if Owen were still here?" The mention of my brother's name made it hard to breathe. Instantly, I felt as if my room was closing in on me. "What did you want to be before he died? Before you went on this ridiculous quest to live the life intended for him?"

I stared out the window, and the first tear dripped down my cheek. I heard Parker stand behind me, but I didn't turn to look at him. Instead, I peered downward at the pile of clothes in my hands. Suffocating clothes. My chest tightened further until my lungs were desperate for air.

"Ari." Parker paused and rested his hands on my shoulders. His voice was soothing. "I remember the girl who wanted to travel. The girl who pretended to be a princess. Who wanted to see the world with me. The one who came over every day and stuck yellow pins into the map pinned to my wall. Do you remember that girl?"

I shook my head, my vision blurry from unshed tears. "I—I don't," I finally cried. I didn't remember that girl anymore. She died a long time ago.

"That's why you need to get away. All those dreams we had . . . Travel with me, Ari." Parker turned me toward him. His eyes were bright, and a full smile covered his face. "Let's finally do it. You don't need to be this person. It's time you be the Ari that Owen loved." His words hung in the air, like a storm waiting to hit landfall.

"Don't bring Owen into this." I shook my head. "I'm doing this for him."

"You're not doing this for him." He almost seemed offended. "You're doing this for them." He snarled at the mention of my

parents. I wasn't doing this for them. This was what I wanted. Wasn't it?

"You don't know anything." I wiped the tears from my face and moved back toward the bed. I had made my decision.

"I might not know anything, but I know you don't need to kill yourself for your parents' approval. You're not Owen. No matter what you do, you will never be him." Parker paused, and I let his words seep deep inside me. "They might not see you, but I do, I see everything. Be the Ari we both loved."

"I don't even know who that is. Who I ever wanted to be," I sighed. I had no clue who I was anymore.

"Don't think about the past, then. Start from the here and now. Make the change. Everest always says to stay in the present, don't live in the past. Be strong. Be you. Be you, Ari." My anger rose. Of course he brought up Everest. Why couldn't I just have one minute with Parker without Everest being present? What the hell did he know about me anyway?

"Me? Who the hell is that, Parker? Who do you—or should I say—Everest—think I should be?"

"Just be who you want." His fingers ran through his blond hair, pulling as he found his words. "You can be so much more than what they want from you. Come with me," he blurted, and his gaze softened as it met mine. "Aria, let's finally do this. Let's go see the world—together. Let's find ourselves—together." It was everything I wanted. Everything I always wanted to do with him.

"I . . . I can't." I bowed my head. I can't go with you." I couldn't think about a life with Parker at the moment. I had to make something of myself first. "I'm not ready, I—" He stepped forward. His hands caressed my cheeks, and soft fingers lifted my eyes to meet his. "I just don't . . ." I stumbled over my words. My mind ran a mile a minute as my heart slammed against my *chest. "I need to do this, I need—"*

"You don't need those things. You don't need their approval. They should love you unconditionally."

"What do you know? What have you ever had to do for your parents' love? I have to show them. I have to be—"

"Have to be what?"

"I just have to be. I have to succeed. I can't go off on some whim."

"Some whim? We made plans, Aria. We said we would do this." His shoulders lifted, tensed. On an exhale, he continued. "You think your job will make them love you? It won't. I love you. You hear me, Aria? I love you, and I want to be with you. I want you to come with me."

"You don't love me, at least not like that." My arms crossed protectively over my chest.

"How the hell do you know what I feel?" His brows snapped together. My gaze lowered, and I eyed his Adam's apple repeatedly bobbing as he tried to regulate his breathing.

"How can you love me? All these years you treated me like a sister. All the girls, all these years you rejected me, Park."

"I know I did, and I'm sorry. I've been doing a lot of thinking, Ari, and this whole time, the reason none of those girls mattered was because they weren't you. None of them were you."

"You sure it wasn't because you were out partying with Everest?"

"What does Everest have to do with this?" Parker began to pace the room.

"If you don't know that answer, forget I mentioned it." Everest had everything to do with it. Anytime I got closer to Parker, there was Everest dragging him off on another adventure. Another mountain that needed fucking climbing. He could show

Parker the world but what did I have to show him? Nothing.

Parker paused in his steps, glanced up at the ceiling, then back down. His brows knit together when his gaze met mine. "Do you love me, Aria?" His words ripped through me. "Do I mean anything to you? Does this mean anything to you?" His eyes pleaded, but I couldn't find it in me to calm down. How could he do this to me today, when I finally let go of the idea of being with him? When I finally decided to move on. How could he do this to me when I was finally about to make something of myself?

"Please tell me what you're thinking, Aria."

I wanted to cry. I wanted to tell him the truth. I wanted to tell him I loved him. I wanted that so badly, but my wounded heart wouldn't let me, and it angered me that he did this to me. That he put this fear there.

"What am I thinking? God, how can you do this to me now? I'm trying to make something of myself. I can't just leave. I'm sorry, but you can't just show up and tell me you love me. How can I believe you after everything that's happened? You say you love me, but you expect me to change. How is that love?"

"I know I don't deserve you after never admitting this. For making you feel like I never saw you, but I've always loved you. I'm so sorry I never told you before."

He loved me? He loved me! No, I couldn't let myself believe that. I couldn't be hurt again. "How could you love me? You rejected me." My words trailed off as I remembered the near kiss, as I felt the memory of his refusal flood over me. As my heart shattered all over again from only the recollection.

"At first I didn't know what I wanted. I was too scared to take a chance, but how can I not? Not one day has gone by without me thinking of you. I think I've loved you since the day I met

you. I love what you are. I love everything about you. I love your kindness. I love your smile. I love you, Aria. All of you. You're all I ever think of. Look at me, please. Do you love me?" He exhaled, and his eyes searched mine. Looking for my answer.

"I can't. I don't. You never chose me. It's always been about—"

"I've always loved you. This feeling has been embedded in my soul. Do you love me, Aria?"

"I . . . It's just—" I cover my face. I can't look at him anymore. His eyes tear me apart.

"Do you want to be with me?" he asked, and my heart stopped from the pain in his voice. From the pain I'd put there. I'd waited so long to hear those words, but now that they hovered over us I couldn't. I couldn't admit the words. Fear held me prisoner.

"No, Parker. I don't want to be with you," I replied. My eyes remained closed. Even as the words left my mouth, I knew they were a lie.

"Fine, I get it. Now you're scared," he exclaimed. My eyes popped open and bore into his. "Do. You. Love. Me?" His words echoed through the room. I didn't just love him. It was so much more than that. So much more than love. He was my rock, my friend. He was the lifeline that ran through me. But I couldn't take that chance. I couldn't give up everything. I just couldn't. So I lied.

"No, I don't love you."

I had never felt so helpless.

I'd destroyed him.

There was nothing I could say to fix this.

The look in his eyes would haunt me forever. "Park . . . "

"Oh sweetie," The old woman sitting beside me says to every hateful word I utter. Every lie I spew. Her eyes meet mine with sympathy and understanding. But she doesn't see. She doesn't understand that I can never take it back. This is all my fault. Everything is my fault. Everyone leaves me. No one ever stays. "He knows you didn't mean it. You were hurt, confused. You lashed out. He will forgive you, but you also need to forgive yourself. You made a bad choice, and you can live with the regret for the rest of your life or you can forgive yourself and do something about it.

"Of course you will make mistakes. But what I've learned through my years is that no matter what mistake you make, you can't change your past, but you can change your present. Accept yourself, faults and all, and move forward. Forgive yourself, because I'm sure he already has."

My tears fall, misting my cheeks. If she only knew. There's no forgiveness for me. There's no end to this torment. That night everything changed. Everything was taken from me, and nothing I'll ever do or say will take back what happened.

I'm not sure how I make it off the plane. I'm not sure how I find the man standing by the baggage claim. I'm not even sure how I find myself in my apartment, washing off the past twenty-four hours. Nothing is clear. I'm lost. I'm alone. That's all I know.

CHAPTER SIXTEEN

THE SPACE IS vacant of any warmth, cold and sterile. I see him from across the room, and I step closer. His eyes are closed. He doesn't open them. My heart pounds in my chest. The reality of the situation I've been running from crashes into me. Suffocates me. Drowns me.

There will be no talks of traveling, no pinning locations on an old tattered map. No crooked smile that lights up my day.

There he is, my once forever, but forever is no longer.

He won't be mine. He will never be mine. The world from here on out will never be the same. I reach out and take his hand. "Please don't go. I'm afraid of my life without you."

But he doesn't speak.

"Can you hear me?" I whisper.

The voices around me break into my subconscious, but I can barely hear their words. My time is limited. They will want to see him soon.

"I miss you. I miss everything. I miss your voice. Your smell. I thought I could do this but I can't. I can't do this without you. I . . . I can't." Tears prick at my eyes and then proceed to pour down my cheek. "Every day that I was gone, I missed you more and more. But I'm here now, I'm with you."

He's not my Parker.

He's a shell that no longer holds his spirit.

He's broken bones.

And breathing only through a machine.

He's not my best friend.

My best friend left me forty-one days ago.

Hours had passed. Countless minutes since Parker had stormed out of my apartment after our fight. I held my phone in my hands and dialed, hung up and redialed Parker's number so many times I lost track. What would I even say? He would never understand, that much was obvious. He loves me? That's what he said. I loved him, too, but didn't dare utter the words. How could I? How could I trust what he would do with my love? For all of these years I longed to hear those words, but now they were tainted. Did he really love me? Why hadn't he loved me before? Why had he rejected me before? I couldn't stand the idea of opening myself up to him just for him to crush me again. No.

I placed the phone down. I wouldn't call him. This would pass. Parker would realize that he didn't really love me. I would go on with my life as if the confession never happened.

It's funny the things you remember and the things you don't. I remember the outfit I wore the night my life changed, but I don't remember whether I ate dinner. I remember the way Parker's eyes shone brighter when he smiled, but I don't recall how his hand felt when he brushed away my tears. I wish I remembered it. I wish I had memories of everything.

I pulled a white camisole and a pair of white and black polka dot shorts from my drawer and laid them beside a plaid pleated skirt and black summer cashmere T-shirt. As I was placing a long pearl-knotted necklace on top of the outfit to complete tomorrow's ensemble, the house phone began to ring.

It was odd for the house phone to ring that time of night. So odd, as only a handful of people knew that number, and it was past ten p.m.

I remember the sound of my feet hitting the wood floors, but I don't remember the feel of the phone cradled in my hand as my world was crushed. I remember the sensation of my chest constricting. The painful dizzying of my pulse accelerating to the point of pain. Most of all I remember . . .

One phrase.

Three simple words.

A moment that would change everything.

"Parker needs you."

I arrived at the hospital after the phone call and I was shocked by the sight that awaited me. I'd expected to walk into the waiting room and be told there was a giant mistake. Parker would come walking out the side door, pull me into a hug, and apologize for scaring the shit out of me. I would laugh through my tears and apologize for being such a brat earlier that morning. He would hold me close, our hearts would beat in tandem, and he would say, "No need to say anything, baby girl. I know how you feel about me. And I love you, too." That's how my night was supposed to go down. But instead, none of that happened.

When I walked inside the waiting room, I was met with both silence and loud violent sobs. Mr. Stone paced the waiting room, his hands running frantically through his gray hair. Mrs.

Stone wept in a metal-framed chair with red polyester uphol-stery. I sat in an empty one adjacent to hers, placed my hand on her back, and let out another wave of tears.

The lady sitting on my other side was talking non-stop into her phone, arguing about something of no relevance. I wanted to yell at her, but instead I stayed silent and allowed her words to echo through the small space we occupied. She looked up into my dead-feeling eyes. I was barren. My walls were up. Protecting. She shrugged and returned to her mundane existence.

I gathered my legs into my chest and cocooned myself. Waiting. An array of visitors stopped by. We met cries and fran-tic questions and prayers to God. Screams came next. Doctors rocketed in and out. They passed like a blustery day. I couldn't even lift my eyes to meet their gaze. I didn't even hear them. All I heard was the buzzing sound of fluorescent lights above. All I saw was the flickering causing my eyes to cringe.

Flick

Flick

Flick

It was an out of body experience.

Waiting, watching . . . nothing.

Then after hours, a tall man wearing rumpled scrubs stepped into the room, and we all went erect as he approached Parker's parents. Mr. Stone held his wife up. He was trying to give her strength, to protect her from the reality we all knew was coming. Her body began to shake as the doctor started talking. Falling to the ground, she broke. I watched as Parker's father lifted her into his arms, and I then I saw her face, and I broke. She was vacant. Her eyes robbed of all life. She was dead inside.

"What did he say?" I asked, but I didn't recognize my own voice. It was as if someone had jumped inside me and was taking

over my basic impulses. Mrs. Stone couldn't speak. She opened her mouth, but it merely trembled. Mr. Stone spoke instead, cradling her to his chest as he gently stroked her hair.

"Parker's injuries are extensive. They don't know if he'll make it."

Police came to speak to us. Words like 'over the legal limit' were thrown out, and I knew. I knew at that very moment that this was all my fault. I had killed my brother and now my best friend was fighting for his life because of me.

As the days passed, I sat by his bedside. My head rested on the hard mattress as the doctors spoke with his parents.

"Parker, suffered from a traumatic brain injury. He has a subarachnoid hemorrhage. He's currently in a medically induced coma, until we can perform an EEG." A screaming sob broke out from Mrs. Stone's mouth as her body fell into her husbands for support. It was a primal sound that made my body feel like it was being shredded from the inside out. Mr. Stone held her tightly his own tears cascading down his cheeks.

"When?" he choked out.

"Tomorrow," the doctor replied and I gasped for air. Tomorrow, Tomorrow, Tomorrow. The words continued to echo throughout the day and well into the night until the time had finally come and all we could do was wait and hope and . . . pray. As the results came in, all my hopes and prayers were extinguished.

No brain function. But we demanded a second opinion . . . and then a third.

All tests reconfirming the original prognosis . . .

No brain activity.

"Oh God . . . What do we do?" Mr. Stone cried out and the doctor stepped toward him, compassion in his eyes.

"This is ultimately your decision if you would like to keep him on the ventilator, but you need to understand according to the menial standards we live by, he's dead. There is no hope of recovery." Parker's body was here, but he was a vacant shell of what he once was. He would never recover. My heart screamed, that was Parker, my Parker. Not a lifeless body in a bed. It was Parker! But he would not breathe—nor open his eyes—on his own again.

"I won't kill my baby," Parker's mother collapsed onto the floor, her husband beside her.

My chest tightens at the memory. Parker went to a bar after our altercation and, according to witnesses, drank multiple shots, had a few beers, and left. He walked out the door saying he was going to grab a cab back to his place. No one knew why he decided to go back to his parents' house in Westchester that night, instead of grabbing a cab like he said he would. The questions poured in. Why was he coming home? Why was he drinking? But I knew the answer. It was all because of me.

He went out because of me. He grabbed his car to escape because of me . . . and then never made it. He hadn't even made it out of the city before colliding straight into a pole. *Head on collision.*

Sadness engulfs me as I remember that night. My breathing shallows. Everything is fuzzy. I feel dizzy. My hand reaches out toward him. To touch him. I fear I'll pass out from the racing of my heart. It hammers to the point of pain as my small hand makes contact with the soft curve of his jaw.

Even if he's lying here, I know he died the moment he walked out my door. And although I didn't put the bottle to his mouth, and even though I didn't put him behind the wheel and didn't make him wrap his car around a street pole, I was guilty of his death.

The sound of the machine breathing for him echoes in my ears. It drums like a freight train. The sound of life . . . the sound of death. An involuntary sob tears through my chest. Perhaps if I scream, the anguish inside me will subside, but I have no energy, and it still won't change that my best friend is dying.

Now when I look at him, words ring over and over again in my head. They run over me, they suffocate me. They drown me.

Parker is gone.

Three words, it's always been three words.

Parker needs you.

Parker is gone.

Parker needs you.

Parker is gone.

Over and over and over again.

Three words can change your life.

CHAPTER SEVENTEEN

*T*HE SEMBLANCE OF *hope that still lived inside me died. I could feel my chest constricting. The doctors gave the news: he would never wake. Neither parent knew what to do. Seconds, days and then weeks passed, but no decision could be made. What would Parker want was asked so many times I lost count. He had no will. He never spoke of his final wishes. What twenty-five-year-old had a will? What twenty-five-year-old imagined that they would be heartbroken, go out to a bar, and then drive their car headfirst into a pole? There was no way to know what he would want. DNR was an option. He could live for years attached to a machine, but what kind of life would that be?*

From outside Parker's room I heard the screaming. Mr. and Mrs. Stone battling on what to do. They had been battling for over three weeks. My chest constricted and bile ran up my throat. The endless arguing made me need to recede into myself and hide. Each time they battled another part of me died. I needed to flee this hell, but I couldn't leave him. I felt an eternal emptiness in my soul. I had no idea what to do. The one person who could help me make sense of this was no longer able to. My rock wasn't here, and I couldn't do this without him. I didn't know what to do without him.

As I gripped his hand tightly, praying for clarity I heard Parker's words. The words that lead us here. 'And that's why you need to get away.' And I finally understood how to make it up to him. How to make this right. How to show him I loved him and that all of this had not been for nothing.

"Parker? I know you can't hear me, but I'm going to do it. I'm going to go. This is all my fault. If I had just said yes. If I'd just admitted the truth to you. We could have gone together. I was too scared and I lied. But I'm going to do it. I'm going to do all of it . . . for you." I leaned forward and placed a gentle kiss on his lips.

"Goodbye, Parker. I love you."

With moisture streaming down my cheeks, I barreled through the cold of the hospital. Through the confusion and cha-os in my path. Then my arm hit someone and through misted eyes I looked up and my gaze met cloudy steel orbs. His eyes were red-rimmed and swollen. His arm reached out to steady me, but I didn't wait for him to help me. I just ran until I was clear of the doors. Suddenly, the patter of giant rain droplets smacked across the pavement. I had stepped out into a torrential downpour. It was only fitting.

I sobbed. I sobbed right alongside the heavens that wept with me. I embraced the release, and in the middle of the park-ing lot, I let go. Let go of all of it. Picked up the phone and dialed. I knew where I would go. A place where I wouldn't need to be privy to the fighting. Where I wouldn't need to hear them weigh out the pros and cons of keeping an empty body in a bed. A place where Parker always said I should go.

Before I knew it, I was on a plane, on my way to honor Parker's last wish . . . on my way to find me.

———

"It's time." A familiar voice says. Turning toward the sound, I peer through squinted eyes to find Chase standing behind me. I don't know how he's here at the hospital with me right now. When he arrived from Italy. How he got here. But I don't care. All I know is at this very moment, despite everything that has happened, I need him. I need him holding me up. Just as I feel Chase's hand gently stroke my shoulder, the doctor enters the room with Parker's parents.

"Are you ready?" the doctor asks Mr. and Mrs. Stone. I want to scream, "No! I'm not ready!" but it's not my place. They speak, but I can't hear what they're saying. I'm too numb to hear. I feel nothing. Time stands still as we wait for the moment to come. The moment a beautiful, bright light will be blown out.

"Parker. Oh God, Parker, please don't leave me! Please. Please, you can't go. I'm sorry. I'm so sorry! Please don't leave me. No, you can't take him. He can't leave me," I mutter through choked sobs.

I lean over to kiss his cheeks. They're still warm. This can't be real. This is nothing but a bad dream. He was going to Europe with me. This can't be the end. We have so many pins left. So many places on the map we haven't seen yet. Chase speaks in a hushed voice to Parker's parents, but it's hard to make out what he says over the pounding of my heart.

I think he asks if they want us to leave. I wish for them to say yes because I can't be here to see the life leave Parker's body. But if they say I can stay, that's right where I'll be. I will never forgive myself for missing his last breath. I will never forgive myself for missing the moment he went to a better place, the moment he found peace. Mr. Stone shakes his head at Chase and then turns back and nods to the doctor.

"No, they can't do it yet." My words are raspy, hushed, and confused.

"Aria—" Chase's voice breaks through my splintered mind. "His family needs to say good-bye. It's time." I shake my head. Barely audible words leave my mouth.

"I . . . I . . . I can't . . . I can't, Chase," I stutter. He touches me. His fingers softly caress my shoulder. My gaze turns toward him, and he nods in understanding. I need to go with him, but I can't will my feet to move. It's time, I tell myself. I want so badly to object. To argue that they need to reconsider, but there is nothing to be said. It's not my place, and it's not fair for me to interject.

I turn and walk toward the wall, my fingers laced in Chase's. Mrs. Stone's whimpering grows fainter with each step I take. Chase pulls me into him, and I bring my face into his chest, leaving the world behind. I hear nothing but the soft thud of his heart beating. Pulling my head from the warmth of his embrace, the sound of the machine rushes back into my conscious. The room is my worst nightmare, sobs and whimpers, and then I hear the hum of the machine. I welcome the hum. It means for this brief second Parker Stone is still alive.

The hum continues as more people enter the room. A group of medical personnel gathers around now, taking final notes. One of them passes a clipboard to Mr. Stone. His hands shake so badly I fear he will drop the pen. My eyes no longer focus. My body seems boneless. I'm using Chase to hold me up. The sounds are still steady. I breathe in. I exhale.

Parker's chest rises. I memorize the movement, etch it into my memory. I observe as they turn off the ventilator, and I turn away to fight through my tears. This can't be the last thing I see of him. I try to focus elsewhere, but for some reason I can't stop looking.

They take out the breathing tube.

Memories begin to flash, one after another.

Beep

The dimple on his cheek when he smiles.

Beep

The small scar he has above his left eyebrow.

Beep

His obsession with Reese's Pieces.

Beep

The way he would softly say baby girl when I was sad.

Silence

The silence is suffocating.

CHAPTER EIGHTEEN

THREE THIRTY-THREE P.M. I saw the last breath leave his body, and now I stand weighted to the wall as sobs wrack throughout the room. Agony descends upon me. An agony I never thought possible. A part of me died when the machine stopped. The part of me tethered to Parker ceases to exist.

I collapse forward.

I break.

A hand rubs my back. Those hands embrace me. Pull me in. Engulf me.

"He's gone." My whole body shakes as I hold on to him and rock in his arms.

"He's in a better place." His words come out strangled, as if he's holding back his own meltdown. Hearing his voice is too much. The pain is palpable, and my knees buckle beneath me.

"I can't do this. I'm not strong enough."

"You don't have to be. I'll be strong enough for you. I'll hold you up. I'll be your strength." More sobs break. "Shh, it will be okay. Everything will be okay," he promises, but it does nothing to soothe the ache in my heart. Nothing will be okay. Nothing will ever be okay again. My skull begins to pound as sadness clamps down on me. I can feel Chase lift me up, and what's left of me snaps like a twig.

"Please don't make me leave yet," I beg. I'm petrified my memories will begin to fade. "You can't make me," I whisper. I jump out of his lap and push past Chase, who tries to hold me in his arms. Leaning over the bed, I get close to Parker's lifeless body.

"Please, I can't remember the last time we laughed. I'm so afraid of my life without you. I stayed away, and I'm so sorry. I lift my hand to touch him. "I'm here. I . . . I'm with you. Park, oh God, Parker. Please, you can't be gone. You can't have left me. I'm so, so, sorry." Warm arms wrap around me, pulling me gently back.

"No. You can't take me. I'm not ready. I'm not ready to leave him yet. He needs me." I lean over to kiss his cheeks. Warm still. "He's supposed to go to Europe with me." A strangling sound creeps out of my mouth. My hand lifts to my mouth. "Oh God," I choke out. "This can't be the end. So many adventures we didn't take." What little is left of my composure bursts like a balloon filled with too much air and breaks me into a million pieces. Parker had always given me strength. He made me strong, and without him, I tear apart. Chase's arms wrap around my middle.

"No, I'm not ready to leave! Get away from me!" I screech at him just as his arms grasp me. I kick as he lifts me into his arms, scooping me up. "No! You can't take me from him." My arms flail to break loose. "I can't leave him. I can't breathe. Oh God. I can't breathe without him. Put me down! He needs me. I never told him I loved him. He never knew! If I had known—"

My body shudders with another round of sobs. If I had known those were the last words I would hear from his lips, I might have tried to stop him. I might have memorized the timbre of his voice. The way his lips puckered ever so slightly when he was upset. But instead, I let him leave. "Oh God," I cry out while I wipe at the tears trailing down my cheeks. "Instead, I . . . I turned back to my outfit. I turned back to picking out my fucking outfit."

My hands pound against Chase's back as he cradles me in his arms. My body goes slack from the exertion, but my muscles still shake. Aftershocks. Repetitious trembling I can no longer control.

"Put me down." It's a whisper. Barely audible. "I . . . I." My words are lost in an involuntary sob.

"I've got you, Princess. I've got you." The levee bursts. My body crumbles.

"I'm so sorry, I'm sorry . . . I'm not ready to say good-bye. I'm not ready for him to be gone, Chase. Please don't take him away from me! I'm not ready. I can't say good-bye again." Chase tucks me into his lap, cradling me, and I cry. I cry until I think there's not one ounce of fluid left in my body. He glances over to Parker. I watch him and want to reach out to him to comfort him, but I can't. I've got nothing left in me.

Chase returns his gaze to me as he gently lifts me up and places me on my feet. With care, he takes my trembling hand and guides us out the door. We don't say anything as we leave the hospital. Neither of us seems able to speak. Sorrow closes our throats. We enter a cab, and I can barely muster the energy to mutter my address. Then I bow my head.

When we arrive at my apartment, he doesn't move to enter. I silently pray he does, that he takes me in his arms and makes me forget any of this happened. "I—" My mouth opens, but I'm not sure what I want to say, so I snap it closed. He stares down at the floor for a few seconds before he lifts his gaze to meet mine.

"I'll pick you up tomorrow for the funeral," he mumbles. His eyes mist over as he speaks.

"Tomorrow?" I can't believe it's so soon. But I guess it's really not soon. Parker's body might have only died a few hours ago, but his soul left weeks ago.

"Yeah." That's all he says, and right now, I'm thankful. If we talk, who knows where the conversation will go, and right now, I'm just not ready to go there. He stares at me for a few more seconds before he leans in and places a whisper of a kiss on my forehead. It's just what I need, and I welcome the feeling. It soothes me. He steps away and turns with his shoulders slouched forward. I watch him go.

CHAPTER NINETEEN

ANGRY CLOUDS PAINT the distance above us. Tiny rain-drops trickle down from the sky. Rows of tombstones stand before me, liquid collecting on the smooth, dark marble. It's only fitting for a day like today. Chase stands next to me, his arm tightly wrapped around my waist holding me up. I don't have the strength to tell him to stop. To tell him he can't hold me like that anymore. I know if he were to let go, I'd fall.

The pastor is speaking, his words like a soft hymn above the pitter-patter of the soft shower. It drowns out the anguish coming from Parker's mother. It drowns out the screams in my own head.

Parker's father stands and makes his way to the head of the gravesite. My body shakes as he begins to speak. Chase gives me a little squeeze to remind me he still has me. Tears pour down my face.

Mr. Stone's words finally penetrate my mind. He talks of their many adventures and the old weathered map on Parker's wall. All the places he'd been and all the places he'd yet to see.

His words splinter inside me as I consider my planned adventure with Parker. How I went without him. My chest constricts as if I'm being suffocated. As if a heavy boulder lies on my chest and doesn't allow me to breathe.

Chase grabs me closer, pulls me into his chest, and I let him. I don't deserve this comfort. I don't deserve to be the one standing on the wet grass on this summer day. More people speak following Mr. Stone. Each has a reminisce to share-a story, a highlight of the life Parker shared with us. The clouds part as another friend takes the podium and begins to speak. A tiny stream of sunlight breaks through the clouds. The light glistens off the water collecting on the coffin. I stand in silence, grieving to myself as I wait for my moment to walk forward. The sun shines brilliantly as I'm gestured forward.

Turning to Chase, I whisper, "I don't know how to say good-bye, Chase." His hand grips mine as he walks me forward.

"Then don't. Speak from the heart. Don't say good-bye forever, just good-bye for now." He steps away with one final squeeze, leaving me to stand in front of the crowd. A suffocating sensation tightens my throat. My chest heaves from the effort of holding back my sobs. With swollen eyes, I stare at Sophie. She's standing a few feet away, her eyes glistening with tears. My lips quiver uncontrollably, my throat feels hoarse as I begin to speak.

"All of the memories I have with Parker are so vivid so fresh, as if we were together only yesterday. It feels like only a moment ago he held me in his arms. Like a moment ago, he coaxed a smile out of me. Like only a moment ago, he got me to dream again.

"When I was younger, I used to write poetry. One day

Parker found a poem I wrote that was crinkled up. He opened it and read the words—words that I believed were trash. He made me believe in my voice, and from then on, he encouraged me to write those poems. I stopped years ago. Too old to write poetry, I said, but I recently found one. It was Parker's favorite. I wrote it when I was twelve years old."

I pull the torn-up, crinkled paper out of my pocket. The pages are weathered and beaten. The words faded from dried up tears.

My castle in the sky
My world so far away
That's where I can close my eyes
And stay away

My castle in the sky
My home away from home
The world where I can never fail
And always get to roam

My castle in the sky
Where you will never go away
Where no matter what happens
You will always stay

My castle in the sky
Is really in my heart
My soul is very frail
But not with my castle in my heart.

"Thank you, Parker, for always being my castle." Tears shimmer in my eyes as Chase walks forward and places his hand on mine. I move away, let him take my place, and I sob.

I cry for Parker.

I cry for Owen.

I cry for the part of me that longs to be back on that boat with Chase and pretend none of this is happening.

And I cry for myself.

For the empty feeling that I fear will never fill.

My heartbeat is slow, as if I died with Parker.

Numbness.

Emptiness

"Our journey together has come to the end, and although you are gone, you'll never be replaced in our hearts. I promise you'll live on through us . . . Forever. Good-bye, my friend." Chase says to the casket, then the pastor steps forward again.

"The Lord is my Shepherd. I shall not want. He maketh . . ."

I will miss everything about Parker Stone.

Moisture continues to travel down my chin, and my chest quivers. I turn my face toward the casket. He's gone. I don't want to do this without him. I don't want to be here without him.

Mrs. Stone approaches me, pulling me into her arms. Tears stream down my face as she embraces me.

"That was beautiful what you read. Parker would be so proud," she whispers as she holds me, our bodies shaking with sobs. With a sniffle, she pulls away and Mr. Stone grabs her tightly and comforts her. As they begin to recede I turn to Chase. His eyes are red rimmed and his obvious pain breaks me further.

"I can't. When will it stop hurting so bad? What do I do?" I say as another cloud rolls in. Tiny spatters of water hit my nose. Chase takes a step closer. His hand stretches across the space that separates us to collect a drop on his fingertip.

"The best thing you can do when it's raining is let it. Don't fight it. Eventually it will stop. Once it passes, you can dry off." His words mean so much at this moment, and I let myself embrace him. He holds me tightly as I come undone.

No more words are spoken. I melt into him and allow him to comfort me in front of Parker's grave. I find comfort in his embrace, yet I can't help but feel I'm betraying Parker. The one boy I ever loved died because I couldn't take a chance. I fall deeper into Chases' embrace. With his arms around me, the self-loathing lessens, even if only for a brief moment, and I welcome it. I welcome the feeling of him protecting me from the demons within me.

When we arrive at the gathering Parker's family was having in his honor, my phone begins to ring in my purse. I'm in such a daze it doesn't register that it's my mother calling.

"Hello?"

"Aria Bennett, where are you?"

"Mom, I can't talk right now," I say through clenched teeth.

"Where have you been, young lady?

"I'm walking into a gath—"

"You're such a disappointment. You were supposed—"

Before she can continue her disparaging line of thought, I hang up. *I can't do this right now.* I can't believe she can't even give me peace today. I'll call her back when I can handle the words she'll throw at me. Right now I can't.

"Be strong. I can see that you are about to fall apart, but I need you to be strong. Okay?"

Chase is right. No matter what my mother said, I need to hold my head up. I need to be strong and walk in that door. I shove the phone into my purse. It rings and I ignore it. Before stepping into the house, I pull a compact out of my purse. My cheeks are as pale as death. The only color comes from the rivulets of black bleeding from my eyes.

I follow Chase inside. Friends from his travels across the globe have come to pay their respects and come to honor and celebrate him. It's the most beautiful and moving thing I've ever seen. I take a deep breath to calm down. I force my eyes to close, and static white noise hums around me. It's jarring. As I open my eyes, time freezes. It stands completely still. Although the room is busy with people celebrating his life, I'm still stuck in a dark, awful place. It feels as if someone physically ripped my heart out of my chest, and they didn't even have the decency to numb the spot.

I want everyone to stop living, too. But as I observe them gathering and remembering rather than mourning—laughing, reminiscing, telling stories, reliving adventures—I realize that for most, time has, in fact, gone on, and I'm jealous.

I walk past the guests and straight to the liquor cabinet. I numb the pain.

CHAPTER TWENTY

MY STEPS ARE unsteady. The whiskey I downed right before leaving the gathering starts to affect me. I use the wall for stability as we make our way into my living room. Chase is trailing behind me. He reaches out slightly to catch me as I stumble.

"Aria." His voice is tentative. "Are we going to talk about what happened?" I keep walking, not even acknowledging that he spoke. I don't know what to say to him. The last few days he's been my rock, even though it's wrong to lean on him. Why can't he just shut up? Then I can stay in this world of denial a while longer.

"Goddamn it, Aria, I just want you to talk to me," he pleads, and it only succeeds in making me angrier.

"You want to do this? You want to do this now?" I brace the couch for support. The alcohol now coursing through my blood stream hinders my inhibitions. My eyes drift to the side, and we lock stares. "Fine. Let's do this. I don't understand you. You and your self-help crap, be a better person bullshit and for what? You. Are. A. Lie." My words are loud, staccato. "Everything about you is a fucking lie! Was anything true? Because from what I can see," I wave my hand haphazardly for emphasis, "You went against everything you ever said, everything you ever 'preached,'" I say in air quotes, which makes me lose my footing. I turn toward the couch, reaching out my arms to steady myself.

"What do you want me to say, Chase?" I plop down and sit. "You want me to fight with you. Scream? What's the point? For what? There's nothing here." I gesture between us. "Everything was built on a lie. You used me. Forced your way into my life, and for what? You know what, I don't even fucking care about the reason. None of it matters." I fist my hands in my hair. "And you know why? Because I'm a horrible person, Chase. I deserve it. I deserved all of it."

"No, Aria. You aren't. Why would you even say that?" He takes a step closer to the couch. His brows are drawn together.

"How can I say that? Because while he was in that bed dying, I was off, travelling through Italy with you." My eyes flood with tears at my admission of guilt.

"You were living your life. You were doing exactly what Parker would have wanted you to do. And that was the best way to honor him."

"How could I go? How could I be that horrible, that weak, and move on?"

"Letting someone go isn't a sign of weakness. It's the mark of strength."

"What do you know?" I jump up and head to the side table with my decanter of whisky. Reaching for a tumbler glass, I pour the liquid then gulp it down in one swig. The harsh burn coats my throat.

"Let me in. Talk to me," he pleads, but I will have none

of it.

"We are defined by the choices we make. You chose to lie."

"No, Aria. We are defined by our actions. You can choose something but act differently. I might have lied, but my actions told you how I felt."

"No! Your actions told me nothing. The time for telling me was in Tuscany, when you first met me."

"I was trying to help you, but instead I hurt you, and I'm sorry. If I could take it back, I would. If I could . . ." My body tenses as I wait for him to continue. His eyes remind me of a cloudy sky. "It's not like you think. I didn't go to Italy to deceive you."

"Oh really? So you weren't aware that I hated Everest. Parker never told you how I felt about you? Because I know that's a lie. I know you talked about it. I know you knew."

"Yeah, I knew. Is that what you want to hear? I knew you hated me. I knew you guys fought about me. Of course I knew. He was my best friend, Aria. But that doesn't mean I meant to deceive you. I was planning to tell you who I was. That day in the hospital—I passed you. I saw you. I saw the pain in your eyes. I saw how broken you were."

He breathes in and then exhales before continuing. "The next day this postcard came. And fuck if I knew I shouldn't, but I read it, and you tore me apart, Aria. I was scheduled to go to Rome a few weeks later, but something inside of me snapped when I read your letter. I pushed up my shoot, changed my flight and went straight to Tuscany. I never meant to lie. I intended to tell you who I was. To tell you I read your card, to tell you he would never hate you and nothing was your fault. Then I saw your eyes and I couldn't put any more pain there. God, I wanted to tell you so many times. But you don't understand—you seemed alive. At first you were like a shell of the person Parker told me about, and then I just couldn't be the one to take the gleam out of your eye. I'm so sorry, Aria. I should have told you." He sighs and I let out a shaky breath as my chin trembles.

"None of this would have happened if I hadn't fucked up."

"Aria, you never put a bottle in his hand. You never made him drive that car. I should have been there that night. He should never have been driving. Jesus, Aria, if you want to blame anyone, blame me! I was staying at his place, but I felt restless in the city and needed to get away, so when he got into the accident, I was on my way to climb K2. I was fucking climbing and he tried calling me Aria, God —" He places his hand against his mouth to muffle the howl he could no longer hold back. His chest heaving as he tries to calm himself. "I—I had no service. When I finally got a connection, I heard about Park . . . I—I heard the drunken message he left me. I came home as fast as I could. It took weeks to get back down and then I still had to acclimatize myself before I was able to return home. Every moment I wasn't there, a part of me died. But I couldn't change anything. There was nothing I could do to stop this. Just like there was nothing you could have done differently."

"You don't understand . . . I—I told him I didn't love him. Those were the last words he heard me say."

"Aria. I know you feel guilty, but how can you possibly blame yourself?"

"Doesn't matter what you think."

"You need to forgive yourself."

"Forgive myself? I killed my brother and then I killed my best friend."

"You didn't kill anyone." All I could do was shake my head. He would never understand the burden I feel in my heart.

"I told him I didn't want him. I lied. He went drinking because of me. He was leaving because of me." My voice sounds as if I'm being strangled, and I fight to keep my composure. "I miss him every day, every second. I loved him, and he died never knowing." Tears pool in my eyes.

"Aria, he knew. He felt it in every breath he took. He always knew, and he loved you enough to know you never meant anything you said."

"How do you know?" I ask, silently begging for anything to believe.

"We talked about you all the time. He loved you, Aria. You were his world." God, I wish he could just hold me in his arms and comfort me.

"Why couldn't you have just told me the truth, Chase?"

"A part of me already cared about you, even before I met you. The way Parker spoke of you. The fire in your eyes in the pictures he showed me, your conviction, and your tenacity. Yeah, I knew it was wrong to mislead you, but how could I not? I was too far-gone to care. I couldn't put any more pain in your eyes. The more I got to know you, I knew I had to say something, but I didn't know how to tell you. I knew the moment I told you, you'd shut me out."

"You should have."

"Would you have stayed?"

"No."

"Then no, I couldn't. This trip has been monumental for you. You've learned and grown. How could I risk that? How could I risk not being there for you? I'm a selfish bastard, okay? Is that what you want me to say? Over the years and through all the stories I got to know you. My best friend's girl. I needed to be there for you. Park would have wanted me to make sure you were okay. I knew I had to tell you, to come clean but I couldn't. I was too scared to lose you . . ." His voice trails of you.

"This is too much." The pain inside me is beyond anything I ever imagined. I want to bash my hands against his chest and beg him to turn back time. To not have been a fraud because I need him more than ever, but I don't. I turn and walk toward my bedroom.

"Where are you going?"

"Away."

"Aria." I ignore him as my hand wraps around the cold stainless steel of the doorknob.

"I'm not invisible, Aria. Don't walk away from me. God, Aria. I'm falling in love with you! Do you understand me? I'm. Falling. In. Love. With. You." I drop my hand and turn to face him.

"You don't love me."

"How can you say that?"

"You couldn't possibly love me. I can't do this right now. I'm sorry, but I can't." My vision focuses on the floor. I can't bring myself to meet his gaze.

"Please, Aria. I can't stand the idea of not holding you. Please don't push me away. I need you."

"I can't trust you."

"I would rather tear my heart out than hurt you again."

"You don't have to worry about that. There's nothing left for you to tear."

"But—"

"Please go, Chase. Thank you for everything you have

done for me, but right now I want to be alone." I lift my head to look at him.

"Goddamn it, Aria, You're everything to me! You might not believe that right now, but it's true. I can't lose you. I can't." His eyes close and he takes a deep breath. "I can wait. That's what I'll do . . . I'll wait. You're worth waiting for, Aria. Even after all the stars from the sky dim, I'll still be waiting."

I'm not worth it, but I don't have the strength to object. Hell, I don't have the strength to say anything at all. I simply turn back to the bedroom door and walk through.

"Goodbye, Princess."

His voice electrifies the air around me, burning hot currents through my body from the pain in his voice.

CHAPTER TWENTY-ONE

I HAVEN'T LEFT THE apartment in five days. Five days that have blended together. I keep myself busy with endless hours of crime drama and then lying in a bed of tears. I don't even know how to function in my world right now. I've pressed decline on so many calls, I should just disconnect my phone. I break out in a fit of giggles, swaying forward and losing my step. Imagine what Sophie would do if I turned off my phone. I lift the glass to my mouth and gulp the contents. Then I make my way back to the couch. My pajama pants hang low on my hips, so I grip them tightly to stop them from falling down. Have I lost weight? I can't even remember the last time I ate. My head throbs from straining to think.

Last night I had a slice of pizza. *Wait, was that last night?* No, the sun was still out. I glance quickly over to the clock displayed on the TV. Five thirty-five. It's been more than twenty-four hours. Holy shit, I haven't eaten in twenty-four hours? A buzz comes from the intercom, and I stumble over to answer it. "Sophie is here to see you. Should I send her up?" Edward, the doorman, asks. *Speak of the devil.* Edward's voice is tentative, and I know he's waiting for me to say no. I think he's starting to get worried about me, and rightly so. I've rejected all attempts to be visited. Both Sophie and Chase have tried to visit but every time Edward has buzzed, I've either ignored him or outright said no. I want to deny Sophie again, but if I do, she will just come back in a few hours. This has become her daily routine. It's probably better if I let her see that I'm fine and then she can go on her merry way.

"Yes." That's all I say. Then I walk back to the counter, refill my tumbler, and take another long swig. I will need it to get through the conversation.

I hear a rapping at the door as my stomach growls. Stumbling over my feet, I feel empty and drained. My shaking hands crack the door.

"What are you doing here?" I say as Sophie pushes past me and lets herself in.

"Good to see you, too. I tried calling. I tried stopping by every—"

"I figured since I didn't answer, since I told Edward no so many times, you'd understand I want to be alone."

"It's been days. Have you even showered? Oh my God, Aria, have you eaten?" She reaches her hand to me and touches my exposed collarbone peeking out from my camisole. The bone sticks out like a jagged rock.

"I'm fine." I pull away from her and cross my arms in front of my chest to cover myself. This only makes her gasp again. The movement highlights exactly how skinny I've become. From this angle, my arms appear to be merely bones, and I brace myself for the comments I'm sure will ensue.

"You're not fine." Her eyes become glassy, as if she's fighting back tears.

"If I wanted your opinion, I would have asked." My forehead furrows. *I'm fine.* Why can't she just leave me in peace?

"You look like a skeleton. Your hair is a mess." I walk toward the other side of the room and grab my drink. My listless body plops down on the couch.

"Want one?" I point to the tumbler across the room. "Please feel free to barge in uninvited and have a drink with me."

"Look at you. Look at what you're becoming. Look at *who* you're becoming! I know you lost him, but he would never have wanted you to become this." With that, I stand up and move directly in front of her. My eyes narrow, and my disdain for her interference pours out of me. Why can't she just let me be? Why does she have to bring him up? She didn't lose Parker, I did.

"What the hell do you know?" I shout.

"What's with your attitude?" A fine line appears between her brows.

"You won't have a drink with me, and you can see I'm okay. Please feel free to show yourself out." Her mouth opens and closes a few times before she shakes her head once.

"Every day since Parker passed, I see you becoming more and more like your mom. Like everything you hated. Every day you are less the girl I know—"

"You mean the girl Parker loved, the one who crushed him?"

"You think he would want you to be like this? He worked so hard to show you that you were more than Owen's sister, that you were more than the shadow behind the ghost of your brother."

"A lot of good that did him. I killed him, just like I killed Owen." She steps toward me, placing her hand gently on my shoulder. Her eyes soften, fill with compassion.

"Don't do this. It wasn't like that," she says, and I know she's trying to make me feel better, to give me comfort, but I don't deserve it, and it's not true. None of what she says is true. It's my fault. Everything is my fault. "I know Parker loved you, Aria. He would never want you to blame yourself."

"But I crushed him. He never knew."

"He knew." But no matter how her words came out, no matter what she says, she knows nothing of how he felt, and her thinking she does makes the anger inside me simmer. It's a heavy feeling that's brimming to spill out.

"You know nothing at all. Nothing," I snap. I'm finally done hearing her.

"Listen to me. He knew more about you than you know yourself. Don't you think he died knowing that? He knew you loved him."

"What the fuck does any of this matter? Who gives a crap what he died knowing? He's still fucking gone. You hear me? He's dead, so why the fuck does it matter? Nothing fucking matters. You know all that matters right now? That you're ruining my buzz. So either drink with me, or get the fuck out!"

"Aria Bennett, I love you, but you're a nasty drunk. I'm leaving before you say anything else that you can't take back. Sober up and call me." She slams the door behind her, and I crumple on the couch. The alcohol courses through my body, making my mind burn with memories so vivid I want to gouge my eyes out. I thought I could handle this. Fuck, I don't know what I thought. I don't know how to move past this. I'm not any closer to finding out. Every step I take forward, I somehow take two steps back.

I grab my glass and take another swig to hush the voices. I'm desperate to drown them out. I'm exhausted. Even though I've slept for days, I'm so tired my body aches. Parker, Parker, Parker. His name spins through my head like a record on repeat. He echoes through my thoughts. My eyelids become heavy. Visions flash against my lids. One more sip will drown him out. One more sip will make me forget.

Sophie and Chase continue to call the next day and the day after that. My mother and father have also tried to contact me. I refuse them, too. Unlike Sophie and Chase, they aren't calling to make sure I'm okay. Since I declined all their calls they started belittling me through text messages.

Dad: Are you ever planning to come to work?

Dad: It's time to make a decision, young lady.

Mom: You really are a disappointment.

I need to tell them that I've decided I'm not working for Dad. That I'm not taking over the empire. That I'm not Owen. But I just can't bring myself to text them back. Every time a new message arrives, the flood gates re-open, and I fall apart. I have no idea what I'm supposed to do with myself. I know I have to get up. I have to stop this madness, but I can't. Every time I allow my subconscious thoughts to surface, I feel as if I'm being dragged down. It's too much. Feeling is too much. I tuck my thoughts away with one sip. That's all it takes. One sip and the feelings lessen. Eventually they will disappear, and so I wait . . . fading in to the hum of the TV that drones on. It's just a matter a time. A few more burns down my throat. I lay in my bed, and the drowsiness washes over me. It's only a matter time before I succumb to sleep yet again. I dream of nothing when it comes. Pure peace.

Tick

Tick

Tick

My eyes flutter closed later that night. His eyes appear behind my lids. His blond hair is soft. The dimple I'll never see again creases his cheek, and then he morphs. Perfect steel, a five o'clock shadow. Chase Porter. My eyes jet open, and I reach for the bedside table. Warm liquid coats my throat, burns my lungs, and forces out all the faces. Stumbling and sliding, I make it to the bathroom. Vomit splashes against the toilet. I grasp the porcelain as tears begin to stream.

"I can't do this anymore," I say, defeated, through my tears. No one is here to witness my hysterics, but my drunken mind doesn't care.

"I can't"—A sob rips through my chest. My throat aches and burns. I cover my face with my hands and lie down. My body shudders against the cool tile.

I wake up sometime later, still on the bathroom floor. *I must have passed out from the exertion.* The world is spinning. I drape myself over the toilet and let my stomach empty again. All my energy has been stolen. With every bit of strength I have, I crawl across the floor until I make it to the hardwood of my bedroom. I let out a moan that's so loud and primitive, I fear the neighbors will call the cops as I pull my listless body into bed. Wrapping my arms around my torso, I try to cocoon myself, as if my frail limbs will keep the torment that lurks in the corners of my mind at bay. Through deep breaths, I try to calm my body as it shakes uncontrollably. A chill, black silence starts to surround me, and I allow it to cloak me in darkness. I welcome the reprieve.

CHAPTER TWENTY-TWO

HE SLEEP EVAPORATES.

The coolness of the air conditioner hits my limbs peeking out from my sheets. Light bursts in through gaps in the drapes hanging across the room. My eyelids flicker against the brightness. I reach out to swat it away, and my head throbs with the movement. It feels as if a train ran over me. My other senses awaken one by one, and I smell the alcohol lingering in the air. Reluctantly, I force myself to sit up in the bed, but when I'm fully seated, I realize what a mistake that is. My head spins and throbs from the movement.

What the hell do I do to feel better? And then I see it, the bottle of whisky on the bedside table. That will make it all go away. One sip and the hangover will be a distant memory. Swallowing hard, I shake my head. No, I'm stronger than that. As my gaze wanders back to the bottle, I clutch furiously at my chest. I roll over onto my sheets, cover my head, and try to fight the need coursing through my veins. I need it. I can taste it dripping down my throat even from across the room. *No, you can't do this.*

Chase's words rip through me. *"Dig deeper. You can do this."*

I can.

One step at a time.

By slow degrees, I lift myself out of the confines of my bed. My feet hit the cold wooden floors, and I want to seek my refuge under the warmth of my sheets. As I take tentative steps, I groan. It hurts badly, but I need to make it to the bathroom. It's only a few more steps.

"You can do anything for forty-five seconds." That's what Chase said, and he was right. I could and I would.

Entering the room, I make quick work of turning the shower on and stepping inside. The water is scalding. It's so hot that it loosens the muscles that were tense only a few minutes ago.

I feel my soul being cleansed by the tiny droplets hitting my body. It soaks through me to the root of my problem. My shoulders slump forward as I allow the water to wash away my pain.

Chase inspired me. He motivated me to push myself outside of my box. Regardless of what happened between us, I couldn't let those lessons fade away. No. From this moment forward, I will bask in the memories. I will treasure them. I won't let his actions rob me of that. And most of all, I will continue to seek out what he taught me.

Live the life intended.

Inspiration can strike at the strangest times. A giggle escapes, shocking me. The sound is so foreign after everything I've been through these past few days.

Ideas of how to accomplish this goal race through my mind. The first step is to finally come to terms and figure out what I don't want. Chase helped me realize so much, and Parker did, too. My lips turn up and my nose tickles from the familiar feeling of tears starting to brew. Nope. No more tears.

I put on my plush terry cloth robe and make my way to my phone. My heartbeat accelerates with fear. I was pretty awful, but I can't stand the idea of Sophie being angry with me. I don't remember exactly what I said the other day, but I know it was bad. I was drunk, and that's no excuse, but unfortunately, it's the only one I have right now.

"Hello." Even though it's just one word, I know she's still on edge that I'll jump down her throat about something.

"Hey, Soph." My voice is sheepish, and as I wait for her to respond, I stare off across the room and out the window. When she doesn't answer, I continue.

"Listen, I'm so sorry. I never should have . . . I . . ." I grab a piece of hair and twirl it in my hand.

"I know, Aria. I know that wasn't you talking. I know it was the grief. You scared me, though."

"I know, and I'm so sorry for that. I didn't know how to cope, but it's no excuse. I was wrong. I haven't had anything to drink since yesterday, and I'm feeling pretty awful about everything."

"You were scary, Aria. It was like my friend was gone. I know you have been through a lot, but if you feel you're spiraling into self-destruction again, call me. And if you don't want to speak to me, make an appointment to speak to someone. It's not healthy to drown yourself in a bottle." I let out the breath I didn't realize I was holding. "I know. I promise."

"Have you spoken to Chase?" she asks, and I sigh. I was still avoiding his calls.

"No," I admit.

"Are you planning to?"

"I'm not ready for that yet. I have a lot of soul-searching to do. I spent so many years trying to be Owen, to replace him, and in the end Parker was right. I need to learn to be me."

"When you're ready, you should speak to Chase. I think you need to even if only for closure." I can hear the concern in her voice.

"I'm not sure of the point."

"Sometimes people pretend so much it starts to become real. Maybe he intended to tell you, but it just got out of hand."

"I hear you, but in the end he did lie to me. How can I ever know if anything was genuine? If he actually ever cared or if I was, I don't know, some sick, twisted—"

"Don't even go there. Okay?" And with that, I stop myself. She's right. I can't go back to dwelling on that. Not when I finally began to make progress.

"Okay," I mumble.

"So, do you want some company? Can I help you with anything?"

"I was just going to lay low and think about things, but yeah, why not? I would love some company."

"I'm going to stop and pick up a pizza. We can talk about things once I get there. I'll see you soon."

"Thank you." I hang up the phone, and it's as though a weight has lifted off my body. I feel lighter than I have for days. Knowing she isn't angry with me is just what I need to help me start healing.

CHAPTER TWENTY-THREE

THE NEXT DAY I wake up refreshed. We had an amazing dinner of margherita pizza, and I filled her in on everything that happened on my trip. I feel so much better today. So much better that I know exactly what I need to do now—and that's start fresh. But where to start?

Job?

Chase?

Definitely job. I'm not strong enough yet to decide what to say to Chase. A part of me wonders if it's easier to ignore it and go about my life, pretend none of it ever happened, and never confront him. I hadn't known him that long, did I really owe it to him or myself to settle things? But then I realize that if I don't speak to him, I'm doing what I've always done. I'm running. One thing I've realized through all of this is that you can't run from your problems. I could have been with Parker. I could have had a few more moments with him just holding his hand if I hadn't run. I won't let myself regret the decision since Chase and our travels did teach me so much, but from now on, moving forward. No running.

I know for sure I don't want to work for my father. I walk out of my room and sit down on the couch with my laptop. I majored in marketing in college and minored in business. Both would have been ideal if I was planning to take over the marketing department for our future real estate developments, but what else can I do with it? I can get a job working in another field, but that just doesn't appeal to me either. The idea of sitting behind a desk sucks the life out of me. No, a desk job won't work either. I open Google. I've never felt more alive than when I wandered aimlessly with Chase. So that's where I start. Search engine topic . . . jobs for the free spirit. Hits . . . four unconventional jobs with great benefits.

This looks promising. My eyes roam the list, and I laugh so hard I snort. Circus Artist? This is the perfect job for me? Maybe I need to redefine my search. Adventure Travel Trip Leader? Now this has potential. Except for the part about adventure, that's the tricky part. I make a note in my notepad to look into jobs involving travel that would allow me to explore the world and not have to commit to one place for long. The more I think of the idea, the more it excites me. Yeah, I will definitely look into this.

Beer Cicerone? I have no idea what this is and after reading over the description, this is not the job for me. Drinking beers as a profession is not the smartest choice for me. *Next.*

Stunt Performers? Yeah, NO! Hell NO! Moving on . . .

With nothing left on the list, I close the computer and decide to look more into travel jobs that don't need to be performed in an office.

CHAPTER TWENTY-FOUR

TWO WEEKS LATER and I've done more research than anyone should on the world of travel. The only thing that sounds remotely promising is a travel storyteller. As a travel storyteller you basically document your travels and large travel agencies and hotels pay you to stay at the hotel and 'sample' with cash or services. I'm not sure how much money is to be made in this venture, and truth be told, other than the random poem, I'm not very good at writing. I table the whole idea. Which leads me back to travel agent, but that would be behind a desk, and I refuse to do that. *No desk job for me.* I'm back to square one, my hands are in my hair pulling as I try to think. My phone vibrates and interrupts my thoughts.

Sophie: Meet me at Perked by my office for coffee?

Stretching my arms above my head, I let out a large yawn. At only three in the afternoon, I'm exhausted. I could use coffee.

Me: Sure, I can be there in fifteen. That okay?

Sophie: Perfect! See you soon

My steps are sluggish as I straighten myself from my chair

and then leave. Making my way outside, the warm summer air hits my face and invigorates me. In the last two weeks, I've barely left my apartment, and I've missed the sights and smells of summer. My feet slip into a brisk step until I arrive. After placing my order for a cookie and a latte, I find a table in the corner and wait.

Sophie makes her way inside the coffee house a few minutes later. Her hazel eyes peek out from above her sunglasses.

"Hey, girl." Her mouth parts into a huge smile, and she walks right up to me and sits down at the table I'm occupying.

"Hi." She reaches her hand across the table, grabs the cookie sitting in front of me, and takes a bite.

"Anything I can get for you?"

"Nope, I'm good." She smiles while batting her eyelashes at me.

"Yeah, I see that. Want my coffee, too?" She lets out a laugh, reclines her body in the chair, and sighs.

"This summer internship is killing me, Aria."

"That sucks. So what's going on there? I completely forgot to ask."

"Let's just say, my boss makes all other bosses seem like saints. She has me working crazy hours. Don't get me wrong. It's sick experience to be working for the hottest new designer out there. But fuck, Aria. I'm tired."

"How did I get so lucky to be able to meet up with you?"

"Ahh, yes. London is out of the office for the rest of the day. She had a meeting over at *W* with the head of fashion accessories. I guess they are featuring her new crocodile line in next month's issue."

"Wow, that's amazing." Her red stained lips curve upward.

"I know, right." Her excitement is cute. As much as she

complains, she loves it.

We both grow quiet.

"Have you spoken to him?" Just the reference to Chase makes my stomach tighten.

"I hate him," I say under my breath. But I don't. Not really.

"You don't hate him. You're being ridiculous."

"No, I'm not. Okay, fine. I'm being ridiculous. I don't hate him."

"Then you did speak to him?"

"No."

"Ahh, I get it." She nods.

"Get what?" I ask, and I let my eyes narrow.

"You. You're doing your thing." She takes another bite of my cookie and then sets it down in front of me.

"My thing?"

"You're running away yet again. Doesn't it ever get old?" My head starts to pound at her line of questioning.

"I'm not running. I'm just taking care of me."

"And how's that working out for you?"

"Listen. I went on that trip to find myself. I haven't spoken to him because I need to understand who I am before I figure all of that out. I need to focus on me."

"And now?

"I'm starting to." Sophie nibbles on her lower lip, and her eyes squint as her gaze takes me in.

"Then why haven't you spoken to him? I love you, Aria. And I only want you to be happy, but you need to stop being so stubborn. In order to be happy in your future, you need to make peace with your past. Regardless of what happens, you need to talk to him.

"I know, I just—"

"What's this really about? Let me in. What are you so afraid of?

"I . . . I'm scared that I can't trust him. I'm afraid that if I see him, he will lure me in again, and I'm terrified I'll fall for it. But what I'm most frightened of is that it was all a lie, and I'm terrified to find out."

"I can understand your fear, where you're coming from, but you can't live like that. You can't let your life pass you by because you are too afraid to live it. You can't turn a blind eye to something that could be truly miraculous. Every day is a gift. Everyone in your life is a blessing. You know that better than anyone. Treat each day like the gift it is, and don't waste time because you're too frightened to find out. Forgive Chase and forgive yourself."

"I don't know if I can."

"Do you love Chase?" she finally asks.

"I don't know." My shoulders drop as I pull my lip into my mouth.

"It's not a hard question. Do you love Chase?" I run my hands through my hair and tug gently.

"I'm not even sure I know what love is anymore," I breathe.

"Love is finding the missing part of yourself in someone else. Like you found home." My heart hammers at her words.

My eyes well up. "I think I found that in Chase," I admit.

"Then what are you doing here with me?"

"I know what you said before, but I still don't know if I can trust him. He said he loved me, but what if that was a lie, too? God, I'm just so frustrated with everything."

"So scream. Get all your crazy out." She lets out a loud noise in the middle of the coffee shop and everyone turns to look at us. I'm not embarrassed, though. Instead, I shout until we both clutch our stomachs to calm our laughter.

"You think anyone will call the cops?" I peer around the room to see if anyone has reached for their phone. In this day and age, an outbreak like that is liable to land someone on the five o'clock news. We burst into another fit of giggles, and then Sophie stops and grows serious.

"Aria, seriously, man up and call him. Stop being blinded by your grief. He might have lied about a lot of things, but never about his feelings for you."

"How do you know? You don't even know Chase." I squint at her.

"I know you haven't spoken to him or seen him. But have you at least been keeping track? You know, like following?"

"Following where?" *What is she talking about?*

"Instagram." *Why would I follow his Instagram? I want to avoid him, not stalk him.*

"No."

"Are you serious? You don't even know?"

"Know what?" I raise my hands at her, starting to get annoyed.

"It's like global phenomenon," she exclaims.

"What is? Oh my God, Sophie, just spit it out. *What's a global phenomenon?*" I'm almost shaking from annoyance. *What the hell is she talking about?*

"Chase Porter Photo." I don't understand what the big deal is.

"His pictures?"

"His latest collection is more than pictures. He started an Instagram campaign, and it went viral." I stare at her and my eyes narrow.

"Aria, they are a living, breathing story."

"Of what?"

"Of you."

"What? What do you mean?"

"I can't explain. All I can do is show you."

She opens my laptop and logs in to the social media site. I'm shocked to see what pops up.

@ChasePorterPhoto

See the world come alive #ThroughHerEyes

Photos bridge the gaps when you don't have the words to speak

I snap my computer closed. I can't do this here. Not in front of all these people. I need to get home to see what he's done.

CHAPTER TWENTY-FIVE

FEEL LIKE A voyeur. The images I'm staring at are all me. They're so intimate, so real.

Chase saw all of me. Through his lens, he saw everything I tried to hide. It was right there for his discerning eye to capture. I see everything in the pictures, and his pictures see past my eyes, they see into my soul. I start from the beginning, scrolling all the way to the bottom of Chase's Instagram page, this time carefully absorbing every detail. The first one is the view from the top of Giotto Scampanile. It must have been taken before he met me.

"During my journey I dream of conquering the unattainable"

The next few images are city views of Florence. I wonder when we will meet in this sequence of shots and then I see it. Our first 'day' together—the field of sunflowers. My gaze continues to scan image after image, and then I see it all through my own eyes, through his vision of what the world would be like from my perspective. I'm floored. All the moments are there. Moments I had forgotten, but Chase had captured and preserved. *How did he do this?* Then it all comes back. The camera in the crook of my neck. *"Hold still while I take this shot."* Some of the photos were taken from my point of view, others from his. They take my breath away. Each headline, each hashtag, sends more tears cascading down my already moistened cheeks.

The day my world stopped turning on its axis.
#ThroughHerEyes #Wish

An image of me in Rome. My hair wispy against the wind, and if you squint real close, my bunny ears.

Be stronger than your greatest fear
#ThroughHerEyes #Conquer

The journey up the mountain of Ponza.

The moment she realized her strength
#ThroughHerEyes #Embrace

My face dusted in dirt. I had found my strength.

Although weathered and beaten, she still stands strong.
#ThroughHerEyes #Speak

In an instant your life can change
It's time to take the journey of a lifetime
#ThroughHerEyes #Adventure

The moment of clarity
#ThroughHerEyes #Truth

She leads me into the sky
#ThroughHerEyes #Eternity

Finding herself in the darkness
#ThroughHerEyes #Princess

The moment she found peace
#ThroughHerEyes #Tranquility

You are the air that I breathe, that allows my soul to take flight.
A simple moment, but also profound. That was the moment I realized she is my everything.
#ThroughHerEyes #YouAreMyTruth

Sophie's voice cuts through me. *"It's your choice how you spend your life, but if I had this, if someone did this for me. I wouldn't be sitting wallowing in the past. I would be taking steps into my future."*

She's right, and for the first time I finally see Chase with my own eyes. Everything is in focus. Chase Porter gives me more than friendship. More than love. He gives me a part of myself. The part of myself that lives in him. In Chase Porter, I find the reflection of my own soul.

CHAPTER TWENTY-SIX

MAKE MY WAY down the pedestrian path of the West Side Highway, and I'm surprised to see the narrow path choked with bodies. Everyone is enjoying the beautiful Saturday afternoon. It's not overly hot, and there's a beautiful breeze drifting through the air. It's the perfect summer day that doesn't occur often, but when it does, people come out in droves to enjoy it. Holding tightly to the little piece of paper Sophie gave me with Chase's new address, I continue down the path toward the apartment Chase has sublet. After we had returned from Italy, Sophie told me he decided staying at Parker's place would be too hard, so he took a monthly rental in the West Village overlooking the Hudson. Sophie recently admitted that although Chase had given me space these last couple of weeks, they were in constant contact. He was always checking up on me, always making sure I was okay.

As I make my approach, I can see water drifting to the left of me. My gaze skates across the distance, and I feel the water beckoning to me. God, I miss being on the ocean. The salty air lingering on my skin. The fresh breeze blowing against my face. The thrill of the sail catching the wind. And Chase. I miss Chase.

The closer I get to his apartment, the more nervous I become. My heart leaps in my chest, and my pulse thumps erratically. I see the overpass to cross over the highway and once across, I continue to walk. When the street sign for Bethune approaches, the building comes into sight and I head toward the entrance. I hope he answers when the doorman calls up. Probably should have check to see if he was home.

With shaking hands, I open the door and walk to the man standing behind the front desk.

"I'm here to see Chase Porter." I cross my arms across my chest, tuck my hands in close, and hug myself.

"Is Mr. Porter expecting you?" His voice has a hint of an accent I can't place. Maybe Scottish. It's stern, which causes me to bite my lower lip and mumble, "No."

"Who may I say is calling on him?" he asks.

"Aria Bennett."

The doorman, whose name tag reads John, pulls out a black cordless phone from under the desk and dials a few numbers.

"Mr. Porter, I have an Aria Bennett here to see you. Would you like me to send her up?" He's quiet as he listens to whatever Chase is saying. He taps a pen on the counter, which only makes me more nervous. "Yes, sir. No problem. You're quite welcome." He turns to me and hands me the pen. "Please sign your name in the roster. Mr. Porter wants me to inform you that he left the front door open for you, and to please let yourself in. It's apartment Thirteen E." My hand shakes as I try to sign my name. *Breathe.*

Just Breathe. My blood pumps so heavily I feel dizzy, as if

I'm going to pass out. I enter the elevator and almost can't press the button, but I channel all my strength to see this through. I need to speak to Chase. There is no reason to be scared.

With each tentative step I take down the hallway, my heart flutters more and more. Turning the knob is a small feat, but once I'm inside, I see a sight that knocks the wind out of me. I'm so mesmerized by the man standing before me I can no longer be nervous. His brown hair is wet. Little droplets of water trickle down his neck. His white V-neck T-shirt looks like it was just thrown on, his perfect V peeking out from beneath it.

"Hi, Princess." He runs his hands through his newly showered hair. His gaze penetrates me, and I can't pull away. He has me completely enraptured.

"Hey, Chase." My voice is soft, sheepish. Moments pass and we just stare at each other. Our gazes are locked tightly. We're both afraid to look away. Afraid that this is a dream and if we do the other might vanish.

Inhale

Exhale

Breathe

"You saw me," I say, and it's a statement, not a question.

"Saw what?" His eyebrow rises, causing his eyes to widen.

"You saw everything. You saw me. And through your eyes—" Tears prick my eyes. "Through my eyes, I . . . I saw me. I finally saw me." He doesn't say anything. His chest rises slowly. Painfully slow. I watch each movement, waiting for his response.

"What are you thinking, Chase?" At this, his lip twitches, and a smile begins to form.

"Don't you know by now? You are the only thought that

runs through my mind. I'm thinking of you, Princess. Always you." His words make my heart flutter in my chest. My breath comes out ragged as the moment pours over me, as Chase's love surrounds me. He takes two steps toward me until he's standing so close I smell the faint fragrance of his cologne.

"I'm so sorry for shutting you out, for not letting you explain. I'm ready to hear. I don't want to fight, but I do want to talk about it. To put it behind us."

"Every day I wanted to tell you," he says as he moves even closer. His face hovers over mine. He leans in and places a soft kiss on the top of my head. "But to know I would be the one to steal the light from your eyes? I just . . . I just couldn't be the one."

"When I found out, I couldn't see anything but my pain, the betrayal, and then the fear. I was so scared. I lost everyone I loved, and I was falling for you. When I found out, I thought it was all a lie. A scam and . . . and . . ." I stutter, trying to make sense of what I need to say, but it's hard to find the words.

"I'm so sorry. I never meant to hurt you. That was never my intention." I lift my chin and our eyes lock. His peer into my soul and shows me everything inside himself with just one look. I now understand. In his eyes there was no malice, just fear. Fear of losing me, before he found me.

"I know that now. And what I've learned recently is that everyone makes mistakes. It's how we act that defines us. Things sometimes need to fall apart in order for us to put them back together." He nods. These are his own words that he once said to me.

"You're becoming quite smart in your maturity." A small dimple forms as he smirks.

"I had a good teacher." I laugh out then silence as I become lost in his gaze, so many emotions run through me. Mostly I feel love, but a part of me still wavers with guilt. It must show in my expression because he raises his eyebrow slightly.

"What's going through your mind right now?" I take a step back. I need distance to voice my deepest fear.

"I have one question."

"Okay."

"You said you loved me at my apartment. How do you know you love me? We've only known each other four weeks."

"How can you doubt it? Princess, it's hasn't only been four weeks. It's been . . . " His voice trails off as he pulls out his phone from his pocket and types something in. His gaze meets mine again, "It's been 2,419,200 seconds."

"I don't . . . I don't understand."

"Even if it has only been four weeks since I've met you, it doesn't matter because each second I'm with you is another second I fall in love." This man loves me with every breath he has. But why—

"Why did you let me go?"

"I never let you go. I just stepped back. It was never letting you go because deep down I knew eventually you'd find your way back home."

"Home," I say with a smile.

"What?"

"Someone once said falling in love should make you feel like you finally found your place in life. Like you're coming home. That's how I feel when I'm with you, Chase. You are my home. I don't have to worry about pleasing you, about being something I'm not. Because in your eyes, I'm always enough. Whatever I give you, you accept, no strings attached. I love you, Chase. But still, do you think it's wrong that we—" Stepping toward me, he closes the gap between us. He places his hand under my jaw, turns my face up so our gazes meet.

"Stop that thought right now, Aria. I know you love him, but let him go, that's what he would want. He loved you, and he would want you to be happy. Parker would never want you to be sad. Not even for a moment."

"But if I love you—"

"Loving me won't change the fact that you loved him. He'll always be a part of you. He'll always live within you." And he's right. I do still love Parker. I will always love Parker. The love I have for Chase will never take away from that. It's different. Parker was my first love and I would never change that, nothing would ever change that. First loves are special and in my heart I'll forever cherish that love. But with Chase, it might not be a first love, but it's equally as real, equally as true. My need for him comes from a place of necessity. What I feel for him is my now, not my past but my present . . . my future.

I let out my last bit of resistance and finally breathe. Chase Porter has taught me how to inhale life and exhale the pain. He taught me how to live again. My heart beats in tandem with his.

"I love you, Aria. You're my air," he whispers as he walks behind me. His fingers begin to trace my shoulder blades, like feathers caressing my skin. Then slowly they trail all the way down to the small of my back.

"I missed this. I missed you," he says in a gentle voice as shadows dance against the walls. "I could hold you forever. I could kiss you every day until the end of eternity. Love is infinite, Aria. Embrace the endless possibilities of what this could become." His lips trail up my spine. He places small kisses and declarations of love.

"You are my life."

Kiss.

"You are my everything."

Kiss

Chills travel down my body. I shiver with anticipation.

Moisture pools between my legs. I crave him. I'm busting with lust.

"Now, Chase. I need you," I'm no longer able to contain my excitement. Strong hands walk me through the apartment, down the hallway until we reach the bedroom. Soft fingers caress mine as he leads me toward the bed, laying me down gently. Slowly he undresses me. His eyes lock on mine, and sparkle the most beautiful shade of blue. "I want to lick you, taste you." His voice drops to a lower octave. "I want you to come apart, and I want to put you back together piece by piece." My body shivers from the chill of the air dancing across my bare skin and the anticipation of Chase's touch. He leans down and his tender kisses trail down to my most intimate spot. I feel him loving me, cherishing me, devouring me.

His tongue worships me.

Licking . . .

Stroking . . .

Lighting me on fire.

His tongue laps my sweet spot one last time, a soft caress. He hovers above me.

His eyes are soft, filled with emotions no words can describe as he thrusts inside me. "I love you today. I'll love you tomorrow. I'll love you forever," he whispers as we become one.

His breathing becomes slower and slower. After a while, it becomes a steady hum, and I can feel the soft tickle of Chase's breath against my skin. As calming as the cadence of his breaths is, I can't quiet my own mind. My thoughts move a mile a minute. As much as I love Chase and cherish everything that has happened to us, I can't stop thinking about everything that has happened over the past month.

"Chase, are you up?"

"Mmm," he mumbles through sleep.

"Chase?" His blue eyes squint as he yawns. "I'm up. Are you okay?" he asks while running his warm hand down my spine to the swell of my hip.

"I couldn't sleep. I just—"

"What's wrong, Aria?"

"I'm sorry. I didn't mean to wake you. Go back to sleep." I turn away, but his hand stops me.

"You can tell me anything, Aria. You know that, right?"

"I know. I just couldn't fall asleep. I can't stop thinking. Why do you think this happened? Why do you think he was taken from us?" One tear runs down my cheek, and his tender caress swipes it away.

"Sometimes people come into your life for a reason. They aren't meant to stay, just to teach you something about yourself. You're a better person because you knew him. I'm a better person because of him." His words overflow with conviction.

"Do you think it was fate for us to meet?" My heart flutters as I wait for him to respond.

"It was more than fate. We are more than fate. We are predestined. Two parts of one whole."

"Don't let me go," I say through a yawn. My body relaxes into his touch.

"Rest, Princess. I won't let you go. I've got you . . . always." He holds me until my eyes grow heavy and sleep finally finds me.

My arms stretch overhead as my eyes fight to open. The soft hum of Chase's breathing brings back all of what happened last night. Moving toward him, I tuck my body into his torso and listen to steady cadence of his beating heart.

"'Morning." His voice is groggy, still laced with sleep.

"Hi." I place a tiny kiss on his chest.

"How did you sleep?"

"Perfect. Best sleep I've ever had."

"Me, too." His arm runs up and down my arm, and then he gives me a light squeeze. "Do you want me to make some breakfast? A pot of coffee?"

"That would be divine. I'll be right back." Placing one last kiss on his chest, I move to get up.

"Where do you think you're going?" he asks just before two strong arms pull me back.

"Bathroom, I need to freshen up before any of that." I pull myself back up as he groans. A laugh escapes my mouth before I head into the bathroom and turn on the water.

After freshening up, I'm revived. I head into the kitchen where Chase is hard at work making his "world famous French toast" for me. I take a seat at the breakfast nook and fold my arms on the marble counter to rest my head. It's cold to the touch and sends a chill up my arms. I accept a mug of coffee Chase has prepared. It warms me instantly.

"Thanks," I say through sips.

AVA HARRISON

"My pleasure. So, what do you want to do today?"

"If you wouldn't mind, I would love to look over the pictures you took. I saw a few of them, and they are remarkable."

"I would love to show you the pictures."

As we eat breakfast, Chase has the computer on the counter between us. He pulls up his website. I have looked at it many times before, but always alone . . . always wondering what each one meant. What he saw when he looked through the lens? What he sees now? I know what I see. I see a lost little girl who finally found her place in life. I peer in close and signal for him to click on the header labeled My Air. All the images from our trip pop up, each with its own title. Some with quotes, others with passages. I take in the first one, an image I've never seen in the endless hours I spent looking at his work these past few days.

Toxic

#ThroughHerEyes #Toxic

We just have to be happy in the moment. Never regret anything you've done.

Under the picture is a small passage.

How can you know what you want for the future if you can't check off the mistakes you made in the past? No matter how toxic, all mistakes are a lesson.

It's an incredible picture, taken on our last day in Positano. Right before everything went so wrong. My image is captured in black and white, and it appears there is almost a halo above me.

"Chase, that's incredible. How did you make it look like that?"

"It's the shadows from the light."

"It looks magical."

"Seeing the world through your eyes, that was magical. It was a beautiful, yet sad experience. You had no idea how amazing you were. But watching you learn, that was the greatest gift I've ever received." My cheeks warm, and I can feel a smile forming.

"How about this one? Look at my smile." As I continue my perusal, I notice more blog entries with quotes. I remember Chase saying he wrote sometimes, so I wonder if these are his words.

"You are everywhere to me. I see you in the first crackling light at dawn and all the way to where the sea touches the sky."

"Did you write that?" He nods, studying my expression. My eyes mist. "It's beautiful, Chase. Thank you."

"You're welcome." We become silent as we admire his pictures. *How far I've come. How much I've grown.* Everything happens for a reason. Sometimes you are too blind to see what that is, but what I realize is the universe gives you exactly what you need when you need it. Now it has given me Chase. My heart flutters in my chest at the discovery.

"Chase, I think I'm ready to finally let go."

CHAPTER TWENTY-SEVEN

Y FIRST STEP in moving on is facing the biggest obstacle I've had my whole life. After checking the mobile app to locate my Zipcar rental, Chase and I begin our trek up to Westchester. When we pull up to the sprawling green lawn that fronts the giant white Georgian Colonial I grew up in, my whole body tenses. Large windows stretch across the front façade. As the car comes to a stop, Chase takes my hand in his. The soft pads of his fingers caress mine.

"Do you want me to come in?" he asks. Our eyes lock, and I give him a little shake of my head.

"No, I think I need to do this alone." He nods with understanding and squeezes my hand.

"I'll be right here if you need me." Opening the door, I step into the summer heat. Each step I take is hesitant. As I place my key in the door, it clicks once and opens. Squaring my shoulders, I hold my head up high and walk in. I find my mother and father in the living room to the left of where I stand.

"Wow, look what the cat decided to finally drag in," she slurs, and I'm not surprised to see a glass in her hand. Regardless of the time or where she is, it's a fixture. I see what Sophie must have seen in me when I hit rock bottom. Remorse fills me, but I don't have time for regret. I might have hit rock bottom, but I pulled myself back up, learned to accept myself, flaws and all.

Inhale

Exhale

Breathe

"Mom. I'm not here to fight with you. I came to tell you and Dad . . ." I turn to face my father. "That I've decided to not work for you. I'm sorry, I know you expected me to, and I know maybe I didn't go about this the right way, but after doing some soul-searching, I've realized this isn't the right place for me."

"Why am I not surprised? You never were your brother," she hisses. She waits for her comment to cut me, to make me falter, but it doesn't. What she doesn't realize is I've come too far to take a step back. Her words no longer have any power over me. I'm too strong for that.

"You know what, Mom, just stop, okay? I get it. I'm not Owen. But you know what? That's okay. I'm done living in his shadow. I lost the most important person to me because I couldn't see what I had. I'll never make that mistake again. I will never try to alter myself for someone else."

"Altering yourself will ne—" My father raises his hand and cuts her off.

"Very well, Aria. If that's what you've decided," he concedes with a slight bow of his head.

"Don't come crawling back when you fail," my mother

cuts in with a wicked smile plastered on her face, and I turn away. I don't wait for her to continue on her drunken tirade. I don't need her approval, and I realize I never did.

"You know what? I don't need this." I walk toward the door, taking quick steps across the Brazilian cherry wood floors in the foyer.

"Aria," my dad's voice echoes. I halt my steps. I use the handle on the door to brace myself. My body trembles as I wait for him to speak. I hear his footsteps as he walks closer to me. "Will you please turn around, Aria?" Slowly, I face the man who, for my whole life, has been vacant.

"Why are you even bothering, Richard?" My mom's voice shrills from a few steps behind him.

"Enough, Victoria. This is between my daughter and myself. If you could please give us a minute," he says through gritted teeth, and she seems to sense his displeasure. Her face pales as she steps backward and exits the room.

"I'm sorry about your mother," he mutters and takes a step closer to me. My eyes widen. *Did he just apologize to me?* His brow furrows. "I know that must surprise you, but I really am sorry, Aria. I know—" He runs a hand through his salt and pepper waves. "I know I haven't always been the best father. I never stood up for you. I've never been there for you. I know it's not an excuse, but losing Owen changed me." I stand speechless in front of him. My heart pounds in my chest. *Is this really happening?* Is he really seeing me, talking to me? I've waited so long for this recognition, I want to pinch myself, make sure I'm not dreaming. "I just wanted to tell you, today. Your decision . . . I'm proud of you. I don't deserve your forgiveness after allowing your mother to abuse you for so long, but I promise that will change. I know she needs real help, and I'm ready to admit I never got that for her. I promise that I will."

"What . . . I don't understand. Why now, Dad?"

"You disappeared. I realized I spent so much time grieving Owen, that if I wasn't careful I could lose you, too."

"I . . . I," I stutter. I'm not sure how to respond.

"You don't have to accept my apology. I just want you to know that I understand things have to change, and I promise I will try. I want to try to build something with you. Do you think . . . do you think that maybe . . .?" His eyes are filled with so much emotion—pain, fear, regret—and as much as he might not deserve my forgiveness, he's my father.

"Yeah, Dad. I think I can try," I manage through choked back tears. The corner of my mouth curves up. "Goodbye, Dad."

"I'll speak to you soon?" he asks hopefully, and I nod. For the first time, I know we'll be fine.

As I return to the car, Chase raises his eyebrows, and I smile. That's all I have to do, because he knows me.

"You ready to go?" He places his left hand on the steering wheel and shifts the car into drive. "One more stop first, okay?" His head dips down with understanding as we pull out of the circular drive. A quarter of a mile up the road, Chase turns left and pulls into the home that held so many memories for me. Together, our hands encased with one another, we ring the doorbell.

The door swings open, and Mrs. Stone stands before us. She throws her arms around me and then does the same to Chase. Tears stream down her face, and she doesn't speak, simply allows us in.

"Hi." My voice sounds sheepish, and her eyes glisten. "We

were over at my parents' and I wanted to . . . can I have . . ." I swipe at the moisture on my cheek. *I didn't even realize I was crying.* Parker's mother shuts her eyes and nods. Her hand still clutches mine as she wordlessly tells me she understands why I'm here.

I'm not sure how long we stand by the door, but eventually I pull my hand from hers and gesture for Chase to follow me. When we finally inch open the door to Parker's room, my breath hitches. There it is: the map. Every dream we ever had. Every destination we never saw, and I know what I have to do. Not just for Parker but for myself.

"There are still a lot of places to be seen," I say to Chase. His eyes squint, and he moves closer to take in all the locations highlighted with a yellow thumbtack.

"Where should we venture off to first?" My head tilts and then one pops out at me. I remember Parker saying he couldn't wait to explore Base Torres Del Paine . . . Chile. *The only place you can experience four seasons in one day, baby girl.* I let out a chuckle and point to the map.

"Agreed. That's where we'll go." Chase starts removing the pins but replaces the marks with colored ink, each shade symbolizing the pin it replaces. As my hands pulls at the tape keeping it affixed to the wall, I try my best to keep it intact. There are a lot more adventures left to conquer.

CHAPTER TWENTY-EIGHT

Aﬀter leaving Parker's house there is one more stop to be made.

Inhale

Exhale

Breathe

Every breath you take is one step closer to moving forward. Holding Chase's hand, I move my way toward the last bit of closure I need. A shadow looms over us. Streams of light flicker in through a canopy of clouds. The foggy haze begins to lift, and I turn my head toward his. Our eyes meet, his lips part. He gives me a knowing nod and squeezes my hand gently. It's just a small reminder that he's here, but it's enough for me to stay my path. On our way up to the destination in front of us, we pass a mass of trees that darken as the sun drops back behind the clouds. Only a few more steps. I can do this.

I step forward and stare at the headstone. The gray marble with etched words I never thought I would see stares back at me. Tears well in my eyes, and I turn to Chase. "Sometimes I miss him so much I don't know how to breathe. He was your best friend. How do you do it?"

"All you can do is own your pain and grow from it. Remember, sometimes people aren't meant to stay in your life. Sometimes they are meant to pass through and teach you about yourself. You can do this, Aria. You are stronger than you ever thought you could be." He squeezes my hand in his, then steps onto the path, allowing me time alone with Parker. My Parker.

He was all the great parts of me. When I was alone and struggling to find my way, feeling unloved, he loved me. If he could love me, I know I'm worthy of being loved.

"I miss you every day. You were my rock, my shoulder to cry on. You were my strength when I had none. You were the very best parts of me, and I will love you always." In the grand scheme of life, I'd only known him a brief second, but that moment of my life would last me until the end of time.

"When I think of the short time we had together, I don't regret anything except that I never told you I loved you, because I do and always did. Chase says you knew that. That you always knew how I felt. I pray every day that's true. I pray that you did know what you meant to me. What you will always mean to me. You made me change my perspective. You opened my eyes, and I thank you for that.

"I want to thank you for coming into my life and teaching me about myself. I want to thank you for every time you held me and put me back together. For loving me and teaching me, many years ago, that my grief will eventually fade and what's left behind is a beautiful memory to always cherish. I'd forgotten that lesson. Chase has reminded me. Letting someone go isn't a sign of weakness, but rather it's the mark of strength.

"I will always be yours, Parker. You'll always own a piece

of my heart, but it's time I move on. I'll never forget you, and I know it would make you happy that Chase brings me peace. With him, I've finally found the piece of me that was missing. We've decided to give us a try and see where the road takes us. So after long consideration, I've decided this will be my last postcard. Not because I don't still love you, but because it's time for me to move on. I'll celebrate you and honor you in every breath I take for as long as I'm blessed to take it. Thank you for giving me your heart. I will never let it go. I will keep it with me forever."

> *Dear Park,*
>
> *All the things I never said to you—I could fill one million cards with all the words and missed moments between us. But I know you'd never want that. Before I say goodbye, I want to tell you that you were right . . . about everything. Thank you for that. Everything I learned on this journey was because of you. You believed in me before I believed in myself. I'll cherish all the memories I have with you until the end of time. You'll live in my heart forever. I never had time to tell you that I do love you. I have always loved you, and I will always love you.*
>
> *Yours,*
> *Ari.*

EPILOGUE

The greatest journeys in life are those not planned.

THE LAST HALF of a year has passed quickly. Right after saying good-bye to Parker, Chase was asked to do a photo shoot in Portugal. He wanted me to go with him, and at first I was hesitant. I mean, I was still trying to find my place in the world, but then I realized maybe this was my place. After a lengthy discussion in which I shared my travel desires with him, we decided to give it a go. We researched day and night for the first few weeks and soon learned that certain brands and multiple tourism boards paid for exposure, and then we discovered that restaurants and hotel chains were constantly vying for photographers to shoot their products, stay at their hotels, and even eat their food. With a large enough Instagram and blog following, you could earn a living leveraging your follows, as well. So we decided we would travel together. I'd report from our locations, and he would shoot the pictures.

It was everything I dreamed of from a job perspective, and more than I could dream of from a personal one. Every day for six months, we discovered new treasures and fell in love a little more. Every minute we were together was monumental, but even the moments that seemed inconsequential were equally important because we were together. Life was good, and even things with my parents were starting to improve. Dad and I kept in touch. We were working hard to mend the distance between us and mom was finally getting the help she needed. I had faith that in time we'd be able to form some sort of relationship.

He pulls me into him, and the movement makes my loose strands of hair flow against the wind. He begins to snap his camera. I cherish these images most of all. They are intimate, beautiful, and ours.

"There's something about towering peaks and deep valleys that inspire me." His breath tickles my neck and makes tiny goose bumps awaken across my flesh. He's right, the view is spectacular. I can see the sun set on a distant horizon. *The only place you can see all four seasons in one day.*

These days I'm often in constant awe of the beauty that surrounds us. Chase has given me the gift of seeing the splendor around me, and now I can't turn it off. Not that I want to. Snowcapped mountains span the distance. They fade into the horizon, making a path toward the heavens. I feel as if I can touch the sky. Heaven is only a fingertip away

"This is what happiness is." My lids close and the sun lightly tickles my face. "This is peace." He lowers the camera and I turn to face him. Peering up into his eyes, once again I lose myself in his mesmerizing gaze.

"You steal the breath from my lungs, Aria. You like this . . . it's what I've been waiting for. You're truly remarkable." He pulls me into his embrace. His touch is comforting, warm, and tender. "If I were drowning, I would want you to be my last breath of air." His gaze never wavers as he speaks his poetry to me, the depth of his blue eyes endless like the sky.

"What are you looking at, Princess?" His nose crinkles as his eyes peer down at me.

"How beautiful you look."

"Beautiful?"

"Yes, Chase Porter. You're beautiful. Your heart, your love. You healed me one broken piece at a time."

"You were never broken, just a bit cracked." His hand reaches out to stroke my cheek.

"You're really good at loving me," I say as I give him a lopsided smile.

"Loving you is the easy part." His lips descend, and he places a delicate kiss on my lips.

It's funny to think of how far I've come. The change was so gradual I barely noticed it, but before I knew it, like a masterpiece from yesterday's past, he had etched himself into my life.

When I set out six months ago for Italy, I hadn't planned to fall in love, but life doesn't always play out the way you expect. Chase taught me how to fall in love. He taught me how to fall in love with *me*.

"I'm out of my mind in love with you." He peers down at me as I speak, his long eyelashes blinking rapidly.

"Good to know, Princess. Because to me, you're the sun, you're the moon, you're the stars in the sky. To me, you're everything." His eyes sparkle as his lips turn up, the right side a bit higher than the left to bring on the smirk I've loved since the first time we met. His fingers touch my jaw, and he gently tilts my chin up. His mouth covers mine, and I sigh into his breath. *Like coming home.* Kissing Chase always feels like I'm coming home.

"Nothing can be more perfect than this."

"I love you, my beautiful girl. This is the beginning of our latest adventure. Only time will tell where this journey is headed, but I'm excited to find out." My weight softens against him. The future might be unknown as it's not yet written, but mine is crystal clear. Everything is in focus.

Life is tiny hills, giant mountains, and adventures for us to conquer. No matter how big, I know I will conquer them all.

"I love you."

One phrase.

Three simple words.

A moment that changed everything.

Life is measured by all of these moments. That's what it's all about.

The little dreams.

The little flashes of time.

And seeing how beautiful life is . . .

Through your own eyes.

THE END

ACKNOWLEDGMENTS

I want to thank my entire family. I love you all. We're a crazy bunch but I love that about us!
To Mom, Thank you for keeping all my poems

To Liz, Thank you for helping me create my first "book".

To my sister: You inspired this story with your many adventures and the map on your wall! I love you, baby girl.

Thank you to my husband for always loving me, I love you so much!

A special thanks to my "Bears". You're everything!

Thank you to all the amazing indie companies that helped mold my words.

Champagne Formats
Chelsea Kuhel (www.madisonseidler.com)
Write Girl Editing Services
Indie After Hours
Behind the Writer

Thank you Lisa from the TRSOR for being amazing, supportive and helping spread the word!
Thank you to Linda from Sassy Savvy for your help with promo and getting my story into so many new hands.

Thank you to Neda from Ardent Prose PR for your unending support.

Thanks to Jenny Woods for taking the most perfect pictures in the world!

A very big thanks to Hang Le! I adore your work and I love that you get me! Sorry for always bothering you with just one more thing . . .

I want to thank all my friends for putting up with me. I know it's no easy task!

To "My Soul Mate" I don't even know where I would be without you! Can't wait for what the future will bring . . . HS.

To Andie, Your friendship means the world to me! Thank you for inhale, exhale, breath and so much more! This book wouldn't have been written without your endless encouragements.

To Jen, You're the most amazing friend and I truly love when you "rip" me a new one. Excited to see what's in store for us in 2016.

To My "E.S.J." Thank you for always being there for me. Thank you for all your advice and suggestions and being a kick ass soundboard!

To Shawna, I want to thank you for always being there to help me out. I appreciate it more then you know.

To Amy, Thank you for sitting on the phone with me one day and plotting Jules . . . which then became Aria's story. Thank you for all your advice and friendship.

To My "Sisters" Thank you for being there for me. Love you guys!

To Christine Brae, Mia Asher, Leddy Harper, Mara White, BA Wolfe, Livia Jamerlan, A.J. Pryor and all the ladies of Writers Hangout thank you for giving me advice.

My Beta's . . . Lisa, Jamie, Argie, Nicole, Jade and Patricia. Thank you for your wonderful and extremely helpful feedback. I appreciate it more than you know!

To the ladies in the Perfectly Flawed Support group, I couldn't have done this without your support!

Thanks to all the bloggers! Thanks for your excitement and love of books!

Last but certainly not least . . .
Thank you to the readers!
Thank you so much for taking this journey with me.
I hope you will, please consider joining my Perfectly Flawed Support Group on Facebook. The goal of this group and my book is to help women own their imperfections. This group is to help us remember that every single one of us . . . is perfectly imperfect.

BY AVA HARRISON

Imperfect Truth
Perfect Truth

ABOUT THE AUTHOR

Ava Harrison is a New Yorker, born and bred. When she's not journaling her life, you can find her window shopping, cooking dinner for her family, or curled up on her couch reading a book.

Facebook: http://on.fb.me/1E9khDv
Twitter @avaharrison333
Instagram @AvaHarrisonAuthor
Pinterest http://bit.ly/1Qo0Tw1

Made in the USA
San Bernardino, CA
27 October 2016